MURDER WITH A PSYCHIC TOUCH

MURDER WITH A PSYCHIC TOUCH

B.T. ALIVE

VILLETTE PRESS • BACK MOSBY, VA

Murder With a Psychic Touch © 2019 B.T. Alive. (v1.0)

All rights reserved. No part of this book may be reproduced in any form without permission in writing from the author. Reviewers may quote brief passages in reviews. Please do.

DISCLAIMER: THIS IS A WORK OF FICTION. ANY RESEMBLANCE TO ANY ACTUAL PERSONS, PLACES, THINGS, PSYCHICS, SMALL VIRGINIA TOWNS, SMALL TOWNS, SMALL VIRGINIANS, BED AND BREAKFASTS, VICTORIAN ALIENS, INCIDENTS, WORKS OF ART, PRODUCTS, COMPANIES, RELIGIONS, TELEPORTS, OR ANYTHING ELSE, IS COMPLETELY ACCIDENTAL AND UNINTENDED. SERIOUSLY.

For more information, visit:
https://billalive.com/cozy

But not now. Read the book first.

MURDER WITH A PSYCHIC TOUCH

PART I

CHAPTER 1

The letter wafted the scent of old cedar chests, and lilacs, and spring.

The address — *my* address — was penned in a script that was impossibly gorgeous, and the thick, cool, creamy ivory paper gave me a tiny jolt at every touch.

Not a "magic" kind of jolt. I only get *that* if I touch... well, you'll see.

This was just a feeling of excitement, and curiosity, and maybe a teeny bit of dread. There was no return address.

If I'd known that by this time tomorrow, I'd be neck-deep in solving a murder, in some tiny town I'd never heard of, with my whole view of what was and wasn't possible pretty much shattered... would I still have opened that letter?

Are you kidding? Absolutely.

Besides, I'd kind of just burned a few bridges here in Philly.

Not that I was really *worried*. No way.

Hence my decision to drop in here at my favorite hipster coffee joint, just as if nothing had happened. Nothing a late-morning latte couldn't fix.

There was this lady behind me in line, though, and *she* was worried. She was an older lady in a cute spring sundress, and she was clutching her purse and creasing her forehead.

"Hey!" I said, all cheerful. "I *love* your outfit."

Her frown cleared into a gracious smile, and her eyes shone.

Nice.

Honestly, her dress looked a bit chilly for April in Philadelphia. But I had to admit that I might just be jealous. When was the last time *I'd* gotten to wear a sundress?

I hate it, but I've had to get used to long sleeves, long skirts, long pants. To prevent accidents.

Anyway. Just then, the truth was that I *may* have had a *minor* setback, but I was determined to just sit and sip and relax and think, and figure out my next move. Everything was going to be fine.

"Excuse me, Summer?" said the hunky barista behind the counter, all husky and friendly. He had nice eyes and broad shoulders, and I couldn't decide whether it was flirty or creepy that he'd snagged my name off my credit card. "I'm really sorry," he said. "There seems to be a problem with your card."

Oh crud. Not again. Not *now*.

I'll be honest. I did consider giving his arm the Magic Touch.

But I nixed that idea. Sure, the effects might ease my embarrassment, but I'd still have to pay for the coffee.

Besides, I had no excuse. For a sales rep who pulled in as much as I did, it was just ridiculous that I couldn't stay on top of my credit cards.

Plus, I didn't want to try anything fancy in here; the little coffeeshop was packed with too many other people who might see. The nice sundress lady was watching me with increasing concern.

"No worries!" I said, and I flashed my best closer smile. "I *know* I've got cash."

Actually, all I *really* knew was that my other cards were *definitely* maxed out. And the cash section of my Italian leather wallet was currently holding a golden paperclip.

But I cracked open my cavernous purse and started digging. I'm tenacious.

And at the very bottom, in the prehistoric bedrock layer of stained pennies and used-up chapstick and ancient receipts possibly dating back to high school, I snatched out a crumpled ten.

This earned me an approving grin from Mr. Name-Reader. I paid, got my precious change, grabbed the coffee, and scurried to a seat to open my letter.

I know, I know, I should have saved the letter until *after* I'd done some planning to conquer my semi-immediate crisis. That would have been some excellent adulting.

But you've got to understand. I couldn't remember the last time I'd gotten *any* kind of letter. Much less on stationery that could be an invitation to a royal wedding.

It's not like I got Christmas cards. Dad's small family were all dead, and Mom's family, if she had one, hadn't written me. Ever.

Just like her.

I mean, who even sends cards or letters anymore besides family? During the holidays, I almost couldn't bear to check my lonely mailbox. I wasn't just an only child; I was practically an orphan. Aunts, uncles, cousins, grandparents… if I had any, I had no idea where they were. And I'd looked.

The envelope's paper was so thick and high-quality that I had trouble opening the thing. Or maybe it was just the tremble in my fingers.

When I did get it open, the first things to slip out brought a stab of disappointment: folded sheets of ordinary printer paper.

But then I touched a single sheet of sumptuous stationery, also folded once.

As I opened it, an ornate letterhead shone at the top, but what riveted my gaze was the opening line.

My dearest Summer—

Dearest?

My solar plexus tingled down to my stomach. Who *was* this? No one had ever called *me* "dearest".

Then the moment was totally ruined.

At the counter, a harsh male voice snapped, "You forgot your entire *wallet?*"

It was Mr. Hunky Barista, scowling. I'd barely recognized his voice.

The woman in the sundress was bent and digging through her purse, her long gray hair spilling onto cheeks going beet red.

"I already started making your tea!" the barista barked. "Seriously, do you have dementia?"

The woman cringed. Like he'd slapped her.

"Hey!" I called.

The jerk startled and caught my eye. As I marched over, he flushed and looked down. "Sorry, it's just, the manager—"

"Don't you *dare* apologize to *me*," I said. I slapped down the rest of my last ten.

It was a grand gesture, but I did feel a slight twinge, that being pretty much all my cash. No, wait, I had some at home. Probably.

"Come on," I told the woman. "Sit with me." I patted her back (the dress material was thin, but enough to protect her) and I ushered her toward my booth.

Her eyes were wet, and her thin lips were clenched all wrong. I felt guilty for not doing more to ease her pain, but there really were a lot of people around.

"Listen, that guy's a turd," I said. "Forget it."

"I know, I should," she said, and the grief in her trembly voice tore my heart. "But my husband... he did. Have dementia."

That did it.

I whispered, "*Forget it.*"

And I clasped her bare hand.

She had cold, soft, old-person skin. The veins on the back of her hand moved gently beneath my thumb.

But I felt the jolt. Like a static shock.

The woman blinked and looked confused. But her upset flush began to fade.

How did I feel? A little trembly myself… I never get used to the Touch.

Gently I guided her into the opposite bench at my booth. "Thank you for sitting with me!" I chirped, with practiced ease.

She was still looking lost. She glanced down at her tea in surprise; she probably didn't remember ordering it. "You'll have to forgive me," she said. "I'm feeling a bit… spacey…"

I brushed this aside with a genial wave. "I don't blame you, I've been talking your ear off! Don't think I even gave you my name." (Cue the killer smile.) "Summer Sassafras."

"Oh, what a lovely name!" she said, like she really meant it. "I'm Sheila. So nice to meet you." She held out her hand.

But I jerked my hand back, cranking up the smile wattage. "Sorry, I'm still getting over a cold," I lied. "Oh look, your tea's ready."

Thankfully, the barista had slunk off and was nowhere in sight. As Sheila went to retrieve her drink from the empty counter, I finally slipped out the letter.

My dearest Summer—

I know this may seem sudden, but I wish to extend you an invitation. Come to The Inn at Wonder Springs, Virginia.
I would appreciate if you came at your earliest convenience.
The matter is somewhat urgent.
You may be in danger.
And you deserve to know the truth about your mother's family.

—Grandma Meredith

Gradually, I realized that Sheila was talking at me.

"Are you all right? Summer? Hello?" she was saying. Somehow she'd come back and I hadn't even seen her. She looked concerned again, even frightened.

"I'm fine," I lied. "Everything's fine."

"Are you sure? You look like you've seen a ghost."

CHAPTER 2

I tried to stay calm.

Of all the surprises in that bizarre letter, I'd felt the most shock at the final word.

Meredith.

At the name, a strange resonance had quivered in my chest, like the tingle of a long-forgotten song.

Had I heard that name before? Why couldn't I remember?

Somehow it felt like long, long ago... like seeing a photo of your toddler self, and the feeling you get from the old front yard in the photo behind you. Do you really remember? Or is it something else... the memory *of* a memory? The ache for when everything felt real?

If it hadn't been for that wisp of memory, as if this woman might be some ancient family friend from back before Mom had left, I'd have chucked the whole thing as an obvious prank.

I mean, come on. Some random lady just writes me out of nowhere, with hints about "danger" and knowing my mother's family? The whole thing almost *had* to be fake.

And what kind of name was "Wonder Springs"? The town probably didn't even exist.

Except, crud, that printer paper that had fallen out was a printout of directions, printed from an ordinary map website. There it was, ridiculously prosaic: Wonder Springs, some tiny town in the mountains of Virginia.

The directions went straight from my apartment, and the travel estimate was at least *five hours* west and south from Philly. And the wretched traffic through D.C. and Northern Virginia might add hours more.

Oddly, "Grandma Meredith" hadn't thought to leave a phone number. I grabbed my phone to search for this theoretical Inn, so I could at least call and see who I was dealing with.

And... my phone locked up.

I dropped it, instantly, so I wouldn't fry it. My phone clattered to the table.

The Touch thing really hasn't been great with tech. I've burned through way too many phones.

I *can* use tech, sparingly, but when any tech I'm touching locks up, I've got seconds or less to break the connection. Otherwise, I'll do permanent damage.

It's kind of sad that I can function in modern society without skin contact, but if I had to stop using electronics, I'd be done.

I have no idea why electronics are less "sensitive" than people. I can use devices, but only if I stay calm.

Right now, I was very much *not* calm.

If there was even a *chance* this Meredith woman could help me find my family... I would *certainly* drive down to Virginia. I'd do much more than that.

Across the table, Sheila was looking like she really wished she could remember how she'd wound up sitting with this freaked-out Millennial who was now dramatically dropping hardware.

"Sorry," I said. "My phone gets hot. I should probably get that looked at—"

"Is everything all right?" she said.

"Yes, sorry. It's just this..." I touched the letter. "A bit unexpected."

"Oh?" she said. She eyed the letter with interest. "Such lovely handwriting. What's it about? If you don't mind my asking."

Or even if I do, I thought.

I hesitated.

That's the problem with not having actual relatives. You catch yourself running decisions past total strangers.

"It's an invitation," I said. "To this Inn down in Virginia."

"How nice!" she said. "For when? Will you be able to get the time off work?"

"No worries there," I said. "I just quit."

(I *told* you I had a semi-immediate crisis.)

"You *quit?*" Sheila said. She pursed her lips with disapproval. Her whole friendly demeanor cooled considerably. "My son's been trying to find work for months."

"Trust me," I said. "He wouldn't want to work with Nyle."

Nyle.

I could see him now, grinning his scrawny grin through his overstyled, graying beard. Of all my work rivals over the years, Nyle Pritchett had been my arch-nemesis. The sneaky little creep had been #1 sales rep in our region for eons, probably since I was in high school. And I'd come so close to beating him for the top spot... *so close...*

"No workplace is perfect," Sheila said firmly. "Was this man your boss?"

"Not until this morning," I said. "Seriously, he got *my* promotion. I should have been *his* boss! I *had* the numbers. I'd *finally* beaten him in sales."

Her frown was skeptical. "Then why did *he* get promoted?"

"Politics!" I said. Which was true, partly.

Nyle was a wheedler, a crooner; I couldn't understand the power he had over people, ranging from women who should have been way out of his league to alpha male clients at the top of their game.

But power he had. That scarecrow with his padded suit shoulders could close a conference room packed with A-level executive piranhas without breaking a sweat. I hated that I'd had to work twice as hard just to be the silver medal to his gold.

That, and maybe bend a few rules.

Whatever. At least I'd never have to see that dude again.

"I see," said Sheila. "And how will you support your way of life?" This from the woman who would never remember that I'd spent my last few bucks to pay for her tea.

"Listen, I *couldn't* keep working there," I said. "Taking orders from *him?* Watching *him* ride a rocket up the corporate ladder? I'd rather die."

"There's always *someone* to envy," Sheila intoned.

"Yeah, but I don't have to live with them," I said.

I got up. I reached for my phone, then remembered about the Touch and, using the letter, pushed the phone off the table into my purse.

Sheila raised her eyebrows.

"Thanks for the chat," I said. "I've got to go, but this has been *super* clarifying."

That was one advantage of running your questions past strangers instead of relatives. You could keep running.

"And if your son's any good at selling incredibly complex software contracts to mind-numbingly boring government managers," I said, politely, as I hoisted up my massive purse onto my shoulder, "I'd be happy to give him a recommendation."

"He's a foot model," she said, shortly.

"Oh," I said. "In that case, I'd be happy to give him my spare toenail clippers. I don't know why, but I'm always buying an extra pair—"

"He's *following* his *dream*," she snapped.

"I hope he's wearing comfortable shoes," I said.

"*Excuse* me—"

"Sorry, that was mean," I said. "You must get stupid jokes all the time."

"I'm *very* proud—"

"Goodbye, Sheila," I said. And I touched her cold hand.

The jolt hit me harder this time. I'd expected that; I didn't know much about the Touch, but I'd learned it was better to wait as long as possible between uses to avoid... unpleasantness.

I decided to jet while she was still sitting there dazed, instead of waiting until she blinked and looked around and wondered who I was all over again. It might seem harsh to leave her in a booth by herself, but it was better this way. In a minute or two, she'd blink, look around, and assume she'd been daydreaming. Alone.

I'm always amazed at how scary fast we can explain away what we don't understand.

Which was maybe what I'd almost done with this letter.

As I fought the midday traffic back to my apartment, I started to see the bright side of a drive down to the country. True, I knew I should probably be setting up job interviews. Especially considering my maxed-out credit cards and empty purse.

But what if this nice old Meredith lady was for real?

I glanced at the letter, which lay where I'd tossed it on my passenger seat.

And you deserve to know the truth about your mother's family.

Come on. Would *you* have started scouring the job sites?

Besides, I was getting too excited. If I tried job hunting now, I'd probably fry my laptop.

I decided to head out right away. I had a full tank of gas, right? Well, enough to get down there. And I *had* to have some cash in a drawer *somewhere*. Enough for a short trip. I'd swing home just long enough to pack the essentials... in particular, my cat, the esteemed Mr. Charm.

I've never figured out whether all animals are immune to the Touch, or if it's only my personal, wonderful cat.

When you can't even hug your friends without making sure you don't brush cheeks, you really appreciate your fat, lazy, snuggly cat. His breed is literally called "Ragdoll", and he's like a sentient white lap blanket. When I touch him, I don't feel a jolt, only a warm, soothing calm. And *he* only seems to relax even *more*... if that's physically possible.

Anyway, I was all worked up thinking about the trip, so of course I missed my exit, and then there was this crazy accident that made the beltway a parking lot. It was well past lunchtime and my stomach was howling by the time I finally parked at my apartment and clattered up to the glass entrance in my stupid heels.

I checked my reflection in the door. The spring humidity was frizzing my bounteous red mane, but only slightly. I'd come to accept that what my hair might lack in finesse, it more than made up for in volume and attitude. My dress jacket and long skirt were classy and confident, and though I was never going to be some twiggy starving model, I decided that between working out and cutting carbs, I was looking pretty darn good. Mostly.

One more girl in her mid- (okay, late) twenties, out to conquer the world.

As I rode up the elevator, I got even more excited wondering how Mr. Charm would react to the countryside. Who knew? He might even *move around.*

"Charm?" I called, as I unlocked my door and bolted it behind me. "Road trip! We're going to Virginia!"

"I think not," said a complete stranger.

He was a cadaverous old man in a black suit, tall and lean and sinking into my couch.

He held Mr. Charm on his lap, and his strong, thin fingers rested close around the furry neck.

CHAPTER 3

Normally, I loved that first step into my apartment. The living room glittered with my exquisite taste, and a wide bank of windows revealed a gorgeous view of the water.

But now my velvet curtains were closed, and the lights were off. On my couch sat a tall man I'd never seen, shrouded in shadow.

He was old, with a gleaming bony head, but he was impeccably dressed in a black pinstripe suit. Though his weight was crushing the cushions, he sat straight up, and his posture radiated power. My precious cat was trembling in his grip.

"Who are you?" I gasped. "If you hurt him, I swear—"

"Let's not be hasty," he said. His voice was cold, smooth, and polished as a new gravestone.

"Hasty?" I said. "You've got ten seconds to get the hell out or I'm calling the police."

"I wouldn't do that," he said.

His thumb and forefinger tightened, ever so slightly.

I *might* be able to unbolt the door and run, but I couldn't risk this lunatic killing Mr. Charm. He didn't seem to have a gun... if he did, wouldn't he be pointing it at me instead of clutching my cat? I loved that cat... I could barely think, but I managed to tell myself, *get this man talking*. The second he got distracted and let go, I could grab Mr. Charm and run for the cops.

"What do you want?" I said.

His thin lips stretched into a smile. It sliced across his pale face, like a surgeon making the first cut.

"Please," he said. "Sit down."

Warily, I came toward him, but with a firm nod, he indicated a chair at a distance, well out of lunging range.

"You really should let him go," I said, as I sat. "That's a nice suit, and you're freaking him out. He's totally going to pee. Big time."

He frowned, with a visible flicker of concern.

Unfortunately, I was lying. Unlike me, Mr. Charm could hold it through a barrel plunge over Niagara Falls.

"Look, let him go, and you can make your pitch," I said. "I'll give you ten minutes. I promise."

"Do you?" he said. "And will that promise hold when you disrupt my memory?"

My stomach clenched, like I'd swallowed ice. I couldn't speak.

I'd been using the Touch for almost twenty years. Maybe longer. No one had *ever* guessed what I could do.

Not once.

Not even Dad, and we'd lived in the same house. At least, officially.

I'd stopped even worrying whether anyone would figure it out. People might catch me and think I was slipping my "victim" a pill or something, but the Touch itself had been *beyond* secret.

Until this leering stranger broke into my locked apartment.

"I see we understand one another," he said. His smile-gash twitched with amusement. "I'll take my chances with the cat."

"Who... *are* you?" I said.

"That is of no consequence. For the moment. The far more intriguing question is: who are *you?* And are you living to your full potential?"

My hyperalert brain jolted out of its panic tunnel vision. Potential? Really? This creep was here to *recruit* me?

Yes, I was technically back on the job market. But would I sign on with the sort of Mr. Cadaver Guy who would ferret out my lifetime secret, break into my apartment, and threaten to throttle my cat? Not a chance. The last thing I needed was a Boss From Hell. Possibly literally.

"I'm listening," I said.

He sighed. "No. You're watching. Let us give you something worthy of your attention."

Keeping one hand clutching Mr. Charm, he lifted his other hand and slowly reached for my end table. "You may not be aware of this, Miss Sassafras, but you are not the only individual with a gift."

I didn't have time to process what the man might mean before I realized what he was reaching for.

On my end table was a spider plant, one of those exuberant houseplants that spills out in every direction like enchanted ivy. The man frowned, squinted, and touched the nearest tendril.

The entire plant withered.

Or even... *bubbled*. It happened so fast that I couldn't be sure.

My mind stopped. Total terror override. I was staring at the impossible, the living green dried to crackled gray in seconds.

You might think that since I personally had the whole Magic Memory Touch thing, I'd have been more prepared for this.

Nope.

I'd never met anyone else demonstrate anything *close* to real magic. I'd gotten used to my own "gift" ages ago, and I'd lived a mostly normal life, thank you very much.

Now I was five feet from some lunatic who could kill with his touch. With his hand on my sweet cat's neck.

I'd never felt this level of full-body fear. But I could also feel the adrenalin rush, my senses kicking into high gear. And if there was one thing I'd learned from a gazillion sales calls, it was this: when you get scared, get loud.

"So! You're a magician?" I blared. The blast of my voice actually made Mr. Cool Cadaver startle. This was absurdly gratifying. "You rigged up that whole trick just for me?"

His eyes blazed with offense. Ice cold, he said, "Do you require a demonstration more impressive?"

"No, that was fantastic," I said. "I hope you do birthday parties. The kids must go *wild*."

He scowled.

"You are destined for a great work, Summer," he said. "You cannot escape the fate for which you were born."

A shiver crept down my back. No one had ever said anything like that to me. Ever.

But what I said was, "You talk a pretty big game for a guy who dresses like a substitute butler."

That did it.

When an old man spends that much money on his outfit, he's walking around with a neon sign advertising his weak point. He growled, and he clenched both hands into fists.

Meaning, he let go of my cat.

In one instant, Mr. Charm lunged, clawed the creep's face, and bolted. I'd never seen him move so fast.

The man shrieked and clapped a hand to his bloody cheek. I jumped up, grabbed my chair, and swung it into his rib cage. The thud made my stomach turn, but he gasped and doubled over, coughing.

I tried to run, tripping across the room in my stupid heels but too frantic to think of kicking them off. I still had my purse on my shoulder, and I swung it off and scrabbled through the junk to get my phone to call the cops. Minutes seemed to crawl before I found it, but the second I finally grabbed my phone, the damn thing sparked and started smoking. Dead.

I hoisted my purse back onto my shoulder and lunged for my landline. (Yes, I kept a backup.) My old corded phone was mounted by the front door. I seized the handset... and the line was dead.

What? I'd hardly *ever* fried the *landline*.

Then I saw. The phone wire was neatly cut, limp on the floor.

Then his bony fingers gripped my right wrist, cold and strong as iron.

The skin contact should have jolted me hard, but I was so amped-up that I barely felt a prick. I expected the man to step away, dazed by my Touch...

... but to my horror, he leaned close, *completely unaffected*, grimacing with rage.

I cried out and slugged him with my other fist. The blow was awkward and I missed touching his face, but my sleeved forearm slammed his neck. Even through my long sleeve, his skin chilled me like ice.

He let go and clutched his neck, gasping. "You... are wanted..." he choked. "At the... highest levels..."

I hollered for my cat, but Charm was already crouched behind me, ready to make another lunge. I scooped him up, struggled for awful seconds with the door bolt, and then finally escaped into the hall.

I tripped again on my detestable heels, and this time I kicked them off and ran. My stocking feet pounded on the thin apartment carpet, but I didn't feel a thing. I was down two flights of stairs before I realized that my wrist felt wrong. It was hot. Burning.

I looked.

Where he'd wrapped his fingers, my skin was dark and mottled. Like cancer.

CHAPTER 4

For the first couple of hours, I just drove. South.

It was a long time before I calmed down.

With my phone dead, my cards maxed, and no cash, I was very thankful that "Grandma" had had the foresight to print out directions. Most of this trip was going to be highways, and after a solid hour or so of monotonous driving on the interstate, I started to feel normal enough to think again.

I glanced at Mr. Charm in the rearview mirror. He was cuddled in the backseat, a big white ball of comfy calm, watching the world with his usual lazy grace. As if nothing had happened.

Just looking at him eased my heart rate. I really do love that cat.

"Thank God he didn't mess with *you*," I said.

Mr. Charm blinked. His big blue eyes vanished into his cute black mask of facial fur, then opened again, bright as ever.

I took this as a sign of placid agreement. I like to tell myself that Mr. Charm tends to agree with me. Also that he likes to hear me talk.

Even in my frantic rush to get in my car, I'd checked the cat's neck where the creep had been holding him. The fur was white and pristine, with not a hint of hurt.

My wrist, however, still ached. I let my long sleeve hide it and I tried not to think about it, but every time the rash caught my eye, I creeped out.

Shouldn't I be going to the hospital? Or the police? What the heck was I doing?

I did finally stop at a rest area and call 911 on an ancient pay phone. This was my first time calling the police, and I felt super anxious, like I might say the wrong thing and they'd be like, *while we have you on the line, we're going to go ahead and pick you up for that jaywalking last Saturday.* The laconic dispatcher didn't help when he kept asking why I was reporting a "break-in" that was already hours ago and over a hundred miles away.

By the time I got off the phone, I had zero interest in going to some emergency room and talking to a fresh round of total strangers. I hate hospitals anyway. And it's not like I had health insurance anymore.

I'll be honest: a woman who ran an inn and called herself "Grandma" sounded about a million times better just then than any other alternative. I wanted to crawl into a cozy bed and have some nice old woman bring me milk and cookies. I know it sounds childish, but I'd never had anything like that in my life. Not even close.

I mean, seriously, I'd been *attacked*. In my own home. A normal person would go and stay for a few days with family. Friends. Someone.

The hard truth was... I had no one like that.

I kept crazy busy with work, and then spent it all faster than it came in. Not a great recipe for social connections. The few old friends who might really have cared, I hadn't talked to in years.

(To be fair... it definitely doesn't help a long-distance friendship when you can't get emotional without shorting out your phone.)

Over the years, I'd tried to find Mom's family, but I'd always drawn a complete blank. If this Grandma lady really could tell me how to find them... real *family*...

I might finally find home. For the first time.

Of course, a few concerns did nibble at the back of my mind.

I mean, aside from the obvious issue of *magic really exists, it's lethal, and some assassin magician dude is obsessed with making you his minion.*

There was that.

But even with Grandma's letter... why had she just *happened* to write me right *now?* With hints about *urgency* and *danger?*

Had she *known* that this creep would come find me? And if so... what did that even mean? Could she possibly be... dangerous?

Nonsense. No way. That was *preposterous.* Just look at the woman's handwriting!

Okay, yes, I *wanted* to believe that everything was going to be fine. Maybe I *needed* to believe it.

But I could still resolve to stay alert. Despite her stunning penmanship, this woman was a total stranger.

"Good thing I've got you," I said aloud, glancing in the mirror at Mr. Charm. "Who knew a Ragdoll could be so good in a fight?"

Mr. Charm purred.

Around D.C., I hit some truly epic traffic, but I finally escaped onto a highway heading west into Virginia. At first, it was a slow slog through nasty sprawl and even more traffic, but at last the road cleared, and I was roaming free between the gentle Blue Ridge mountains. Up north in Pennsylvania, the April weather had been chilly and brown and bare, lingering in late winter, but down here, the slopes were green with spring.

Following the printout, I took an exit onto a country road. It was a two-lane ribbon of pavement, and although it snaked and twisted along steep slopes, pickup trucks zoomed around me at highway speeds. The dented guardrails looked like they might not save a scooter, and every so often, a roadside cross with a wreath of fake flowers marked a fatal accident. So much for the calm countryside.

But the natural landscape *was* soothing. The sun was setting, bathing mountains and valleys in a golden glow, and the space and the sky opened around me like I could finally breathe.

"Are you seeing this, Charm?" I said. "There are so many trees in bloom... blossoms are *everywhere!* White, pink, purple..."

But he was asleep.

That was the only real downer with all this country expanse and beauty. All this space seemed a bit lonely.

Then I crested a ridge, and the sudden view caught my heart.

Below me, the road sloped down to a small river that was sparkling in the sunset. A two-lane covered bridge arched over the water, complete with a wooden roof. Across the bridge, on a gentle slope, sat the loveliest little town I'd ever seen.

I'd seen other small towns on the way here, and they were mostly depressing. The country highway would blast past a few cruddy franchises, a decaying church or two, and maybe a post office from the Truman Era and a courthouse from the Civil War. The places seemed haphazard, accidental, unloved... like the crook of a stream that gradually gathers trash.

This was different.

Even from afar, you could see for sure that someone loved Wonder Springs.

Of course, it helped that the place was a sheer riotous garden of tree blossoms. I recognized the ethereal clouds of dogwoods, both white and pink, but there were also those purple blossom trees I kept seeing along the road, and trees that drooped and swayed like willows, but cascaded with white blooms. There were other kinds of trees too, more than I could recognize at this distance—trees in bloom were truly everywhere, festooning every street.

The shops and houses blended a quaint old-fashioned style with immaculate upkeep; even from here, the stone walls and wood siding sparkled pristine. The wide main street seemed to be paved with brick, or even cobblestones. I couldn't tell for sure, but there wasn't a car in sight, only people walking peacefully, many holding hands.

At the far end of that street rose a matriarchal mansion, brooding over the town like a mother hen. The mansion was a paradise of nineteenth century whimsy, with crenellations and towers and high windows aglow.

That had to be the Inn.

I drove down the hill and across the covered bridge, and the roof above and the river below made it feel like some fairy passage, both inside and outside at once.

On the far side of the bridge, the road ended in the pedestrian mall I'd seen before. The main street really was cobblestone. A pretty welcome sign politely guided me to drive around to a side street, and I followed more signs down a few blocks to the Inn.

Even the side entrance where I parked was gorgeous. A wraparound porch with a low, sheltering roof seemed to shimmer with hospitality, as if the empty rocking chairs were just *begging* you to sit and share a sweet tea.

In fact, two figures were already sitting there in chairs. But the sun had softened into twilight, and what with the high porch railings and the bushes of azaleas that were just starting to open pink, I couldn't quite make them out. One of them wore a strange high hat, oddly shaped but vaguely familiar.

I pulled into a spot, parked, and grabbed the letter.

When I looked up, one of the porch people had risen, the one without the hat. She stepped toward me, showing the face of a woman in her early fifties, with wide, dark eyes and a bright smile. She didn't seem like a "Grandma"; it was possible, maybe, but something in her expression just seemed too young.

Her smile was so friendly that I popped open my door and jumped right out.

Behind me, Mr. Charm hissed.

Because out of nowhere, a huge bloodhound had shown up.

The thing was enormous; its head in particular was somehow too big, its massive nose a couple feet from my thigh. It was sniffing hard, growling, and glaring right at my face with eyes that were just *wrong*. Uncanny.

I froze and clutched my car door, gripping it like a shield. My heart was thudding hard... the creature was so *intense*.

From the porch, the woman's nice smile snapped into frustration. "Jake! Scat!" she called. "She's one of us!"

The dog glowered, but it backed off and trotted away into the twilight.

Which would have been a great cue to relax, except that now the *other* porch person stood. And he looked like freaking Gandalf.

That familiar high hat? It was a *wizard* hat. He had a white beard that billowed all the way to his waist. And though the woman wore a light spring dress, perfectly normal, this old dude was rocking a freaking *robe*.

They both came toward me, creaking off the porch.

I don't know about you, but for me, a big scary dog and a big tall bearded wizard dude are not my idea of a welcome committee.

"Hold up!" I called, still hiding behind my car door. "Stay back."

But the woman's hand flew to her heart, and she caught her breath. "Oh," she murmured, talking not to me but to Mr. Wizard. "Oh, she looks just like her."

"Like who?" I said. "Are you Grandma Meredith?"

"No, Summer," she said. "But—"

"How the hell do you know me?" I said. "Who are you? Stay back, I mean it!"

They both stopped, and she winced, like she'd had a sudden cramp. But she smoothed her face back into a smile and then spread her hands, palms up.

"Summer, please, you're safe here," she said. "Are you hurt? What happened?"

How had I ever thought this woman looked friendly? Her dark eyes were *earnest*, boring into me like she could see behind my deepest lies.

"I'm fine!" I snapped. "I mean, yes, some random magician broke into my apartment and might have given me skin cancer—"

"Magician?" rumbled the wizard wannabe, speaking for the first time.

"You *are* hurt!" the woman exclaimed. "Please, we can help—"

She stepped toward me, but I shouted again and waved her back. The gesture yanked my sleeve up my arm, exposing a full view of my injured wrist.

I gasped.

The rash was spreading down my arm. At least two or three more inches of skin were blotching purplish-black. Toward my heart.

And I'd been blocking out the pain, but now that I looked at it… my skin felt pricked by an itchy swarm of little needles of ice.

Both the wizard and the woman were grave with concern.

"We need Cade," the woman said.

The wizard frowned. "He won't—"

"He'll have to," she snapped.

"Who's Cade? Is he a doctor?" I said. Their obvious worry was freaking me out. "It wasn't like that this morning. I need to get to a hospital." I ducked back into my car and fumbled the key into the ignition.

"Summer! Wait!" the woman called. "Please! They won't know what to do."

I paused, my fingers trembling on the key.

The woman still stood at a distance in the twilight. Her palms were up, but her voice and her face were imploring.

"I'm so sorry, Summer, but there's no time," she said. "If you drive away, that could go to your heart."

I didn't want to trust her.

In that moment, this whole trip seemed like the stupidest, most reckless mistake I'd ever made.

But there was something about the way she said my name.

When you live alone, people don't really say your name that much. Not like that.

Then, from the backseat, Mr. Charm crawled into my lap, purring hard. I rubbed his warm, furry back, and my breathing slowed a bit.

I pulled out the key.

The woman exhaled in a massive sigh.

"What exactly do you all suggest?" I said, quietly.

"You need rest," she said.

"*Rest?*" I cried.

Beside her, Mr. Wizard spoke a single word in a low groan. "*Sleep.*"

A wave of exhaustion hit me like a smothering fog.

I fought it off, choosing not to analyze how the hell this could be happening. "What are you *doing?*" I snapped. I tried to jam the key back in, but my arm felt like lead and I could barely lift it. "This is better than the hospital? Some *nut* who likes to dress like Gandalf—"

The wizard raised his hands. "*SLEEP!*" he thundered.

I passed out.

CHAPTER 5

I woke up slowly, gradually feeling the sunshine on my face and the warmth on my chest from a quilt and Mr. Charm. I was looking up and out a window, into bright clouds and a sky of endless blue.

Then I freaked. WHERE WAS I?

I sat bolt upright, sending Mr. Charm flying. As always, he landed easily on his feet. Then, with an arch look my way, he scampered up a quaint old dresser and curled up in a basket bed that was pretty much adorable.

Actually, that went for the whole tiny, gorgeous room. It was like all the bed and breakfast selfies in the world had died and gone to heaven.

Seriously, the place was a Regency refuge. Hardwood floors, deep-silled windows with diamond-paned glass, pretty wallpaper and trim with tiny flowers… and one whole corner was a reading nook, with a built-in seat and shelves by a sunny window. You could curl up on that cushion and reach for any book you liked; the shelves were well-stocked with old hardcovers that looked scuffed and loved.

Usually, I'm more into people than books, but that nook called to me. The whole room was wooing me; this was edging perilously close to love at first sight. My apartment was packed with expensive decor in the finest taste, but this felt like home.

I fought the allure. "What happened, Charm?" I demanded. "Who are these people? Did you see anything?"

But the little luxuriating sybarite just curled up in his new boudoir. Great.

Then I remembered. My wrist! That rash!

I looked.

My wrist, my whole arm, was perfectly clean and smooth.

A memory flashed, confused and jumbled. Someone's hands were hovering over my wrist, not quite touching, but so close that my skin tingled with his warmth.

His warmth? Yes. The hands were male, strong but also gentle, and his voice was soothing and low.

Then I got another flash, a glimpse of his face. His eyes were so... *kind*... and he was both scruffily handsome and also watching me with total selfless concern. Talk about a combo to make you ache.

Three sharp knocks destroyed my reverie.

"Summer?" said a crisp, mature woman on the far side of the door. Her voice was Southern, but aristocratic, and even in that single word, she was soft as sweet tea and hard as nails. "Summer, it's Grandma Meredith."

I jumped out of bed, heart pounding. I caught a glimpse of myself in a full-length mirror and winced. I was still in my stupid dress suit! I was glad that no one had messed with me, but they could at least have taken off the jacket. The wrinkles were hopeless; I looked like a used lunch bag, and I didn't even want to think about how I smelled. Oh, and I had no shoes, of course, and standing there in my stocking feet made me feel about twelve.

I ran my fingers through my wild disaster of hair, hoping no passing birds would try to nest.

"Summer?" she repeated, with a harder edge.

"Come in!" I squeaked. I cleared my throat and tried to sound more like a grownup. "I'm ready!"

Maybe *ready* was optimistic.

The door opened, and in strode Grandma.

What struck me first were her eyes. Large, light, and striking, they were still and calm, yet they seemed to take in everything at a glance.

She was short and old, but crackling with energy. At first, I pegged her in her early sixties, but on a second look, I couldn't be sure. She might be in her seventies, or even eighties. It didn't seem to matter.

Her outfit was both super practical and super flattering on her trim frame. Her short and styled hair was dyed a graceful light blonde, and her makeup job was amazing. But it was all accents; she wasn't hiding her age like some injected celebrity. Age was irrelevant.

Not quite the comfy old darling I'd imagined. No milk or cookies in sight.

Behind her came a woman who looked younger than me. She had cascades of jet-black hair, and her cute bangs bounced over wide, dark, laughing eyes. Her heart-shaped face was bright with a perky smile; she had one of those faces that *had* to smile.

"Hi!" she chirped, and she actually waved.

Then, as she looked me over, her eyes went even wider with delight. She covered her mouth and basically squealed. "Oh my *gosh!* Look at you!" She raised her arms and rushed toward me for a tackle hug.

"Tina!" Grandma snapped.

The woman, apparently Tina, stopped short in surprise. She stood between me and Grandma, looking back and forth in confusion. Then her face cleared, like she was remembering something, and she sadly lowered her arms.

We all stared at each other.

Wait. Had this Grandma woman stopped that hug because she *knew*? About… my Touch?

No way. I was not going to go there. I really, really needed these people *not* to be on Team Magical Creep.

Of course, Grandma could have found out some *other* way than whatever magicky method Mr. Plant Killer had had at his disposal. But that option was almost worse. Wasn't I safer if you needed *magic* to know my big secret?

Anyway, whether she knew or not, she clearly hadn't lured me down here to trap me in an underground government lab or whatever so I could spend the rest of my life getting tested to death. (I hadn't really worried about that scenario since high school, but let's face it, I can wipe short-term memories. Imagine the potential uses that a government would see for "enhanced interrogation." When I'd first realized what might happen if I ever got caught, I'd had insomnia for weeks.)

Whatever the *real* reason was that this woman had asked me down here, I was going to focus on what she'd promised. The truth about my mother's family.

And, I hoped with a fervent ache, whatever I'd need to find them.

"So," I said. "I got your letter."

"I gathered that," she said, with a twitch of a smile.

"Should I call you 'Grandma'?"

"Certainly," she said. "Everyone calls me 'Grandma.'"

"Grandma!" cried Tina.

"See?"

"But you are *my* Grandma," Tina said, in a plaintive tinkle.

"True enough, child," Grandma said, with her first slight hint of affection.

To my shame, the corners of my eyes misted, threatening sudden hot tears. Wow... apparently I was feeling the lack of family support even harder than I'd realized. Was I that fragile?

I mean, it's not like I was hundreds of miles from home, the day after a freak attack, with total strangers who might know my deepest secret, or anything.

Watching me, Tina winced.

Oh, please, I thought, and the anger helped me get back in control. *Stop trying so hard to be nice.*

Or maybe she really *was* that nice. Like it wasn't already enough to be such a cute and gushy Southern belle that, even though she was wearing a regulation employee polo shirt and khakis, any male in the surrounding square mile would succumb to an instant crush.

I guess that sounds awful. But she *was* the one in the room with an actual grandmother. It's just hard when people make it look effortless. She probably had a high metabolism, too.

"May I see your wrist?" Grandma said.

"Oh! Sure," I said, like this was a completely normal routine when two people first meet. I pulled back the rumpled sleeve of my jacket, and both Grandma and Tina studied my smooth wrist with care.

"It's perfect," Tina breathed. "I *knew* he'd be amazing."

"Indeed," Grandma said, but she flicked Tina a sharp glance, and the younger woman fell silent.

Turning to me, Grandma said, "Thank you. And how are you feeling?"

"Oh, I'm fine," I said. "Mainly just... curious."

"I'm sure," Grandma said. "We have a great deal to discuss, Summer. But if you don't mind, may I first ask you to tell us how you came by that injury? I want to ensure that you've received proper care. The details matter."

I hesitated. It was surreal, this professional "bed and breakfast" lady asking me about a magical wound with the same calm seriousness as if she were taking a customer complaint about the service. I still resisted trusting her, but after all, my wrist was perfectly clear. If she wanted to know the details, I at least owed her that much.

As quickly as I could, I gave them a play-by-play of yesterday's encounter. I liberally paraphrased what the man had said—I didn't need to actually *tell* them about the Touch—but I did leave in his grandiose ramblings about my Great Work and Fate. Both Grandma and Tina listened with serious attention to everything I said, but at the bits about being "wanted at the highest levels," they both looked especially grim.

I also didn't see the need to get into the backstory of how I'd, you know, just quit my sales job.

Somehow, standing in this luxurious room in an Inn that was bound to be enchanting, I felt that the proprietor might be less than sympathetic with my choice. If Grandma Meredith had been in my shoes, I was pretty sure that she'd have beaten Nyle for that promotion... and she'd probably be running the company.

When I finished, there was a long pause.

And my stomach chose that moment to rumble like a dying hog.

"My goodness! Where are my manners?" Grandma said. "You haven't eaten since yesterday afternoon, at least! Come along down to the dining room and let us give you a proper welcome."

"Oh, that's all right," I said, though now that I thought of it, my stomach was aching with hunger. "I can wait. I'd really rather—"

"You're starving," Tina said. "I can tell."

"Really?" I said. Her certainty was slightly unnerving.

Grandma flicked Tina another strange little glance, and Tina said smoothly, "Sure! I see hungry people all day long. I work in the dining room. And sometimes the front desk. All over the Inn, really. Wherever I'm needed."

"Speaking of which," Grandma said. "We'd better go down and see how Hamish is holding up. We're getting on to the breakfast rush, and we've got a huge party this morning, a whole family reunion." She started walking toward the bedroom door.

"Wait!" I said. "You can't just... I mean, what *is* this place? How did you heal my wrist? I *passed out* last night. From this creepy wannabe wizard—"

Tina snorted. Even her snorts were adorable.

"That's just Uncle Barnaby," she said. "He's an—"

"Eccentric," Grandma said.

"He does say the hat helps him focus," Tina said.

"*Tina*," Grandma snapped, with a sharp twang.

Tina tried to look repentant, but her eyes sparkled.

Grandma turned to me with a courteous smile. "I assure you, Ms. Sassafras," she said, and her voice was honey-smooth, "you are due for a long and most enlightening conversation. But not on an empty stomach. Allow me to offer you a complimentary welcome to the finest dining in Wonder Springs."

At the word "complimentary," I relaxed a bit. As you may recall, my cards were maxed out, and my purse had about forty-seven cents.

"Thank you," I said. "But—"

"Excellent," Grandma said, and strode for the door.

Then I looked down and wailed. "Oh *no!*"

In the doorway, Grandma turned back and frowned. "Yes?"

I quailed a bit. Clearly, Grandma Had Spoken, and she was used to getting her way.

So was I.

"My *shoes*," I said, firmly. "I can't walk around in my stockings."

"Hmm," Grandma said, and she eyed my feet with grudging agreement. "Tina can take you past the Lost and Found. We have an astonishing supply of abandoned sneakers."

"Sneakers?" I said. "With *this* outfit?"

But she had already strode away.

"Is she always like that?" I asked Tina.

"Oh no," Tina said. She winked. "Sometimes she gets bossy."

"Tina, listen," I said. "You've *got* to fill me in here."

"I know, I know," she said. "I can't *imagine* what this must be like for you. But I know Grandma. She'll want you properly fed, and us past this morning rush, so we can all give this conversation our full focus. You know?"

"Not really," I said. "I've been trying to find my mom's family for, like, my whole adult life. Can't she just give me a name and address?"

"Oh, *no*," Tina said, horrified. "That would be awful, Summer. It's... it's really complicated."

"Great," I said. "I get it. They're all dead."

Tina laughed. "You're a real optimist," she said.

"So they *are* dead?"

"No! I mean, I don't know *all* the details..." Tina groaned in frustration. "Can we *please* just get some food in you? You are *so* hungry. Seriously, I can *feel* it."

She fixed me with those dark eyes. Playful, but pleading.

I sighed. "Fine."

"Hooray!" she said, completely free of irony, and practically glowing with happiness. "Oh, Summer. I'm *so* glad you're here."

"Um," I said. "Thanks."

Did she expect me to reciprocate with a mutual gush? I'd known this woman for less than fifteen minutes.

Right then, Mr. Charm perked up, and he leapt lightly to the floor.

"Oh my gosh!" Tina said. "Your cat!"

"Careful," I said. "He's sketchy around..."

But he was twining around Tina's legs, purring like a motorcycle.

"... strangers," I said.

"OH MY GOSH, he's ADORABLE!!" she gushed. She scooped up Mr. Charm and nuzzled his neck. Huh. That cat had always resisted nuzzling... with me. Now, in Tina's arms, if he tried to purr any louder, his ribs were going to crack.

"Traitor," I said. Then I caught myself and flashed Tina my best fake smile. "I'm totally joking."

"Oh no... you're *not*," she said, with infuriating compassion. She reached out to touch my arm, then awkwardly stopped herself and tried to fake like she'd meant to pet Charm. "Anyway, I *love* your cat, but we'd better hurry. Let's get you *both* some food."

And she walked off, carrying *my* cat.

I padded after her on the cool smooth floor, smoldering with pet envy and my growling empty stomach.

But as she led me through a fantastic warren of old halls and stairs and nooks and corners, I pretty much forgot to be mad.

Every room in the Inn was unique. I'd walk through a light-filled ballroom with a dome ceiling and a glittering bank of windows, then cut through a low cozy tavern room made *entirely* of brick: the walls, the floor, and even the ancient built-in hearth. The Inn seemed to have grown by fits and starts across time warps, like an English manor house. You could live here for decades, and never reach the end of its secrets.

The place had a kind of beauty magic. I'd spent my short adult life thus far in bleak conference rooms and offices and gridlock, but here it was all hardwood and brick and windows you could actually *open*, to cool spring air and the scent of blossoms.

And as we walked into a wide, tiled lobby, heading toward a hall with the oaken doors of the dining room, that scent was enriched with the luscious aromas of *breakfast:* the bite of bacon and the waft of fresh bread, the seductive promises of dark coffee and the forbidden delights of… *pancakes*.

How long had it been since I'd allowed my low metabolism to indulge in such a perilous feast?

"Wait here," Tina said, slipping behind the front desk with Charm still in her arms. "I'll be *right* back." And she vanished through a door into a back office.

The front desk here on the main floor was like a time travel machine to a classic movie. I half expected to see Humphrey Bogart and Ingrid Bergman trading sultry quips at the wooden counter, or a mysterious shady figure sneaking a note into one of the cubbies on the wall behind the desk.

I wasn't thrilled to be standing around basically barefoot in public, literally salivating outside the gates of breakfast paradise. But before I could get *too* frantic with hunger, Tina emerged. Instead of my cat, whom she had presumably deposited safely with some gourmet meal, she carried a pair of sneakers with roughly the appeal of bowling shoes.

"Sorry," she said. "It's all we had in your size."

"It's fine," I said, resigned. It wasn't like I was going to know anyone. And I slipped on the hideous sneakers and hustled after Tina into the airy, oak-paneled dining room.

Where I promptly spotted Nyle Pritchett.

Yes, *that* Nyle Pritchett. The bug-eyed tool with the styled beard who'd stolen my promotion.

Right here in Wonder Springs.

CHAPTER 6

My mind reeled. This couldn't be happening.
What the *heck* was Nyle *Pritchett* doing *HERE???*
The odds were... unfathomable. I stared, transfixed, fighting to persuade myself that it must be some *other* middle-aged white dude who thought he could still pull off thigh-high khaki shorts on the weekend.

"WAITER?" Nyle bellowed, in his wheedling whine, trying to get the attention of a lone, gaunt waiter who was drooping over a nearby couple like a depressed vulture. "HELLO?" Nyle added, and he actually *snapped*.

Okay, that was definitely Nyle. Crud.

Ahead of me, Tina startled and turned back. "Summer? Are you okay? What's wrong?"

What was *wrong?* What was I supposed to say to *that?*

Oh, nothing, nothing at all... except the guy who just *humiliated* me and *torpedoed* my career just *happens* to be RANDOMLY HERE, of all possible places on Planet Earth! No biggie!

Wait, wait... he was *here*... oh *crud*...

If he saw me, he might freak out too. He might start talking. That would be bad.

I'd avoided telling Grandma and Tina about my quitting for a reason. The situation had been... complex.

If Nyle started braying all the gory details... yeah, no. Not going to happen. I could totally see Grandma revoking her "complimentary" breakfast and booting me right out on my broke backside. At a minimum.

I had to avoid him seeing me. No matter what.

Even as I thought that, Nyle twitched at his table across the room, and began to sweep a glance that was coming right for me.

"What's *wrong*? Nothing!" I chirped at Tina, with manic cheeriness, as I twisted my back to Nyle and tried to position Tina between us. "I *love* this *room!*" I gushed. "Look what you've done with this... corner!"

I scurried toward the corner table that was farthest from Nyle. In a snug, paneled nook that was lit by an old sconce, a mousy blond woman sat alone, fiddling with a laptop.

"The corner?" Tina said, confused.

"Sure!" I said. "So few decorators understand the importance of—*GYAH, you look just like him!*"

That last bit came out as a shriek, and the mousy blond jerked up and stared at me in shock.

This only gave me a more thorough view of her face, which, as I had shrieked, looked *just like Nyle*. The bulging eyes... the thin, sallow cheeks... they could have been brother and sister.

How was this possible? Was I losing my mind?

"Who does she look like?" Tina asked me, at the same time giving the woman a reassuring nod, like, *Hi, we're normal! And it is totally okay that my friend here just walked up and yelled at you.* "Someone you know?"

"Yes. No! Just... that guy." I jerked a nod back toward Nyle, who was now waving his arms at the waiter like a castaway at sea. "Sorry," I added, with a contrite glance at the blond. "I just... happened to notice a resemblance. Startling."

"Oh, you mean Nyle?" Tina said. She giggled in a high, merry tinkle of glee. "Of *course* Kitty here looks like Nyle. So does half the room. It's the Pritchett family reunion."

"*What?*" I gasped.

My disbelief tilted into nightmare. It was true.

There were *more* Nyles. Wherever I looked, Nyle, Nyle, *Nyle*…

At the nearest table to Nyle sat an older, heavier Nyle clone, arguing with a woman who was either his wife or his irate boss. Probably both. At another table, a late middle-aged clone had attempted to hide the awful family resemblance with an extra twenty years and a bushy mustache, but to no avail. The Nyle stamp remained blinding. Finally, I spotted a young, horse-faced edition in a black turtleneck, who was hovering by the empty hostess stand and eyeing Tina as if he hoped she might come over. (Of course.)

Maybe that old magician creep had actually killed me. I wasn't sure what I believed about the afterlife, but if it was going to involve torture, this was looking excessively appropriate.

"This is the first year we've had the Pritchetts," Tina went on, chatting as if the three of us were old friends. "But I can *totally* see why Nyle caught your eye. Quite a looker."

I gaped. She was serious.

The laptop woman—Kitty?—cringed a little, then gave me a smirk. "Please don't let her near him," she said. "His ego's already the size of Texas."

"I know," I said. "I mean, I'm sure. With that… beard, and all."

"You have no idea," Kitty said. "I should know. I'm his cousin."

"I'm sorry," I said.

She shrugged. "Family's family, right?"

"Sure," I said.

Great. Nyle *also* had a devoted extended family. Of course he did.

Just then, the horse-faced Early Twenties Nyle clone strode up. He wore trendy glasses with those thick frames that are considerably cooler in moody stock photos than in real life, and his black turtleneck hinted that he either thought he was the next Steve Jobs or else he'd just never learned how to knot a tie.

"Need some technical assistance?" he blared down at Kitty. "I've got data on my phone."

He pulled out a *gargantuan* phone—had that thing been in his pocket? He was going to need a hip replacement by the time he was thirty.

"Thanks, I've got it," Kitty said, in a strained voice. "The wifi here should be fine for a video call." She gave Tina and me a tired smile. "Aunt Delilah couldn't make it."

"Oh, that's so sweet of you to call her!" Tina said.

The tech guy made a show of "seeing" Tina, like he hadn't happened to stand right next to her. "You again!" he brayed. "Are you following me around?"

Tina *giggled*.

What was *wrong* with this woman?

The tech genius, grinning at his own prowess, turned back to Kitty and leaned toward the laptop. "Are you sure you've got that data? You need to click the little icon—"

"Bryce!" barked a testy old woman's voice from the screen. "Get back from the camera! Your nose hairs are the size of pipe cleaners!"

He jolted back, flushing red to his tight black collar.

Tina blushed too.

The tech dude turned to me, unconsciously pulling at his nose. "So!" he said, with blustery fake confidence. "What do *you* do?"

"Sales," I said, without thinking.

"*Really*," he said, glancing at Tina as if this were one more magical connection they shared. "That's so funny, my cousin *Nyle* is in sales. And he just got promoted." He turned toward the center of the room and raised his arm. "Hey, Nyle—"

"No, no!" I blurted, and I pressed his arm back down.

To my surprise, even through the fabric of his long turtleneck sleeve, an odd energy prickled into my skin. It wasn't as strong as the jolt I'd have gotten with skin contact, but it was more than I expected through a sleeve.

That was weird.

But this was no time to ruminate on the vagaries of the Touch. I started backing away, keeping my back toward the center and Nyle.

"It's been *lovely* meeting you both," I said. "But Tina promised to feed me."

"Don't worry, I will," Tina said, with a longing look around me, presumably toward Nyle. "But we *could* just say *hi—*"

"Tina!" I snapped, still backing away.

Tina frowned.

From the laptop, the voice of Aunt Delilah crackled, "Who are you all talking to?"

"Sorry, Aunt Delilah!" Tina chirped, popping in front of the screen and waving. "Hi, I'm Tina!"

"Well, *hello* there, darling," Aunt Delilah said, warmly.

Tina bid both Kitty and Bryce a cheerful goodbye, smothered one last giggle at Bryce, and then pranced over to me.

"Thanks," she said to me, as we walked across the room. "I needed that."

"What?" I said. "Look, I know we just met, but I have serious concerns about your taste in men."

"I know, right?" she said, and she walked a bit faster. "Don't worry, I just need to get some distance. It'll pass."

"Distance? What are you *talking* about?" I said.

"Nothing. Sorry," she said. "Did you know you're walking backwards?"

"Tina!" snapped Grandma Meredith, who somehow materialized right behind me. I jumped, and I nearly crashed into her, which would have been bad, because both her arms were loaded with plates full of food. "Hamish is floundering," Grandma said. "I need you out there."

"Right," Tina said, with a glance at the gaunt waiter, who was now drooping over the older gray Pritchett with the mustache. "But what about Summer?"

"I'm fine!" I said. "I just want to hide in the bathroom. *Go* to the bathroom. Where's your bathroom?"

"The hall by the kitchen," Grandma said, with a curt nod across the room.

"Perfect! Thanks!" I said, and I backed away in the exact opposite direction, so I wouldn't have to walk past Nyle.

Both Tina and Grandma watched me go, nonplussed.

I worked my ridiculous way around the wide, busy room, turning to walk forwards as soon as I could. I made it to an archway in the far wall, which opened into a dark hallway. The far end of the hallway led to the kitchen door; I could hear dishes clanking and some dude bellowing in what sounded like Russian. (Russian?) The near end offered a quaint door with "RESTROOM" painted with a flowery script and ivy. I dove in and locked the door.

Safe.

Maybe I could just stay here. Until Nyle left. And/or I died.

"This doesn't mean you win, dude," I muttered. "Just because you got the promotion. And I quit. And now I'm hiding in a bathroom."

I sighed, avoiding my reflection in the little round mirror.

It was the kind of moment where one reflects upon certain life choices.

Also on creepy magicians breaking into your apartment, being immune to your Touch, and giving you accelerated skin cancer. And total strangers knocking you unconscious and healing you overnight.

"Breathe, Summer," I said. "You can do this. All that really matters is finding your family. You get those addresses out of Grandma, you win. You get home. All the rest of this weirdness can fade away."

Would this Grandma Meredith woman *really* refuse to tell me about my family if Nyle recognized me and started mouthing off? Maybe I was being paranoid, but after the last twenty-four hours, I was no longer placing bets on the universe acting sane.

She'd called that wizard guy "eccentric", but despite her polished exterior and aggressive Southern charm, I knew in my bones that Grandma Meredith herself was more "eccentric" than all the rest of her clan put together.

She had her own strange reasons why she'd written me out of nowhere, and she was clearly bent on keeping them secret. The slightest glitch might reverse her decision.

Hiding in the bathroom wasn't such an awful plan.

Thud. Thud. Thud.

Three dread knocks exploded the silence.

"You are kidding me," I muttered. "Watch this be Nyle."

It was not. It was the Sheriff.

CHAPTER 7

And I do mean *Sheriff*, with a capital S, all decked out in the full Sheriff Regalia. His righteous gray mustache could probably halt a bank robbery all on its own. The man might even have been handsome once behind that stern glare, but age and beer were taking their toll.

I might not have thought a tiny town like Wonder Springs would even *need* a sheriff. But he stood here now in the dark hallway with his arms crossed, glowering down over his massive chest. From his expression, you'd have thought he'd just caught me in there cooking meth.

And yet… something about his face was strangely familiar. Which was disturbing.

"Bathroom's all yours," I said.

"Much obliged," he said. "And you are?"

"Um, Summer?" I said. And then, keeping up the pretense that this was an actual social introduction, I added, "Nice to meet you…" I checked his nameplate, and I caught my breath.

His name was *Jake*.

Like the bloodhound last night.

With the weird, uncanny eyes. Eyes which, as I looked closer at this strange old man…

He frowned. "Is there a problem?"

"No! Sorry." I really *was* losing my mind. Yesterday morning, the very *idea* of a…. of a what? shape-shifting man-dog?…

wouldn't even have *occurred* to me. I needed to eat something. And maybe sleep for a week.

"Hmm," the sheriff said.

And then he *sniffed*. Like, way harder than ordinary people use their nose, however prominent.

"Hey!" I snapped. "I didn't have time to shower!"

"Excuse me?" he said, confused.

"Never mind," I said. I strode away toward the archway, but as I stepped into the light of the dining room, I remembered about Nyle and ducked back into the shadows.

Then I realized that the Sheriff had been watching me. He cocked a bushy eyebrow.

"Hmmmm," he said again, and he lumbered into the bathroom and closed the door.

"Great," I muttered. Oh well. How much harm could some random suspicious sheriff do to me? I'd be out of Wonder Springs by nightfall, as soon as Grandma Meredith told me what she knew.

For now, I just needed to get out of this freaking dining room.

But Nyle was all animated, waving his arms and arguing with the woman at his table. I hadn't noticed her before; I couldn't see her face, but her hairstyle seemed edgy for corporate Nyle—dark and long on top and pinned back, but with the sides shaved short and dyed... hot pink?

Anyway, whatever he was arguing about, he was looking all over the place. If I tried to make a break for the entrance, odds were high he'd spot me.

I was trapped.

And any second, that stupid sheriff was going to lumber out from the john and... what, arrest me for loitering?

Relax, Summer. Sometimes, even sheriffs just had to use the bathroom.

Even snuffly, suspicious sheriffs who'd probably come out and insist on standing there, and asking me a bunch more questions, and attracting Nyle's eye...

This was truly getting ludicrous.

But then, over a matter of seconds... almost every diner in the room turned toward the entrance.

I did too, and I forgot about Nyle.

The Matriarch had arrived.

I had never stopped to wonder how Nyle's face would look on a woman who'd had an extra fifty years or so to layer scowl wrinkles and overeat. Now I knew.

She crossed the room slowly on thick legs, huffing like a dowager processing at a royal wedding. When she finally eased herself into a seat, there was a collective exhalation of relief.

She swept the room with a gaze like that flaming eyeball tower in *Lord of the Rings*. When she spotted the gaunt Hamish, she skewered him with a glare, and she didn't even have to call him, because he was already trotting over like a disgraced puppy.

The closer he got to this woman, the deeper she scowled. By the time he reached her table, I thought her face might implode.

"What can I get you?" he bleated, with a solicitous droop.

"The chef," she bellowed, in a piercing bray that filled the crowded room.

"To *eat?*" he blurted.

"I wish to speak *directly* to the *chef*," she announced. "I will *not* entrust my digestion to the mental capacity of anyone working for half the minimum wage."

He gaped.

"Now!" she barked.

Hamish the waiter skittered away. I couldn't see where he went, but the next thing I knew, the massive chef exploded from the kitchen door and barreled right toward me.

"This is joke!" he growled, as I leapt sideways to dodge the man. He covered his face in thick fingers, growling further expostulations that I was probably glad were in Russian. But he dropped his hands as he lurched through the archway into the light, unleashing a forced, beefy smile that was fairly ghastly.

As the ancient Pritchett berated the chef with her order in endless, exquisite detail, I watched in utter fascination.

The woman could easily be in her eighties or nineties, which meant she was probably Nyle's aunt, maybe even his grandmother. The German word *schadenfreude* bubbled up from some long-ago course I'd taken in college: the pleasure of savoring another person's pain. I had to admit that I was enjoying this. For all his lucky breaks, Nyle seemed to have inherited one truly horrific grandmother.

As she droned on, something unsettling happened.

A faint tingle prickled along the hairs of my arm. I startled, assuming someone had touched me.

"Hello?" I blurted.

But I stood alone in the empty hallway.

The sheriff still hadn't emerged from the bathroom. At the other end, the kitchen sounded silent; without the chef clattering around in there, the emanating quiet was bizarrely unnerving.

No one could have touched me.

Whatever, I must have imagined it. I needed to get out of here.

Besides, I could see that Nyle was just as engrossed in the chef drama as I had been. It was the perfect time to sneak out and make my escape from this dining room before he saw me.

I edged out, working my way around the back of the room toward the entrance. I almost made it, too.

But I got snagged by Grandma.

"Summer!" she said, dashing in between me and the door with full plates balanced literally up to her shoulder. "I am so sorry to ask you this, but it's a madhouse this morning. I need another pair of hands. Would you go see Vladik and take those last plates?"

"Vladik?" I said, bewildered.

"The chef!" She nodded back across the room, to a wide, low window in the back wall that opened into the chaos of the kitchen. A jutting metal counter held several full plates.

"Oh," I said. "Um..."

Grandma squinted. "Is that a problem?"

"No! Totally fine," I said. "Glad to help."

"Excellent," she said. "You're a peach." And she shimmered away.

I fast-walked back to the metal counter, basically staring at the wall to hide my face. As I approached, I could see (and hear) that Vladik the chef had been released and was back thrashing around his kitchen. I tentatively reached for the nearest plate.

"No touch!" he roared. "Is not for you!"

"I'm not trying to *eat* it," I snapped, although despite the man's rudeness, the scent of his handiwork was certainly torturing my empty stomach. "Grandma told me to take these out."

"Is true?" he said, and he raked a skeptical glance down my wrinkled dress suit. Then he jabbed a thick finger at the two rightmost plates. "Those two. Getting cold. Table ten."

"Um," I said, looking around the room. "I don't see any numbers—"

Vladik burst out in a torrent of Russian, eyes raised to heaven, like Tevye imploring what he'd done to deserve such torment. At last he pointed out to the diners. "Right there," he growled. "Man with beard."

"Oh," I said. "*Oh.* You know, I think Tina wanted to do this one—"

"Pink hair lady," he snapped. "*Go!*"

A few tables away, I caught Grandma watching us as she lowered plates. Her face was a mask, utterly without expression.

Was this some kind of test? What was *up* with this woman?

"Unbelievable," I muttered. But I grabbed the two plates and marched right to Nyle's table.

I told myself to relax. I'd eaten out with Nyle. The guy hardly looked at the wait staff. This would be over in ten seconds.

I clanked down the plates. "Enjoy your meal!" I gasped, at double speed—I'd considered disguising my voice, but it wound up happening anyway—and I turned to sprint away. See? Done. I had totally nailed it—

Except, I tripped.

Yes. For real. The freaking shoelaces had come undone.

I hate sneakers.

I tried to scramble up, but Nyle's bony hand had already closed around my sleeve. As he half-yanked me to my feet, asking if I was all right, a strange minor jolt rippled through my sleeve, like I'd felt with his cousin Bryce. But given that his huge eyes were bulging at me like ping pong balls, another weird jolt was the least of my concerns.

"*Summer?*" Nyle shrieked, and all the surrounding diners startled and stared. "What are you *doing* here?"

Not far behind him, Grandma gasped in surprise.

CHAPTER 8

There were several ways I could have played this.

Here's what I went with.

"Summer?" I said, sounding confused. "Oh! You must mean my twin! Ha!"

I'm not going to say I'm proud of it.

"Twin?" Nyle said, baffled.

"No worries," I said. "Happens *all* the time. It's fine, I'm flattered. She's the hot one, really—"

"Summer, you don't have a *twin*," he said. "You gripe about being an only child at least once a week."

"Oh," I said. "Wait, did she say that? The *nerve*—"

"Do you know this woman?" said a deep, throaty voice. It was the woman sitting at his table; I'd been so laser-focused on Nyle that I'd barely noticed her.

Now I almost blasted out laughing, because she was such an absurd mismatch.

Not only was she lean, and attractive, and no older than her early thirties (so, at least ten years younger than he was), she was also *wild*. From the front, that combo of dark long hair and pink short sides looked even more rocking, and her makeup was dark and defiant. She wasn't exactly a Goth, but she could easily be a punk rocker, just starting to age out but still looking good.

I checked for a ring. What? She had a rock the size of the Epcot Center. Nyle had a *fiancee* who looked like *this?* Come *on.*

Maybe he'd sold his soul to the devil. No… by now, the devil would have wanted a refund.

"Of course I know this woman! We work together," Nyle told her. "I mean, we did. Yesterday, she quit."

Grandma frowned, with deep displeasure.

I knew it.

"How do you already have a new job?" Nyle asked me. He stepped away from me and back toward his seat, looking me up and down with growing distaste. "You didn't even *change*."

"Okay, look," I snapped. "I have had a *very* long twenty-four hours."

"Clearly," he said. "Did you… did you *follow* me? I didn't even tell anyone at the office I was coming here."

"*Follow* you?" I cried. "Oh my gosh, *really*? You think I would lose a promotion we *both* know should have been *mine* and then I'd *follow* you down to *Virginia* so I could, what, beg you to gloat?"

"So this is actually your next career move?" he said. "A waitress? In… rural Virginia? Huh." He shrugged his scarecrow shoulders, and he sat down to his plate. "I can see it," he said, with a sneer.

That's really what did it.

Very few people can pull off a legit, blood-boiling sneer of utter contempt. The kind of look that makes you feel like they're watching you clean out their toilet with your own toothbrush, and they're looking forward to seeing you brush your teeth after. It's a rare talent. Nyle was a master.

But it also didn't help that his gorgeous fiancee looked up from her phone and said, "Oh wait, it's the *promotion* girl? The one who was cheating the clients with dementia?"

Behind her, Grandma's eyes went wide.

"I did not *cheat* anyone!" I said.

"No, it was just *coincidence*," Nyle said smoothly, as he picked up his fork and started to dig in to some unholy custom special order of eggs and bacon and white sauce. "We just *happened* to have to cancel half your contracts in the last six months, because clients kept calling and saying they didn't fully remember reading what they'd signed."

"It's not my fault they had a few senior moments," I snapped. "That's not *dementia*."

Of course, they hadn't really been "senior moments" either.

That's the problem with the Touch. You get two or three hours into one of these epic sales meetings with a risk-averse bureaucrat, and it's like, we both know you're planning to sign this. Can we just pretend we *already* did the extra five hours of "due diligence" to cover your butt?

Maybe I'm being too vague here. To be one hundred percent clear: yes, I'd started wiping people's short-term memories to close deals. (Also lying. Slightly.)

Especially in the last few months, when I'd *finally* started to close in on this tool's numbers. After years of watching him win.

Am I proud to admit this? Not at all.

But in my defense...

... um...

Hmm. I used to have something. It'll come to me.

"You can call them 'senior moments' if you want," Nyle said, talking through a mouthful and chewing with gusto. "Point is, the rest of us seem to hit our targets without taking advantage of mental lapses."

"You *trained* me to take every advantage I could!" I snapped. "You had me read *The Art of War!*" Which was true.

Nyle's eyes flicked toward his fiancee, but he didn't look at me, just shoveled another bite and shrugged. "I don't remember saying that."

At the next table, Nyle's heavier alter ego and his wife/boss were openly staring at me, and I could feel the glares of others around the room. I probably only had seconds before Grandma or even Sheriff Jake escorted me out the door, but I didn't care. This guy was going to walk away with my career; the least I could do was wreck his precious breakfast.

"I was finally going to kick your skinny butt," I said. "And you *knew* it."

"Maybe," said Nyle. He met my eye and cracked another sneer, this time with bacon bits stuck between his teeth. "But you quit. So now we'll never know. And I'd like to finish my breakfast in peace."

"I hope you choke on it!" I spluttered.

He grinned, swallowed, and forked a giant mouthful.

Then he frowned. His face creased with a spasm of pain, like he'd suffered a sudden cramp and expected imminent intestinal difficulties.

"Nyle?" said his fiancee, sharp and frightened. "Nyle, what's wrong?"

But Nyle writhed, sucked one harsh gasp, and then pitched forward onto his plate. The dish clattered, and then was still.

At the sound of the crash, everyone in the dining room went silent and stared. Slowly, his gray beard began to sop up the wet remains of eggs and sauce.

Then everyone went nuts.

People were yelling, screaming, crashing out of their chairs to get close or get away. A ring of stricken Nyle clones surrounded me, hemmed me in, everyone talking at once.

"Did he choke? Is he choking?" bawled the wife/boss. Her beady eyes were raking across my face, and her breath was onion sour. "I heard you tell him to choke!"

"I didn't... he's not..." I stammered. Shock made me stupid; I was still staring at the back of Nyle's head, willing him to sit the hell up and quit freaking us out.

"He didn't choke," growled Sheriff Jake, as he shouldered his way in through the ring.

The family went quiet as he bent over Nyle, nostrils flaring, and sniffed hard with that huge nose. He sniffed around his head, then bent further and got several deep whiffs of the demolished breakfast.

"Should I take that... plate?" I said, on some obscure idiotic impulse, the Worst Substitute Waitress to the last.

"Don't touch *anything*," he barked. "This is a crime scene."

"Crime? I don't understand—"

"This man is dead," said Sheriff Jake. "And my best guess is poison."

Nyle's family murmured in surprise and shock. *Poison? Nyle? How can he tell it's POISON?*

"We'll need tests to confirm, of course," the sheriff announced. "But if he *was* poisoned..." The sheriff fixed me with a piercing glare. Softly, he said, "Now I wonder who could have done that."

I froze. "You don't... you can't actually think that *I* would..."

He did.

PART II

CHAPTER 9

Sheriff Jake scowled hard over that massive mustache. He looked ready to arrest me right there in the dining room, surrounded by the stares of irate relatives and Nyle's marinating corpse.

Panic tightened in my chest. The creep who'd grabbed Charm and tried to give me skin cancer had been bad enough, but this was The Law, a whole new level of threat. I couldn't just slug a sheriff and run.

So much for being safe in Wonder Springs.

"Sir, I assure you," I said, and my voice sounded calm, almost mechanical, "I don't even work here. I was asked to bring out this man's plate. I'm not aware that he had any health issues, but—"

"Why would *you* know anything about *his* health?" said the sheriff, arching his wild eyebrows. "Unless you did, in fact, already know 'this man'?"

"She worked with him," said his fiancee (ex-fiancee? was Nyle actually *dead*?) in a dull monotone. The black-and-pink-haired woman was rooted in her chair as if frozen, a few feet from Nyle's side. She was staring at her fingers, shredding a straw wrapper into bits. Her bleak face looked ten years older. "And she just quit yesterday because he got her promotion."

"*Did* she?" said the sheriff, with elaborate curiosity, as if he and the whole room hadn't heard the whole fight. "And now here you are, with exclusive access to the man's breakfast. Isn't that… convenient."

"It's not like that!" I sputtered, as the ring of hostile gazes prickled deeper into my skin. "I had no idea he'd be *here*! I only came to this stupid town in the first place because of Grandma!"

At the mention of Grandma, his eyes flickered, but he cocked his head with a scoff. "Is that so?" he said. "I hope you'll pardon my skepticism, young lady. I may need to take steps to make sure you *stay* in our stupid little town for the duration of the investigation."

He stepped toward me, hand outstretched and reaching for my arm.

I backed up, but the ring of relatives closed behind me. My pulse was spiking, throbbing through my neck. Any second, one of these idiots was going to grab my bare arm, and then I'd *really* have some explaining to do. Like the whole "revenge murder" thing wasn't already plenty.

"You mean jail?" I chirped. I hate when I chirp. I tried to bring my voice back down to normal. "Aren't we jumping the gun a bit here? Don't you need a warrant? A trial? All that good stuff?"

"You're an out-of-town stranger and a clear flight risk," he said, still advancing with slow caution, like *I* was the wild dog. "I'm sure the judge will agree that you require supervision."

Five more feet, and I was going to downgrade from "complimentary lunch guest" to "murder suspect being held for interrogation." Possibly even "future government experiment", depending on who would find out if I unwillingly wiped the memory of a small-town sheriff in public. I had no idea how the chain of command worked in law enforcement. For all I knew, this guy had a panic button to the FBI. What was I supposed to do?

No idea. My mind went blank.

Thanks, mind.

But behind me, Grandma Meredith spoke.

"That won't be necessary, Jake," she said, in her crisp Southern lilt. "I'll vouch for this woman. She's not going anywhere."

The sheriff stopped short and glared over my shoulder.

The ring of relatives had parted for Grandma, and she stood beside me, arms crossed, glaring right back up at the big burly man.

The two faced each other in bristling silence, unsaid words sparking across the space. Ancient feuds and secrets roiled between them, and for a second even the murder faded away, upstaged by the mystery of long lives entwined.

Then the sheriff snorted. In a low voice, he said, "No offense, but you don't have the best track record in this department, Christina."

Grandma's eyes flared, with an anger so sudden that it made me flinch. Whatever he was referencing, the sheriff had struck a nerve.

Or maybe Grandma just resented mere mortals hearing that she had a first name.

She spoke with icy calm. "This is not the proper venue to exhibit our respective histories," she said. "Unless you've developed a taste for excruciating shame." The sheriff jolted, but she smiled with lethal sweetness. "No offense."

The sheriff scowled. He drew closer to Grandma, though he also seemed to hold back, like they were two magnets flipped wrong and repelling. In an even lower voice, he growled, "I don't care why you brought her here. No promises."

"Of course," she said, with sharp annoyance. "If you get actual *evidence*, do what you will. I wouldn't harbor a murderer."

Ouch, I thought. *Thanks for the vote of confidence.*

The sheriff nodded, then turned to the ring of relatives. As he belatedly went into Officer Mode, offering his stiff condolences and formally requesting them to retire to their rooms and await questioning, Grandma finally turned toward me.

I cringed. In a flash, the woman had turned furious.

"Ms. Sassafras," she said, with cold control. "To my office, please." She swept her gaze around the room, eyed Tina, and snapped, "You too."

As she marched off, and I hustled after her like a shamefaced kitten, I realized that I was worrying less about the possible murder charge and more about getting Grandma's opinions on everything Nyle had managed to say about what I *had* done.

Maybe I should have taken that jail cell while I had the chance.

CHAPTER 10

Grandma's "office" was more like a castle turret.

A wide bank of windows with deep stone sills offered a spectacular view of the main street and the whole town as it sauntered down to the bridge and the river. If you sat on the cushioned window bench, you could see *everything*, down to the tourists strolling along the cobblestones.

To one side of the windows, a massive old roll-top desk stood at the ready, every little compartment pristine and tidy. I had never seen one of these desks in actual use, but as Grandma sat in her leather executive chair and swiveled to pluck a folded paper from a cubbyhole, she seemed to have the entire town (at least) at her manicured fingertips. The overall tone was godlike surveillance.

But a few vases softened the effect, perched here and there on the wooden antique furniture and fresh with branches of lilac or cherry blossoms cut from the trees below. The scent was pure soothing spring.

"Did you kill Nyle Pritchett?" Grandma snapped.

So much for soothing.

"Of course I didn't kill anyone!" I snapped right back. "Not even Nyle!"

Grandma flicked a questioning glance to Tina, who stood to the side between us, watching with anxious care.

"She's telling the truth!" Tina said. "Totally. No doubt."

"How would *you* know?" I said.

"Enough!" Grandma cut in. She lowered her eyes, and thoughtfully tapped her knuckles. In a softer, grimmer voice, she said, "This is unprecedented."

"Don't blame yourself, Grandma!" Tina said. "You couldn't have seen this coming! Well, I mean, *technically*—"

"Quiet!" Grandma barked.

Tina flinched. "Sorry."

Grandma swiveled toward me, eyes blazing. "I have not yet heard your *full* history with this Nyle person, but thanks to your inability to hold your temper—"

"I did *not* start that—"

"*Excuse* me," Grandma intoned, in a voice that could shrivel granite.

I shut up.

After a taut pause, Grandma continued. "Thanks to your aggrieved theatrics, our local sheriff now has it in his thick skull that you're a murderer. I know Jake; the man's only got one slot in his head. Once he gets hold of an idea, he'll worry it to death like a dog with a bone."

"Speaking of which," I said, "what's with all the sniffing?"

Tina's eyes twinkled, but Grandma scowled. "Don't torture the simile, child," she snapped. "The point is, until the real murderer is found, you're in serious danger."

"I know," I said. "So how do we catch him?"

Both Grandma and Tina gaped.

"Or *her*," I added. "Though I'm pretty sure the statistics are way on the side of *him*."

Grandma found her voice first. "What exactly are you proposing, child?"

I bristled. "First off, I'm *not* a *child*."

Her lips tugged in a half-smile. "Everything's relative, sweet pea. But, duly noted. You're a grown woman, Ms. Sassafras, and I believe you said your expertise is… sales?"

"I'm not going to just sit around trapped in Wonder Springs, shopping the boutiques!" I shot back. Although now that I mentioned it, a few of those stores through the window *did* look super cute... oh right, my current net worth was less than the loose change under a couch cushion. Focus up, Summer. "That snuffly sheriff wants to throw me in jail, and you said yourself he's got a one-track mind."

"I'll handle it," Grandma said.

"No, *I'll* handle it!" I said. "I don't even know you! You're a total stranger to me!"

She arched her eyebrows. "Oh?"

"Aren't you?" I said. "I appreciate the night's stay and the free breakfast you didn't actually give me—"

"You did also have that wrist problem," Tina put in, mildly.

"Right! What is *that* about?" I said. "You wrote me this random letter that you'd tell me all about my mom's family, but you haven't said *anything,* and then you made me take that *stupid* plate and now I'm going to wind up the freaking *prime suspect* in a stupid *murder!*"

"Pardon me," Grandma said. "Are you saying it's *my* fault that you chose to defraud your clients with your gift?"

Silence.

Now that I *knew* that this woman knew, I was much more frightened than I'd expected.

"Who are you?" I said quietly, fighting the shake in my voice. "How do you know about that?

"In light of recent events, I'd prefer not to say." Her eyes went narrow, and she crossed her arms. "You may handle this yourself."

"*May?*" I said, piqued, even if I was scared.

"Yes," she said. "And until you clear your name of this crime, we can set aside the question of your mother's family."

"Grandma, no!" Tina said.

"You can't be serious," I said. "You're *still* not going to tell me *anything?*"

"I don't believe you quite understand our position," Grandma said. "You just handed one of our guests a dish, prepared in our kitchen, which most likely killed him. The publicity from this may shut us down. And not only us; the Inn is the heart and soul of this town. This crime puts us all at risk."

"I'm really sorry to hear that," I said. "It's not super great for me either."

She glared. "I'll give you one week."

"One week!" I cried.

"I consider that more than generous," she said. "I don't want you anywhere near the kitchen. But you may keep your room and eat with the staff. At no charge. All I ask is that you prove your innocence." She sighed. "I doubt I can hold off Jake for more than a week anyhow."

She frowned, fiddling with the folded paper she still clutched between her fingers.

"That... *is* generous," I said. It was, but I hated that I couldn't pay my own way, that I had to take favors from people... especially this woman. "Thank you," I ground out.

I realized I had to be scowling, because I noticed that Tina's brows were hunched with sadness. Man, she was sensitive.

"And if I don't successfully complete my first amateur murder investigation within a single week?" I added.

"Then, Ms. Sassafras, you're out of my inn. We can't be seen as harboring a murder suspect. You'll have to take your chances with the sheriff."

"He can't *actually* arrest me without proof, right?" I said. "I *could* just leave this crazy town and go home."

Grandma sighed again, with a note of real sadness. For the first time, she looked hesitant.

A pang of fear pricked my neck. "What?"

"I'm sorry, Summer," she said, and she handed me the folded paper.

It was an ordinary piece of printer paper, but as I pried it open, my fingers shook. The single page was a short article, printed off from some news site, but what first caught my eye was the single, grainy graphic. It was a photo of an apartment building... *my* building. Or what was left of it.

"FREAK FIRE DESTROYS APARTMENTS," the headline yelled. "ARSON SUSPECTED."

I tried to read the text, but I thought I might puke.

Softly, Grandma said, "You don't *need* to do this all alone."

But I crushed the article into a ball of trash, and I pitched it at her elegant little wastebasket.

"I'm fine," I said. "A week will be plenty."

I met her gaze, and I was surprised to see that she looked concerned. Almost as concerned as Tina, who also looked so upset that she might be nauseous herself.

I felt the impulse to reach out, to touch these women who might actually care.

Instead, with a polite nod, I walked out. This was no time to risk trusting strangers. I might get hurt even worse.

This was me, remember? Touch just wasn't my thing.

CHAPTER 11

Honestly, right then, I was feeling pretty wiped. Between inadvertently killing a dude, getting accused of murder, and finding out some sorcerer creep had fried everything I owned, I was ready to curl up with Mr. Charm and take a long nap. Like, until Christmas.

But that was no way to catch a killer.

Come to think of it… how *did* you catch a killer?

As I walked away down the hallway from Grandma's office, running my hand along the cool, smooth polish of the hardwood trim that ran waist-high along the walls between the thick old doors, I ransacked my mental store of mystery shows and novels. What exactly did detectives do?

Hmm. Mainly, they seemed to snoop around and bug suspects with trick questions.

In other words… this was basically a sales job. Entry level.

And I was already a pro.

No, seriously! Swap "suspects" into "prospects," and you had yourself a sales detective. What else did we warriors do all day but poke and pry our targets to yield up their secret yearnings, hidden motives, true desires? How had I never seen this parallel?

Granted, there were minor differences. Closing a sale was usually far more pleasant for the client than getting hauled off to prison. (Though with some of the long-term contracts I'd seen, prison might be a tempting alternative.)

Also, in sales, if you pushed a bit too hard, you generally didn't have to worry about a cold prospect turning into a cold killer.

That thought froze my warm enthusiasm for a sec. If I actually did this detective thing, it would eventually mean talking to an *actual murderer*.

This was legitimately creepy.

On the other hand… this *particular* murderer was the sort who snuck around lacing breakfast platters with poison. The danger level seemed several notches down from, say, some ax murderer who collected severed toes. Or a housebreaker who threatened to choke your cat and could magically kill your plant, give you cancer, and burn down your house…

… which was now apparently part of my life! Yay! So compared to thinking about *that*, plus the rest of the pile of recent trauma that was waiting to pounce the second I stopped to breathe, one-on-ones with potential sneaky poison people would be just fine. Avoidance was my specialty.

Besides, at my peak, I'd wined and dined CEOs who called the shots on sweatshops. If I could split a Merlot with a man who'd pay starvation wages to kids and take a million-dollar bonus, I could definitely handle some small-time measly poisoner of one.

It's amazing what can give you confidence. At the time.

And just as I was rounding a new corner and striding along through that maze of hallways, with fresh energy and zest for my brand new job description, whom should I see struggling to unlock her room door but that mousy blond Kitty woman who'd been running that video call on her laptop? A suspect… meaning, a warm lead.

"Hi! How are you this morning?" I said, with my best bright smile that oozed rapport.

"Well, my cousin was just murdered," she said, frowning at her jammed key. "Not super great."

I resisted the urge to palm my face.

"I'm so sorry," I said. "If there's anything you want to talk about—"

"What? With you? Why?" she said. "Are you a cop?" She looked up and eyed me, seeing me clearly for the first time. Her eyes widened. "You're the *waitress*," she gasped.

Crud. Of *course* she would recognize me as the person who'd *actually brought Nyle the fatal plate*. This could prove a major roadblock in the whole murder investigation plan. I should probably think about at least scrounging up a different outfit. And maybe shaving my head.

"You poisoned him!" she said. "The sheriff said—"

"Let's start over," I said, and I touched her wrist.

The pain stabbed me hard, catching me by surprise. Normally, touching one person wouldn't hurt worse than a static shock. This felt more like I'd touched both prongs of a plug. What the heck?

Kitty had jolted and staggered back, leaving her key ring dangling in the door. Now she swayed and teetered, dangerously close to tipping… this was why I usually made sure people were sitting first.

I tugged off my wrinkled jacket and rolled it under one arm, and I twisted my hair in a loose, sloppy bun behind my neck. It would fall out in five minutes, but at least she *might* not recognize me in the first instant.

Then I carefully steadied her from behind, with a hand on either sweatered hip. The trick here is to avoid the person accidentally grabbing you when they come to, but to also let go in time, so they don't feel some unseen person gripping their waist.

In my experience, this is often trickier with dudes, who tend to have a lot less experience with random people feeling entitled to handle their body.

Unfortunately, some women are hypervigilant. For instance, Kitty.

"What the—?" she snapped, twisting back toward me and catching me by surprise. I was spooked; she was fully alert again way earlier than most.

"Are you all right?" I said, trying to act like it was totally natural to be adjusting her posture in the hallway. Casually, I patted her shoulder and retracted my hands. "You looked a bit dizzy."

"Huh," she said, frowning. She looked around and spotted her keys in the door, then placed a hand to her forehead. "I do feel... off."

"Can I get you anything?" I said. "I'm Summer, by the way."

"Kitty," she said, automatically. "Kitty Carter."

"Oh, you're not a Pritchett?" I said, all chatty. "I thought I saw a family resemblance."

As soon as I said it, I knew I'd goofed. Of *course* she was a Pritchett; hadn't she just told me that her *cousin* was murdered? True, the Touch had probably made her forget she'd said that, but she'd also told me the same thing hours ago, when we'd first met in the dining room. She couldn't have forgotten *that*.

Did I explain this part yet? Long-term memories were always safe from the Touch. However it worked, the Touch had *never* erased more than the last few minutes of memories. It was often less... especially when someone recovered this fast.

Honestly, for a secret superpower, the Touch was pretty darn glitchy.

Anyway, to my mild shock, Kitty *smiled*. For someone who looked like Nyle, her smile was surprisingly nice.

"Of course I'm a Pritchett," she said, proud and beaming. "My dad remarried into the family, so I'm not *technically* a blood relative. But people always say I look like family, and my grandmother says I'm more Pritchett than any of them."

"Wow!" I said, hiding my surprise. So she was actually his... step-cousin? Or maybe "second cousin, thrice removed, with a side of bacon" or whatever... the point was, I had trouble believing she didn't share any genes with Nyle. She looked like she could be his sister. It was uncanny.

I tried to steer back toward safer ground. "That's right, I remember, we spoke earlier. You were doing that video call with your aunt."

"Yes," she said, and her smile faded.

"I'm sorry," I said. "You were probably still doing that call when... it happened."

"She heard it all. My aunt," Kitty said, her eyes dull. "She could have missed this whole thing... she *would* have... if I hadn't broadcast it right onto her screen."

"Oh no! You couldn't have known," I said. I wished I could give her a hug; I'd braced myself to face a possible murderer, but I'd forgotten all about grief.

Kitty rubbed her eyes with both hands, suddenly weary. "Of course I couldn't," she snapped. "But she still heard it. I was even *recording* the whole call... oh my *gosh*... in case she wanted to watch it again later."

"Wait, you were recording? That whole time?" I said. "That's fantastic!"

"Fantastic?" she said. She eyed me in disbelief. "There's going to be... screaming..."

"But that's just it!" I was so excited, I started pacing in the narrow hall. "Whoever poisoned Nyle had to do it *after* he placed his order, but *before* I brought his plate. You've got a video record of exactly who *couldn't* have done it, because they were onscreen talking with your aunt! You might eliminate *multiple* suspects here... who knows, your family's not *that* big, we might even figure out the killer..."

At this point, I remembered one of the golden laws of salesmanship, namely, Do Not Start Pacing And Ignoring Your Prospect's Face, Especially If She Gets Really Quiet.

Too late.

Kitty was glaring with cold suspicion.

"*You* brought out his plate," she said. "And then you told him to choke... *that'll* be on the video too."

"Oh, you heard that?" I said. "I'm so sorry... it's a long story... if there's any way you could just share a quick copy—"

"*Copy?*" she said. "My cousin just *died*, and you want a *copy* of his final moments?"

"Only when you get the chance—"

"Who *are* you?" she demanded. "Some sick pervert? This is my *family*. I'm not going to put them on display for a total stranger! Especially the stranger who might have killed him!"

"I did *not* kill Nyle," I snapped. "I'm trying to *catch* his killer."

"What? Why?" she said. "Are you with the police?"

"No, the police think I did it," I said. Brilliant, Summer.

She gasped. "That's right! I heard that sheriff—"

"You know what?" I said. "I think we got off on the wrong foot." I reached for her wrist.

But she yanked it away.

That creeped me right out. People don't usually remember the Touch, not even on some unconscious instinctive level. I mean, maybe she just didn't like me, but in the moment, I had this irrational fear that she had somehow sensed my secret.

I guess I could have lunged and tried again, but I was too caught off-guard, and worried that it might not work at all. Kitty seemed like the type who might press trumped-up charges for assault, especially if she thought you'd killed her cousin.

I lifted my hands in a peaceful gesture of surrender. "Please, I apologize," I said. "I can't imagine what you're going through, but even in my own way, I'm just very upset by this tragedy. I want to see this killer brought to justice."

"So do I," she said. She grabbed her doorknob, fumbled with the keys, and finally creaked the door open. She darted behind the door, then peeked out with a fierce glare. "And I'm sure the sheriff will be interested to hear that you're fishing around."

She slammed the door in my face.

CHAPTER 12

I decided to take that nap.

I slunk up to my room, crawled into that comfy bed, and slept like the dead. l mean… poor word choice… whatever. When I woke, the sun was low and the shadows were long, but I still felt groggy and weary to the bone.

Project "Keep Summer Out of Prison" was already crashing and burning.

It was the kind of lonely moment when a girl reaches for her trusty cat, the one companion who will never leave her side, no matter what. Even when creeps attacked, or killers struck, Mr. Charm would always, *always*.…

… never mind, he was all curled up and snoozing in his stupid new perfect cat bed.

At least one of us was settling in at Wonder Springs.

Now what was I supposed to do? If Kitty was any guide, the rest of the suspects were going to run screaming when they saw me.

Then I noticed something on the floor. It was a slip of stationery, and it hadn't been there when I came in to sleep. Someone must have slid it under the door.

I picked it up. The paper had a print of little pink flowers, and it smelled of simple roses. Inside, a note in a pretty, girly hand read:

Hey Summer! Do you want to borrow some clothes? Come to my room, it's up in the East tower. Just go to the top floor, end of the hall, turn right, and open the little white door with the red begonias. No need to knock, the ladder creaks. Please come, this'll be super fun!
—*Tina*

Ladder? That sounded intriguing...

But wait, did I *really* want to start sharing a wardrobe with Tina? That was something you did with close friends. Or so I'd heard.

She was totally rushing things, trying *way* too hard to prove how nicey-nice she was. In reality, she was probably looking forward to how flagrantly none of her clothes would fit me. Who was I kidding? There was no known universe in which I could squeeze into that woman's pants.

Then my eye caught my reflection in the full-length mirror. Yikes. No matter how much I resented Tina's pants, I couldn't walk around interviewing suspects in the same trashed dress suit they'd seen me wearing with Nyle.

And even if Wonder Springs had a thrift shop, I wasn't going to find anything special for forty-seven cents.

Oh well. Maybe she actually *was* just being thoughtful. And maybe she had a pair of super stretchy leggings. And a huge (for her) sweater with long, protective sleeves.

Plus... I just might be able to maneuver the friendly Tina into slipping me a few answers. Chatty types can be fountains of information. She might be on orders from Grandma to stay tight-lipped about my family, but at this point, I would savor even the tiniest crumb of information about pretty much anything... the weird sheriff, or how they'd known about my Touch, or who *exactly* that handsome dude had been who I remembered singing over my wrist.

I was getting desperate to know what the heck was up with Wonder Springs.

Desperate enough to ask Little Miss Nice.

I checked that Mr. Charm was still sleeping and cozy, and left the door open a crack so he could roam if he woke. And by "roam", what I meant was, "poke his head out the door and see whether a bowl of cat food had magically appeared." There's a reason they call the breed "Ragdoll".

I didn't love leaving my door unlocked, but I slipped on my purse, and then there was nothing left to steal anyway. Destitution has its perks.

I made my way to the end of the old hallway, but I had to hunt around a few turns before I found the elevator.

It was *ancient*.

You know those elevators in really old movies where there aren't even walls, just a filigreed grating and a chipper bellhop? This wasn't *quite* that old—there were definitely walls, with thick solid wood that trapped the air stale—but as the doors creaked shut and the box groaned and shuddered upwards, I found myself eyeing the faded emergency escape hatch in the ceiling. There was so much *noise*, clacking and straining and… was that a faint *sloshing*? Elevators were *not* supposed to slosh.

Basically, I felt like I was riding in a coffin. In a hearse that was about to break down. On the highway.

By the time the thing had crawled to the tippy-top floor, I had promised myself I'd take the stairs next time. And for the rest of my life.

But when I rushed out of the elevator, I was instantly reassured.

Like every other area in the Inn, the top floor had its own quirky style. Even each hallway was unique. Here, I found a lush, thick carpet that led down a row of imposing doors, each with an elaborate lintel that writhed with carved leaves like a Corinthian column.

But at the end, I turned into a bright alley of bare white-painted wood. The high windows on either side were small, but the late afternoon sun still filled the space and lit up the simple lines of Shaker elegance. A short row of tall thin doors were narrow enough to be linen closets, but each had its own little painting of flowers, set in the white like a jewel.

I felt a sudden urge to try every door, as if each might lead to a separate fairyland. But I squashed that silliness, and opened the door in the corner with the red blooms.

Inside was a tiny room, not much wider than a phone booth. Against the boards of the back wall, a ladder reached up at least two stories to a round glimpse of light.

"Tina?" I called. My voice sounded jarring in the stillness, like a sneeze in church.

At the top, Tina's head popped into the halo. "Oh, hi!" she said. "Come on up!"

"Thanks!" I called, then eyed the long ladder and muttered, "No wonder she's so thin."

Despite the grump, that first hoist onto the ladder raised a little, long-forgotten thrill of fun. I wondered if Tina had lived here since childhood; I would have done *anything* to climb to bed like a pirate when I was twelve.

The buzz lasted about halfway up. Then I started to notice I was winded, and how old the ladder wood was and how much it creaked. So much for me not being a real adult.

When I got to the top, the hole opened near a curved wall with a window bench, and beneath the bench, at eye level as I climbed in, was a rack of shoes. I was anxious to respect her space, and since her feet were bare, I perched on the bench and pried off my sneakers.

Then I looked around and stared.

The room was round, with wide windows set in every corner of the compass. In the late afternoon sun, the town spread beneath us like an enchanted quilt, and beyond the bridge and the river, the blue-green mountains cascaded like waves in a still sea.

The room itself was a bright little paradise of nooks and built-in furniture. A curved wardrobe here, a lean curved single mattress there… the sweep was only slightly marred by a discreet stall that seemed to be a later addition. For her sake, I hoped that thing had a toilet. The romance of the tower was great and all, but I knew I wouldn't want *anyone* to face a four-story round trip for a midnight pee. Not even Tina.

All this, I took in with a single glance. But what *really* caught my attention...

"You have a *parrot?*" I said.

CHAPTER 13

Tina laughed. "Meet Keegan. He's a sweetie."

Keegan the parrot was massive. He was housed in a huge cage on its own antique shelf. I'd never seen a parrot in real life, not even at the zoo. I'd always thought parrots were mainly red, with accents in a tropical rainbow, but this bird was metal gray, with a face of white feathers and accents in black, plus a gray tail with a streak of red. Was he really supposed to be this big?

"So big!" he chirped. "Why so BIG?"

I blinked.

"Keegan!" Tina chided. She turned to me with a glance of apology. "I'm so sorry, that wasn't me. I don't know why he'd say you were *big*; you're in fantastic... shape..."

She trailed off, clearly realizing that I hadn't assumed the parrot was commenting on my size.

No. I had panicked because a *bird* was *reading my freaking mind.*

It didn't help that his voice sounded *nothing* like the classic pirate accessory squawking for a cracker. This was freakishly human, reedy and high-pitched like a soft-spoken male soprano.

"Tina...?" I managed to say.

"Don't mind him," she said, with an airy wave. "He'll say any random thing that pops into his head."

"Cracker!" Keegan chirped.

"See?" she said. "Classic parrot!"

"I was just *thinking* 'cracker'," I said.

"So was I!" she said. "That explains it."

"Explains *what*?"

"Let's get you some clothes," she gushed, and she skipped past me to her wardrobe. "This will be fantastic! I *love* your hair, and I have all this stuff that'll look *so* much better on you than me. We're totally the same size!" She flicked me an appraising glance. "I mean, I think you'll look *great* in these peasant skirts—"

"Skirts?" I snapped. I hadn't worn any big flowy skirts since college. Those things were just a public admission that you'd look enormous in anything snug.

But this was getting off-track. Forget my look. This parrot was *not* normal. Tina was straight up lying.

"Lying!" Keegan chirped.

"I am *not!*" Tina snapped, giving the bird an angry glare. "She is *absolutely* going to look *super* cute. Look at the golden embroidery on this skirt, they'll totally match her eyes. I know they're blue, but they have flecks of gold—"

"He's not talking about the outfit!" I cut in. "He's talking about me!"

She frowned, confused. "*You're* lying?"

"No, I *thought* 'lying'. This bird is *reading my mind*."

"Oh," she said. "Hmm."

"*Hmm?*" I cried. "I just claimed your pet has superhuman magical powers, and all you're going to say is *hmmmmmm?*"

"It's not *magic*," she said, irritated. "It's more like magnets."

"He can read my mind with magnets?" I said.

"No, not magnets *specifically*." She sighed. "Grandma really didn't want to get into this yet."

"Oh right, everything's got to stay *top* secret," I said. "Maybe you should have thought of that before you got a mind-reading parrot!"

Tina shrugged. "Why do you think we keep him up here?"

"Tina, you and your grandmother *promised* me we were going to have this Big Amazing Talk and All Would Be Made Clear."

"I know, I know," she said. "But Grandma—"

"I'm not completely *stupid*, okay?" I said. "I came here in the first place because some creep wilted a plant right in front of me, then gave me some kind of skin cancer which then, poof, you all magically remove."

"It wasn't exactly *cancer*—"

"Then I come here, and there's this guy in a wizard hat who can magically knock me out on command—"

"It's *not magic*," she insisted. "Magic is its own thing."

"Whatever!" I said. My mind was racing now, making new connections even as I ranted. "The point is, there's something off about *all* of you. Even you, it's like... whatever I'm feeling, you anticipate. I feel sick to *my* stomach, and *you're* the one who squirms. Nobody's *that* sensitive—"

"Empath!" Keegan chirped.

I gaped.

Tina rolled her eyes at Keegan and heaved a dramatic sigh.

But her eyes had a certain sparkle... and I had a sudden stab of suspicion that she'd planned this all along. Grandma couldn't blame *her* if the parrot said too much.

Even if what he said was... insane.

"Hold up," I said. "*Empath?* Are you saying you can... feel people's emotions?"

Tina brightened into a sunny smile. "Yes! That's awesome, most people haven't heard the word."

"But you mean, like, *actually* feel? Not just imagine, or infer? You can *feel* the secret emotions of total strangers? In your own body?"

"Sure," she said. "All the time."

Somehow this seemed much stranger, even disturbing, than a parrot who could guess a random thought here and there. Maybe she was lying. For real.

"Lying! For real! Stranger danger!" Keegan chirped.

Tina shrugged again. "And the parrot's a telepath. Welcome to Wonder Springs."

Inside me, something flipped. I sensed inside that I was ready to believe.

By which I mean, my stomach lurched, and my knees trembled.

"I need to sit down," Keegan chirped.

CHAPTER 14

I did sit down. I might have been in mild shock.

True, you might think that I, of all people, should have been most ready to discover that I wasn't the only one out there with magic. (Or whatever Tina wanted to call a one-of-a-kind superpower that no one else had.)

But that was just it. Until yesterday, *no one else* had had anything like me. Not even close.

Now? Now I was arguably less interesting than a parrot.

Yes, I knew these thoughts were beneath me. But I *also* knew that I had to face this. This was my new reality. Other people had powers.

Okay, Summer. Breathe. I'd have to save the existential crisis for later. My *immediate* question should be: how could I use all this to catch Nyle's killer?

"Are you all right?" Tina said. She studied my face and winced. "Oh, no! You feel like *that*?"

"Like what?" I snapped, instantly on guard.

"Like you're not… special. Oh, Summer, don't!" She leapt toward me, reaching out to pat my arm. Then, at the last second, she remembered and stopped short. But she still said, "Please. You're amazing."

Right, I couldn't help thinking. *Just ask my mom.*

"How'd you all know about my… Touch?" I said.

"Grandma," Tina said. "I think it's fascinating! Half the time, I *wish* I could make people forget what they're *feeling*. Maybe more than half."

"It's not like that, exactly," I said. "But *how* did Grandma know?"

"I'd better leave that to her," Tina said. "She's going to be peeved as it is."

She pranced over to a mini-fridge that I hadn't noticed, elegantly tucked beneath a shelf. "Can't I get you anything?" she said. "It's way past lunch. You never did eat, did you?"

"I'm fine," I said, as my treacherous stomach rumbled.

"I ate, but I'm already hungry again." She opened a cabinet, slid out a pretty tin, plucked a huge, luscious muffin that was clearly homemade, and took a long, lingering bite.

I hadn't tasted a muffin in over three years.

(Stupid low-carb diet. Why did *that* have to be what had finally worked?)

"Empathy is *super* draining," she said. "Plus, my metabolism is crazy high."

"Shocker," Keegan chirped.

Tina snorted.

"Is there anything we can do about the parrot?" I said.

"Sometimes if we use the cloth, he'll fall asleep," she said. She crossed to his cage and draped it with a large square of flowered velvet. "But if he doesn't, blocking out the distractions seems to heighten his... skills."

"Great," I said.

"*Please* let me feed you," she said. "It's all from the kitchen; I've got my personal pantry up here. Fruits, veggies, dairy, soy, nuts, grains, eggs, cold cuts, tofu... seriously, you're making me *starving*, it's like I have *two* empty stomachs—"

"Okay, okay!" I said. I wasn't going to solve any murders with a hunger headache. "But is there anything *you* can do about your... um..."

She laughed. "Sorry. I know it must seem super invasive. I'm so used to it, it doesn't even feel like snooping anymore. It's more like the weather... and when there's more than one person, I'm getting this mix, so it's kind of more anonymous, unless I really focus. Half the time, I'm not even sure where *my* feelings start and the rest begin."

"Really?" I said. "That sounds horrible. I can't even handle my own feelings."

Her smile made a wry twist. "It's got its pros and cons," she said. "In theory, there's this technique called *shielding*, but so far, I'm not that good. Mom's always telling me I've *got* to get better, that I could really get hurt if I can't shield in a crisis. Of course, *she's* a pro—"

"Wait, your *mom's* an empath *too*?"

Tina's face clouded. She crouched and opened the fridge. "You're low-carb, right?" she said, in a breezy, stalling voice. "I've got hard-boiled eggs, fresh peppers, oranges... I promise to skip the muffins next time."

"That sounds great," I said. "Please eat whatever you want. I'm totally fine."

She sighed. "Summer, listen... it's all secret." Still squatting, she fixed me with a pleading look. "All this stuff about powers, it's *got* to stay secret. I can't say why yet, but—"

I arched an eyebrow. "But it might connect to strange men who wilt plants and burn down apartments?"

She smiled. "Wouldn't that be a coincidence?"

"Eerie," I said, and was surprised to find myself returning the smile. "Believe me, secrecy suits me fine. Who would I tell, anyway? And... I hope you all are treating my thing the same way."

"Absolutely."

She brought my food to a little table by the eastern window. We sat together, and I started to eat.

Wow.

Maybe I was just famished, but her food tasted *phenomenal*. Even the plain hard-boiled eggs seemed to burst with flavor and life. The yolks were so vibrant they were nearly orange.

But despite the amazing food, I couldn't stop brooding.

And from Tina's watchful look, I could see that pretending to be polite would be pointless. Maybe an empath friend wasn't an entirely bad idea.

"It's the killer," I said. "We've got all these powers; we ought to be able to catch him."

"Hmm," Tina said, noncommittal.

"Like, that woman who was making that video call, remember? Nyle's cousin? Her name is Kitty, I talked to her—"

"Already? Awesome! Did you use your power?"

"Um," I said. "Somewhat."

"Oh."

"Listen, the point is: she was *recording that call*. It's all there, a record of the entire thing! We just need to get it!"

"Didn't you ask?"

"Of course I asked! But she thinks I killed her cousin!"

"So what are you suggesting?"

"I don't know!" I said. "That's what I'm saying, there must be some other power we can use—"

"Like what?"

"I don't *know*."

"Well, you can forget telekinesis," Tina said, sharply.

"Teleki-what?" I said. "Is that the one where you can make objects fly around? Like the Force in *Star Wars*? Oh my gosh, one of you can *do* that?"

"Seriously," Tina said. "Forget it."

She looked so stern that a few hairs prickled at the back of my neck. "Understood," I said, though I didn't. "But don't you see it's a waste not to use our advantage? Can't we do *something*?"

"Sure," she said. "Let's get you some new outfits."

I sighed, and I finished my lunch. But as Tina started rifling through her wardrobe, pulling out shimmering skirts and loose embroidered tops, and chatting all the while about color and complexion and the precise shade of my eyes, I couldn't quite share her enthusiasm. Somehow, everything seemed to work against me.

The more sensitive she was to my whims and inclinations, the more perversely I resented this woman. She was practically acting like the mother I'd never had.

She didn't even bother to show me short-sleeved shirts, because she knew without having to ask that touch magic meant all long sleeves, all the time, even at the height of humid summer heat. Yet her peasant-style tops were airier and more soothing than any camisole. And I found myself resenting *that*.

A sudden fury struck me, standing there at her antique full-length mirror, seeing myself in her cute flowy top and skirt… because I looked *good*. Even Tina's castoffs were an improvement on me.

My old fancy sales suit lay on the floor, wrinkled, abandoned, and dead.

For so many years, I'd exulted in the Touch as my glorious secret, the one thing about me that at least was *unique*. But Tina's empathy was *way* more meaningful… and even the damn parrot could freaking *read minds*.

And on top of all this… I squinted at my face in the mirror…

"Oh my gosh," I said. "I have a *zit*."

It was a whopper, white and red and swollen, perfectly placed on the tip of my nose. Hello, Rudolph. I knew it wasn't ripe enough to pop, but I touched it anyway, triggering exquisite pain. What was this, high school?

"It's just the stress," Tina said.

"You think?" I said.

I thought I sounded light and snarky, but Tina's face flashed with real hurt. Her pain startled me out of my self-centered funk... she really could *feel* how angry I was, even if I tried to hide it.

Wait.

That was it.

"Tina!" I said. "I've got it! You're perfect!"

She frowned. "What are you talking about?"

"You know what people are feeling *even when they try to hide it*, right?"

"Kind of," she said, wary. "It depends on the person. Some people are natural shielders—"

"But most of the time, you can tell?"

"Sure. At least, I pick up *something*."

"Perfect. Let's go." Still wearing my new outfit, I scooped up the other clothes she was loaning me and strode to the ladder. "Hey, how do you carry stuff down?" I said.

"Backpack," she said. She handed me a worn leather pack embroidered with vines. "Where are you going now?"

"Not *me*. Us."

"What? Why me?"

"You're an *empath*, Tina! I need you in the room with these suspects."

"You mean, like... spy on their hearts?"

"Oh, come on!" I snapped. "You said yourself you do this all day long. I can't even *try* to be nice around you. You pick right up on my true self... the whiny inner jerk."

"That's not true," she said stoutly. "You're strong, Summer. I sense all kinds of good things, and anyway, that's different."

"Why?"

"Because I'm not doing it on *purpose*. It just *happens*," she said. "Mostly I try to ignore it, unless I think I can help."

"Of course you can help!" I said. "You can help catch a killer!"

Tina cocked her head. "Really?"

"Think about it! If the sheriff's fixated on me, that doesn't just mean I'm in danger. It means the *real* killer is loose, and free to kill again. Maybe even here in the Inn."

Tina frowned.

It was time to close.

"Please, Tina," I said, with my best vulnerable plead. "I... I need your help. I can't do this alone."

She totally bought it. It occurred to me that fabricating emotion might not be the smartest move with an empath, but her eyes were moist, so I guessed it had worked. This meant we'd have to be careful; if I could come across as way more vulnerable than I actually felt, couldn't a suspect trick Tina too?

Maybe. But most people weren't a sales goddess. Unless this murderer was also a method actor, Tina might just be the secret weapon to bring him down.

"You're right, Summer," she said, with a little catch in her voice, and those big dark eyes glowing with innocent concern. "No way you should have to do this alone."

I felt a twinge of guilt, which I promptly smothered. I really did need her help, and with an empath on board, this killer was history. No question.

The *real* question was: how long I could stand to be with someone so sincere?

CHAPTER 15

We decided to start with Nyle's brother, the heavier guy who'd been bickering with his beady-eyed wife. Right away I realized another asset Tina brought to the team: she not only knew everyone's names, she even knew how to find their rooms.

The brother's name was Lionel. ("Nyle" and "Lionel"? Really? Maybe Nyle's parents were more to blame for how he'd turned out than I'd thought.) He and his wife Deanna were staying in one of the more posh suites on the ground floor, but as we approached their filigreed door, the sharp sounds of an argument erupted into the empty hall.

Shoot, so they were both there. With the Touch, one is always best, because if you try to touch two people at once, one might recover first and see the other one all dazed. (Plus, a double jolt hurts like crazy.)

But I had Tina, so I wouldn't even need the Touch. I hoped.

I knocked, and the voices died at once. After a long pause, the door opened. I wasn't expecting a warm welcome, but I was still startled at the cold contempt of Deanna's glare. She stood gripping the door handle, and behind her, on the nearer bed, Lionel sat slumping sideways, his shoulder against the headboard. He looked haggard and wretched, like he'd aged ten years since breakfast.

Were those the ravages of guilt? Or just that, you know, the dude's brother had just died.

"Who are you?" Deanna snapped. She had the flat, petulant voice of a bureaucrat, like the DMV lady who can't *believe* you forgot to bring your fourth proof of identity.

I was about to say something about catching Nyle's killer, but Tina cut in.

"We're hotel staff," she said, with a warmth that would have gotten a hug and a tip from Ebeneezer Scrooge. "Is there anything we can do to help?"

Deanna's glare flickered with a hint of humanity, and she grudgingly beckoned us in.

Well played, Tina.

The room was wide and light, with a matching antique night table beside either bed. The table near Lionel was a teetering pile of papers, knickknacks, and outright trash, but the table by the other bed was a pristine arrangement of a purse, a hardcover romance, and a high-end water bottle that all seemed to be posing for a magazine cover.

"You can start with making the bed," Deanna said.

"Of course," Tina said, with a demure nod of deference.

"Our pleasure," I said, and I moved toward the bed where Lionel sat. Unlike the extra bed, which was still made, this bed really was a disaster. How could grown adults make such a mess of the sheets? This guy looked like he might not have the energy to roll over.

"Sir?" I requested, in my best courteous tone. "I'm afraid I'll have to ask you—"

"Not *his* bed," Deanna sniffed. "*Mine.*"

"Really?" I blurted. That other bed looked *perfect*. If I messed with it, it'd be like giving the Sistine Chapel a touch-up.

But Deanna took my surprise in a more personal vein. "My husband and I have *very* different sleeping styles," she snapped.

"Oh, right," I said. "I didn't mean—"

"Are you in the *habit* of probing your patrons with invasive personal questions?" she said.

This was getting off to a fantastic start.

Before I could make it worse, her husband rumbled for the first time. "Let her be," he said. He turned and faced me with bleary eyes. "Sorry about that. We had a personal tragedy this morning."

"I heard," I said. "I'm so sorry."

Technically, I'd done way more than just hear, but neither Pritchett seemed to notice. Wow, were people really that unobservant? Changing my outfit had worked like, um, magic.

"Thank you," Lionel said, with gruff force, and suddenly he clamped his meaty hand around my forearm. Like, from sheer force of emotion, supposedly? Nice try, late-forties married dude with your wife standing right there.

He was lucky that the thin sleeve pressed in his sweaty palm seemed to be doing its job, sparing him a jolt of short-term memory loss. Though I wouldn't have minded him forgetting he'd pulled this move.

"I can't imagine the shock," I said, extracting my arm with an expert twist, and resisting the urge to "accidentally" knee him in the groin and then wipe his memory. That was an ethical line I didn't want to cross. Especially with his wife right there watching. "And during a family reunion!" I added.

"Indeed," he said, still fishing for soulful eye contact.

On the far side of his bed, Deanna scowled and crossed her arms. "I don't know why the *reunion* makes a difference. Dead is dead!"

"True," said Tina, who was close by her side, industriously remaking the perfect bed.

"Of course," I said, trying to sound chastened. "I just mean, to have his own family all around, right there. It's so cruel. Even his own fiancee—"

Tina gasped.

It was more than a gasp. As I flicked her a glance in alarm, her face was *contorted*. Rage, jealousy, hatred... she looked like a different person, an evil Tina twin.

Beside her, Deanna's face was smooth and cold.

A shiver iced down my spine. This empath thing was real.

Seeing Tina sense *my* emotions was one thing; weird, yes, but it was mirroring feelings that I knew firsthand. Seeing her manifest this secret loathing that would otherwise have festered under Deanna's cool frown... that was like prying open a grave.

Deanna eyed Tina. "Are you ill?"

Tina's face cleared, and she managed a smile. "Thank you, I'm fine. I'm sorry. I just have a... condition."

Deanna blanched. "I hope it's not contagious?"

Tina's smile went bright, and her eyes twinkled. "Not at all."

"As long as you're sure," Deanna said. She frowned toward me. "I thought that thing on your nose might be an open sore."

I seethed; I'd forgotten all about that stupid zit. "It's not," I said. "But I was saying, about Nyle's fiancee..."

Tina winced again, but this time she quickly masked it. I felt bad for her, but I had to pry; this was our first big clue. Why was Deanna so jealous of the woman? Was Lionel always comparing them, rating his older wife against his future in-law's implausible hotness, relative youth, and impeccable pink and punk style? Could Nyle's catch have precipitated a marital crisis?

"What about her?" snapped Deanna. "What do you care about Mercedes?"

Mercedes, eh? Classy name. Somehow I wasn't surprised.

"We're concerned," I said, playing for time. Trying to work this woman was like pulling teeth from a peevish crocodile. With toenail clippers. "We can check on her ourselves, but perhaps if one of you—"

"Did you *pay* this woman?" Deanna barked at Lionel.

"Don't be asinine," he growled. "I've never seen this woman in my life."

"Oh really?" she said. "Your brother's not even buried yet, and some 'random stranger' just *happens* to *urge* you to go *console* your grieving *ex*."

"Ex?" I cried. "Mercedes was with *you*?"

I know, I know. You'd think that after years of sales calls, I'd be a bit more suave. Thing is, suave was never my strong suit. Besides, when you're talking about features and monthly fees, most prospects avoid dropping revelation bombs.

Lionel glared at me, his face twisted with an offense so fierce that he nearly snarled. I flinched; he looked ready to slug me.

"What did you say your name was?" he said, slow and seething. He squinted, and he seemed to really *see* me for the first time. "Wait. Aren't you—"

"Summer," I said, and touched him.

His closer hand had been resting on his lap, but when I palmed it, gripping the hairy back, the jolt shook us both. He lurched back against the headboard, and I nearly tripped myself.

Damn, that hurt. What was *up* with this family?

"I'm so sorry!" I gasped, as he panted and looked around with glazed eyes. "These carpets, they really can carry a static charge."

He still wasn't talking, just gaping and struggling to blink.

Tina was gaping too, but with surprise. Her jaw had literally dropped, and her eyes were wide. I admit, it was pretty gratifying.

Then I saw Deanna. Her lips were clamped tight, and she was glaring down...

...at her husband's hand, which I'd forgotten to release. Great.

On the plus side, maybe she was so fixated that she hadn't noticed how long it was taking her husband to recover from a "static" shock.

I let go. "Mr. Pritchett?" I said. "Did you need anything else before we head out?"

Lionel furrowed his brows. "Need anything?" he said slowly. "No. Thank you. Were you saying something about our reunion?"

"Wow," murmured Tina.

"Forget it," I told him, with a smooth smile. "We'd better not trouble you and your wife any further."

I glanced at Deanna to include her in the smile. Instead, I cringed.

We might have found ourselves a major clue, sure. But judging from her scowl, Mrs. Pritchett had found *herself* a whole new "rival" to envy.

Great.

CHAPTER 16

"That was *amazing*," Tina gushed, as we hurried off down the hall. "I've never seen anything like it!"

"Thanks," I said. "Coming from you, that's… significant."

"I mean it! You just *zapped* that guy."

"Zap?" I said.

"Totally!"

Huh. I guessed I had. I'd always focused on the memory loss aspect, but maybe the jolt "side effect" had its own potential uses.

Zap. Interesting.

Except, the "zap" usually seemed to hurt *me* worse. And even if the "touchee" did feel anything, they promptly forgot.

I might have to refine my technique here.

If I ever had any idea what I was doing.

"Didn't it hurt?" Tina said.

"Not too much," I lied. Then I remembered who I was talking to. "I mean, it's been worse," I added, sheepish.

"Really?" she said. "You haven't done that to me, have you?"

The question was so sudden that it was sheer luck I could blurt the truth. "No! No way."

"Would you?" She wasn't even pretending like this wasn't a big deal.

"Of course not," I said easily. "That's the first rule of psychic detective work. Never zap your partner."

She beamed, clearly relishing that magic last word.

I kept talking, avoiding her face and looking off down the hall, as if we were driving instead of walking. "What about you?" I said. "You read that woman like a book! I could see it on your face."

"I know. I try not to show it like that."

"No no, it was great," I said.

"But she *noticed*."

"It's fine. She explained it away," I said. "She had no idea you were reading her mind."

"I wasn't!" Tina said. "I didn't know *why* she hated Mercedes. I wasn't even sure it was *about* Mercedes. It was just this awful, awful wave. Like nothing else existed but the craving to destroy."

"Wave?" I said.

"We call them *waves*. When you pick up emotions," Tina said. "Partly because they're like radio waves; it's like tuning in. But they're also like ocean waves, when you're surfing. Most waves are gentle. You might not even notice. But even if it's huge and scary and overwhelming… a wave will always pass."

"Unless you drown," I said.

She frowned.

I sensed a story here, but I decided not to probe. For now. I wasn't sure I'd want to hear it.

"When you say *destroy*," I said, "do you think Deanna really felt capable of murder?"

"I don't know!" she said, more snippy than usual for Tina. "It's not like I'd have a standard to judge that."

"Then guess," I pressed.

She hesitated. "I'm not sure. It's… possible. But why would she kill *Nyle*?"

"Good point," I said. "Maybe she thought Nyle was the real insult. Like, it was *his* brother, *he* should have known better than to chase the guy's ex."

"Yeah, that makes sense!" Tina said. Her eyes were bright with excitement, like we were already snapping on the handcuffs. "And Mercedes, who cared about *her*? She was just some bimbo."

"Exactly," I said. "And I love that you just said *bimbo*."

"What?" she said, confused. "Is that like, not a thing?"

"It's precious," I said. "This whole place is like a time warp."

"I know I've heard people say *bimbo*—"

"Forget it," I said.

She darted me an anxious glance, and took a step away from me as we walked.

"Hey!" I said. "Come on! I promised!"

"Did you?" She smirked. "I don't... remember."

"Oh *gosh*. Fine, I promise," I said. "You happy? And just so you know, I wouldn't zap *anyone* for something like *that*."

"Sorry," she said. But she smiled with relief, and stepped back toward me.

"What I was *going* to say," I said, as we approached the end of the hall, "was that we've got to go talk to Mercedes. See what you read with her."

"It's really not *reading*—" she said.

Abruptly, she halted, and clapped her hand to her mouth.

"What? What is it?" I said.

"Keegan!"

It took me a second to get her meaning. "Wait. We're already hassling these people out of nowhere to pry about their dead relative. You want to show up with a *parrot?*"

"People love Keegan!"

"I thought you said you had to keep him in the tower."

She flicked her bangs, impatient. "There was this *one* time, and honestly, I think Grandma overreacted."

"To what?" I said. "What happened with the parrot?"

Tina frowned. "He has a name, you know."

I rolled my eyes, but she went on. "Seriously, Keegan is *very* intelligent. And sensitive. I mean, there's other telepathic African Greys—"

"Wait, what?" I said. "Telepathic parrots are a *thing?*"

"Of course," she said. "They've done experiments; you can do a search and see the videos. African Grey parrots are the smartest, and they have to be highly trained. But even among African Greys, Keegan's in a class of his own. I think Grandma's partly afraid, deep down, that if word got out about him, some scientist would whisk him away."

"Right. Plus this incident you're not going to tell me about."

"It'll be fine," she insisted. "We've got your zap, right? And the doctor's on speed dial."

"Speed dial?"

"It's just an expression!" she said, flustered. "I bet lots of people still use speed dial."

"Sure," I said. "So they can call each other up and go to a sock hop."

"Quit it!" Tina said. "Besides, a sock hop would be super fun."

"Would it, though?" I said. "This town's cute and all, but it doesn't exactly seem oversupplied with eligible dudes."

"Oh, you'd be surprised," Tina said, with a mischievous look. "But let me get Keegan so we can wrap this up, okay? You just *got* here, there are *so* many better things to do in Wonder Springs besides this murder stuff! Especially when the weather's so nice!"

I sighed. "Fine. But you've got to keep him under control."

"Totally!" she said. "Stay right here, I'll be right back." And she sprinted off down the hall.

Call me overcautious, but I still had reservations about introducing myself to grieving relatives in tandem with a talking parrot.

But there was no point in worrying, so I strolled a few steps into the strange room at the hall's end. To my surprise, the space opened around me into a wide, high, warm half-circle that was full of light and flowering plants. It was a solarium—a gorgeous sun room with cozy benches. A stream bubbled into a mini-pond, and a wall made entirely of glass offered a sweeping view of the main street.

The place was soothing... magical... simply steeped in peace.

And then *he* had to walk in.

The man who'd healed me. With the kind eyes and the scruffy handsome ache.

Wow.

CHAPTER 17

Let's be clear: I am not usually the type to go all gaga over a dude just at sight.

I've been to meetings where some A-level exec struts in flexing his abs through his work shirt, and I'm thinking, dude, did the orthodontics for that stunning smile cost more than a year of college for your baby daughter? If a man clearly spends more time on his hair than I do, I'm swiping left.

Sure, if some Italian model feels the need to mow his lawn shirtless, I might get a few tingles. I'm human too. But what the hell would we ever talk about?

I've spent my whole career duking it out with males who expected my breathless feminine submission at the size of their bank account, or their title, or their astounding ability to tell people what to do. I'm *really* not into giving some random stranger my instant obsession because he knows how to grow a bicep.

So why was I now staring like an eighth-grader, with a shimmer buzzing from the back of my calves to the top of my head, feeling so light that I might float away?

He just seemed… real.

Too real, like the first red tulips in gray spring. I almost can't look straight at them; it's like they've cut through from a brighter world, too strong for my eyes.

It wasn't that he enthralled you with his lean good looks; sure, I suppose he could grace a magazine cover, or at least a second-tier catalog for sweaters or something, but I don't think he'd catch my eye. Not on paper.

What you first felt about this man was *presence*.

Even with the long solarium between us, he radiated a strength and calm at a level I'd never experienced, not with men running companies worth billions.

And he wasn't even looking at me. A huge bright flower had caught his eye, some tropical bloom that would die outside, and he'd drawn near to study it with intense focus. I studied him, though with quick fitful glances, both yearning he'd look up to catch my eye and also terrified.

His skin was tanned deep, almost brown, with that rich, varied tone you can only get from working in the sun. His shortish haircut looked like it was meant to be low-maintenance, but his tight curls were spurting a bit shaggy. He wore brown work corduroys and a loose linen shirt with patterns stitched in the sleeves and collar.

What was it with embroidery in this town? The shirts Tina had lent me had a similar vibe... oh yeah, I was wearing one now. Somehow this made me absurdly self-conscious, a feeling which only spiked when I remembered that Tina had *also* tried to lend me sandals, but my feet were at least two sizes too big. So here I was about to make my first impression, with a calf-length skirt and... castoff sneakers.

I've heard that men barely notice shoes, but this has to be an urban legend.

As I ransacked my mind for solutions to my footwear crisis (I may or may not have considered kneeling) the outside door opened, and a woman walked in, a mousy blond.

Kitty Carter. Crud.

Considering how our "interview" had bombed, I had zero interest in Kitty bawling me out here in my sneakers, with this guy looking on.

Turned out, I shouldn't have worried. Mr. Plant-Enthusiast-Healer-Dude took up all Kitty's interest.

As she passed him, the mousy little woman couldn't tear her gaze away, trying to catch his look with open hunger. She passed him a lot closer than she needed to, but he still could have pretended to ignore her. Like, say, some jerk barista.

Instead, he glanced up, and his face *transfigured* in a warm smile.

"Afternoon," he said, with a nod, and his voice sent an absurd thrill through my whole chest. I wondered if there was some way to keep him smiling longer, like, forever. If he were smiling on that sweater catalog, I might buy the whole store.

"Hi," Kitty squeaked. She flushed, gave him a tight wave, and scurried away.

Which meant, she scurried *toward* me, but I bent to pretend to tie my shoes, and she rushed past. I was pretty sure she hadn't even seen me.

While I was down there, I took a moment to reflect. Now that I'd broken visual contact, my helpful neocortex was getting her chance to ream me out.

What are you THINKING? You're trying to catch a KILLER here, Summer! This is NO TIME to SUCCUMB to some HUMILIATING COUNTRY CRUSH!

(My neocortex can be emphatic.)

It was true. I don't fall hard very often, especially on sight, but the few times I had, it hadn't ended well. For various reasons.

The thing to do was to *take action*. Just go right up and introduce myself, like any normal adult. Nothing vaporizes an obsession like actual conversation.

Besides, my neocortex added, *you two ALREADY "met". You were passed out and probably drooling. Sleeping Beauty... with a skin condition and a long day's worth of B.O.*

Actually, I'm not quite sure that really *was* my neocortex. I might have just been channeling a dead malicious aunt. If I had one.

Anyway, I'd already decided. I stood, walked right up, and said, with friendly confidence, "Hey! I'm Summer. I never got the chance to touch you."

He startled hard, and stared at me like I might pounce.

"Thank!" I gasped. "Never got the chance to *thank* you. For the other night."

His eyebrows shot right up to his manly curls.

"The healing thing!" I said. I could feel my face flushing to the tips of my ears. "With my wrist?"

I held up the arm in question. The conversation had plunged to a level where we needed to rely on visual aids.

It worked. "Oh!" he said, in that unfairly gorgeous Southern lilt, and his face cleared. "Oh, that. No problem." We had full-on eye contact for a few throbbing milliseconds, but then he flicked away to eye some fascinating spot on the wall. "Glad to help."

"Well, I really appreciate it," I insisted, with a banality that was almost surreal. It felt like I was thanking the guy for changing my tire, not magically healing some disgusting spreading skin blight cast by an assassin sorcerer. "I mean, you took time out of your evening... Friday night..."

"No no, it's fine," he said. "Anything for Grandma."

"Right, of course... I didn't mean—"

"Oh, *ouch!*" he said. He frowned, staring not quite in my eyes.

"What? What is it?" I said, bewildered. "Are you all right?"

"*I'm* fine, it's *you*. That looks *painful*. Hold still."

I had no idea what he was talking about, but he reached for my face, and I instinctively froze. His fingers hovered just below my eyes... we weren't quite touching, but I could *feel* his warmth, smell the sun-drenched fragrance of earth and tree bark and life... and then right at the tip of my nose, a tiny tingle tickled.

"You're *healing* my *zit?*" I cried.

"All done," he said cheerfully, and withdrew his hand. "Small stuff is quick."

"I don't *believe* this!" I said. I felt exposed, humiliated... I couldn't even *see* the damn thing. I had to stand there and rub my nose to confirm it was gone. The skin felt absolutely clear... like, nicer than since childhood. For the next half hour or so, I could probably be a nose model.

He looked confused. "Does it still hurt?"

"Is this your life purpose?" I said. "You go around leaving smooth female skin wherever you pass? You're like a human moisturizer!"

His cheeks tinged, and he flicked his glance away again. "I'm not sure I should unpack that one."

"*I'm* not sure you should mess with people's bodies without asking!"

He raised an eyebrow. "I was removing a zit."

"You should have *asked*," I said. "Maybe I wanted that zit. Maybe I was maintaining it as a spiritual practice, to overcome ancient insecurity from high school."

"You were?"

"No! That doesn't matter! I can't believe you'd just *assume*..."

Now he frowned. "We are talking about a zit?"

"You know, a *normal* person would have been like, 'Hi! Nice to meet you! I'm going to politely ignore your tiny, *temporary* flaw, instead of acting like it's some disfigurement so compelling that I have to instantly bust out my magic, and not even bother to check whether *you* care about how *I* think a woman should look!'"

His frown broke, twitching into a cheerful half-smile. "I suppose that's fair."

"Really?" I blurted, in a breathy, all-is-forgiven tone for which I instantly hated myself. A slight concession wasn't the same as an apology, even if it did come with a mind-altering smile. Not that I could remember the last time *I* had made any concessions in the heat of an argument... no, don't do *that*, I thought, don't you try to *justify* him just so you can keep basking in his smile... wow, that smile...

Behind me, a voice chirped, "You are so crazy hot."

Both he and I jolted, and I whipped around, my cheeks burning, to see who had read my mind.

But I already knew. Keegan the parrot was perched on Tina's hand, working his beak in a silent cackle of glee.

"Cade!" Tina said, with bright eyes and a glowing smile. "What are *you* doing here?"

"Hey, Tina!" he said, straightening and smiling and generally lighting up into a beacon of masculine force. "I just came over to check on Summer."

Oh *really*, I thought, with a sour twinge. It didn't take an empath to see how this Cade guy was reacting to Tina. I bet he'd planned this... he was just using me as a *pretext* to see *her!* Damn it.

"That's so nice of you!" Tina said, and she pounced on Cade with a lingering, *very* friendly hug. Somehow she managed this while still holding Keegan, who wound up giving Cade an affectionate peck on the ear.

One big happy family. Good for them.

I endured this vortex of mutual attraction for as long as I could, which was maybe five seconds (though it felt like five hundred), and then I cleared my throat. "Yeah, thanks, Cade," I said, as politely as I could. "But now that you know my skin is *perfectly* clear... Tina and I do have to get to work."

"Already?" he said, as they slowly disengaged. "It's not the dinner rush yet, is it?"

"Shockingly, I *didn't* mean work in the kitchen," I said. "We're actually working on—"

"Grandma stuff!" Tina cut in. "Summer's right, Cade, we've got to go. Nice to see you! Don't be a stranger!" She tapped his bare forearm for one last touch, then glanced my way and started walking down the hall.

"Thanks," he said, beaming. "I'll be around."

Then his bright smile dimmed as he gave *me* a polite nod.

"Nice to meet you," he said. "I'll try to be less… intrusive."

"Don't worry," I said. "I'm not staying long."

Was that a flash of disappointment that crossed his face?

No. It was me deluding myself. Now I had one more reason to solve this stupid murder and get out of Wonder Springs.

The last thing I needed was to fall for some dude who was Tina's pick. That would be a contest that could only end in pain.

CHAPTER 18

The first thing I noticed in Mercedes' room was a pair of pretentious purple silk boxers. Crumpled on the carpet, clearly untouched since being dropped by Nyle.

I found this unexpected intimacy revolting... and I wondered what trash I'd leave behind one day for the hands of strangers.

I suppose I'd expected Mercedes to have tidied everything up by now, but really, how fair was that? I'd never thought about the endless needling details after death, the widow having to strip the sheets and empty the bedpan one last time.

Mercedes seemed to be avoiding it all, gingerly picking her way among Nyle's detritus as if she were afraid to leave her prints. She had a suitcase open on her side of the double bed, and she was jamming cosmetics into it with quick anxious jerks. Long strands of her dark hair were coming loose and dangling over the shaven pink sides, and the unkempt look made her seem even more... haunted.

She'd flicked us a glance when we'd first knocked and come in, but apparently she hadn't noticed the parrot. Now she did.

"What the hell?" she cried. But then her surprise cleared to admiration. "What a beautiful animal!"

"Thank you," chirped Keegan.

This kind of freaked me out... could he also *converse?* Then I noticed Tina's pleased smile, and I wondered whether she'd *thought* what he said. Or maybe she'd just trained him to reply to standard compliments. Still, if you practiced, could you use this parrot as a sort of telepathic puppet?

And why was I even thinking that? This town was so *strange.*

But Mercedes just laughed, and a few of the worry lines faded from the corners of her mouth. "You are a *cutie,*" she told Keegan. She walked around the bed to where Tina and I were standing at the entrance, and she gently touched the long red feathers in his black tail. "I think I might take you home."

"Home to Lionel," chirped Keegan.

Mercedes startled and scowled at us, hard. "*What* did he say?"

Whoops. I guess if I was going to bring along a telepathic parrot, I had to be a lot more careful what *I* was thinking. Fabulous.

"I'm so sorry," I said. "I can see where that would be startling. We were just up chatting with Lionel and Deanna, that's all—"

"Oh, I *see,*" Mercedes said. "And they must have been thrilled to tell a couple of random hotel staff all about my thing with Lionel."

"No, no, not really," I said hastily. "They didn't get into detail."

"I'm *sure,*" Mercedes said. "Listen, sister, I don't know if you killed him or what—"

"Me?" Rats. So much for a change of outfit being an adequate disguise. On the other hand, she'd actually *watched* me hand Nyle the plate that killed him.

"I said *listen,*" she snapped. "Nyle had his issues, sure. But he was a *saint* compared to Lionel."

"What? How?" I said. "What is Lionel, a mass murderer?"

Mercedes scowled. Too late, I remembered that, oh yeah, she'd been engaged to Saint Nyle. Oops.

"Everyone knows Nyle could be abrasive," she said. "But Lionel? Lionel was the Older Brother from Hell."

"Oh no!" Tina said. She winced, and I wondered what she was feeling from Mercedes.

"Oh yes," Mercedes said. "Lionel was already five when Nyle was born, and he practically tortured the kid from the time he was a baby."

"You mean, like... physically?"

"No, nothing like *that*," Mercedes snapped. "Just someone pounding into his head, over and over and *over*, from before he could even talk, that no one would ever love him, and he'd be better off dead."

"He *said* that?"

"Every single day."

I felt sick. As much as it had hurt me to be alone, with no mom or siblings and barely a father, I'd never imagined a life with a family who *loathed* me.

I imagined a cute little three-year-old Nyle (at that age, even Nyle would have been cute), running to show his older brother a picture he'd scrawled, and Lionel scowling, checking to see if their mom was around, then starting to whisper...

Wait, what was happening? Was I actually feeling *sympathy*? For *Nyle*?

Mercedes kept talking. "Of *course* Nyle grew up all obsessed with success. Except that unlike *some* people, he used his money to help."

My fleeting sympathy vanished. "Nyle?" I scoffed. "That guy's idea of leaving a tip was to toss down his business card."

Mercedes bristled. "I know for a *fact* that his hipster cousin Bryce owed him a huge pile of cash."

My memory flashed the guy with the glasses and the black turtleneck, mansplaining to Kitty over her laptop. "Nyle loaned him money?" I said. "For that stupid app startup?"

"It didn't *start* as a loan," Mercedes said. "First he coughed up big bucks for *multiple* rounds of 'investment'. He was just trying to help the kid; he never expected to see a dime. He only finally made a loan so Bryce would stop asking for more. Not that it worked."

I was stunned. Nyle? A supportive relative? He was old enough to be Bryce's uncle, but still... Nyle?

I glanced at Tina, but she was stone-faced, visibly hiding some strong emotion I couldn't guess. She seemed to be draining her energy just trying to look calm.

"Did you tell the cops all this?" I said. "I mean, if Bryce owed him all that money—"

Mercedes scoffed. "That guy couldn't even organize his sock drawer," she said. "No way he could pull off... this."

Her face crumpled, but she mastered herself. She looked grim, and weary. I wondered how her strange entanglement with these brothers had ever started... and if she'd ever dreamed, in her worst nightmare, that it could end like this.

And then, perched on Tina's hand, Keenan squawked a single word.

"GUITAR."

Guitar? I thought. Great, the parrot had a random streak.

Then I saw Mercedes.

She had *blanched*; her cheeks were chalky white. Her teeth were clenched, as if she were in pain, and she had fixed the bird with a wild glare, like it was some kind of demon.

"He must think you're a rock star," I said, trying to keep it light. "*Do* you play guitar?"

"I have no idea what you're talking about," she said, ice cold. The talkative, grief-stricken Mercedes of ten seconds ago had vanished. It was eerie. "I work with the city government."

"Really?" I blurted. I barely managed not to add a comment about her pink hair.

"That's great!" Tina cut in. "And you must be absolutely *exhausted*."

"Yes," Mercedes said.

I'd never thought that government work was all that, ah, taxing (sorry), but Tina tugged my sleeve and started backing toward the door. "Please let us know if there's *anything* we can do," she gushed. "We'd be happy to move you to another room for free."

"Thanks," Mercedes said, still watching Keegan with a wary eye. "I was hoping to leave tonight, but that sheriff is telling us all we need to stay in town."

"Not for long, I'm sure!" Tina said cheerily, as she pulled the door shut behind us. "Get some rest!"

Then she sprang off down the hall.

"What was *that* about?" I demanded, as I sprinted to keep up.

"Couldn't you tell?" Tina said, over her shoulder. "She wasn't *grieving.*"

"She wasn't? Why?"

Tina stopped running, and she leaned on a corner. Her dark eyes were wide, and she was panting like she'd run a hundred-yard dash.

"Because she hated him."

CHAPTER 19

"Mercedes hated Nyle?" I said. "But she was defending him… she was going to *marry* him."

"I know," Tina said. "It's horrible."

"So was all that stuff about Nyle just lies?" I said.

"I don't know," Tina said. "I don't *think* so. But I couldn't tell. The hate was too hot, and the fear… and then when Keegan said *guitar*, she just flipped. It was too much; I had to get out of there. Sorry."

"No worries," I said.

"Really need that shield," chirped Keegan.

"Keegan!" I snapped.

But Tina laughed. The tension eased… I noticed the delicate pink blooms twining on the hallway's Victorian wallpaper, and smelled the faint scent of strawberry. Seriously, if you ever manage to get bored in the Inn, just look around.

"Fine," I said. "It's true. This empathy thing might be a problem if you need to bolt whenever things get interesting."

"I know," she said. "She was just so… terrified."

"And you don't know why?"

She shook her head. "All I get are feelings. Mostly."

"Great," I said. I eyed the parrot. "And even though you seem to get a *constant* stream of updates from *my* mind, that was all you got from her, just one word? Guitar?"

"Hungry," chirped Keegan.

I sighed. "I *am* hungry. And my cat could probably use a snack too. Let's grab some food and talk this over in my room."

Downstairs, I waited outside the dining room while Tina made a quick raid on the kitchen.

Considering Grandma's insistence that I keep my suspect face far away from the Inn's dining experience, I was feeling anxious even hanging around at the door. It didn't help that Tina had handed me Keegan.

"Stupid parrot!" he chirped, squirming and flapping and clawing my hand. He was heavier and stronger than I'd expected, and yes, parrot claws are sharp. "Hurry, Tina!" he cried. "Help!"

"Is she hurting that bird?" said a teenage boy.

I craned my head around the flailing Keegan. The boy who'd spoken was a beanpole with a dark shaggy boy-band haircut, frowning at me like a judgmental mop.

Beside him, a girl who had to be his sister, or at least yet another Pritchett, looked up from her phone. Her black hair flopped in almost the same cut as her brother's, except longer; I was mildly surprised she could see anything under those low bangs.

"Oh no, he's fine," I said, as the claws pinched the skin between my finger and thumb.

"Ouch! Ouch!" Keegan chirped. "Hurting me!"

"Cool," said the girl. "It talks." And she hoisted up her phone with its giant camera eye.

"Oh, hey, um..." I said, remembering Tina's fears of Keegan getting spirited away by some ambitious neuroscientist. I turned to try to shield the parrot with my body.

"Stupid kids!" Keegan chirped.

"He just called you stupid!" the boy said, and he cracked up.

"Shut up," she said.

"Oh no, we just trained him to say that," I lied. "He does all these tricks."

"Get a haircut," Keegan chirped.

The boy quit laughing, and the girl snorted.

"You too," Keegan chirped.

The girl flipped her bangs out of her face, and for the first time, she fixed us both with a careful stare.

"Hilarious, huh?" I said, eyeing the camera. Desperately, I tried to keep my mind completely empty. I failed.

"Big marshmallow man," Keegan chirped.

The teens looked confused.

I should have been relieved that they hadn't caught the movie reference. The last thing we needed were two camera-happy Pritchetts knowing we had a mind-reading parrot.

But had kids these days really never seen the original *Ghostbusters*? Way to make me feel *super* old.

Just then, Tina finally slipped out, and we beat a hasty retreat. As we speed-walked away, I caught a glimpse of them watching us go, both pairs of eyes following our every step.

At last we turned a corner, and we rushed up to the sanctuary of my room, where we nearly crashed into Sheriff Jake.

Yes. Sheriff Jake was freaking *in my bedroom*. He was crouched by a window, nostrils flaring as he noisily sniffed around between the wall and the nightstand by my bed.

"What are you *doing* here?" I screeched. "I swear, if I have to walk in on one more old dude creeping around my room—"

"I have a warrant, Ms. Sassafras," he said, utterly unruffled. In fact, his eyes were bright, and he looked, if anything, happy to see me.

"I don't care," I said. "You can't just walk in and search my room!"

"I already did," he said, and he held up a clear plastic evidence bag.

At the bottom of the bag lay a small glass vial.

Tina gasped.

"I'm screwed," Keegan chirped.

"That's not mine," I said, as calmly as I could. "What is it?"

He smiled. "Well now, I believe that's the sixty-four-thousand dollar question. But my *hunch*, Ms. Sassafras, is poison. The poison you used to murder Nyle Pritchett."

I gaped.

His smile died. "Naturally, we'll have to run a few tests," he said. "I'm sure I can count on you to stay close by?"

I nodded, dazed.

"Run!" Keegan cried.

The sheriff narrowed his gaze.

My mind was racing, jabbering with panic. But it all came down to two simple facts.

One: the second those tests came back, I was done. Arrested. On track for conviction for murder. That gave me, like, a day. Two at the most.

Two: the *real* killer had thought to plant the poison in *my* room. The murderer was after me.

PART III

CHAPTER 20

So, I admit, I kind of freaked out.

On the outside, I semi kept it together. "You're not serious, right?" I said, giving the sheriff my best thoughtful, intelligent, confident frown. "If I really *had* killed someone, why would I *save* the poison?"

"I wouldn't presume to know," he said. "Maybe you had plans for other victims."

"Maybe someone *planted* it," I said, the edge of panic creeping into my voice. "Isn't that an option?"

"Not possible," he said. "No one's been in this room since yesterday besides you, Tina, and the feline." He nodded at the cat bed, where Mr. Charm was, of course, managing to nap through this entire crisis.

"How can you say *no one*?" I said. "The door wasn't even locked; I left it open for my cat."

He frowned. "If anyone had walked in here…" he said, and his nostrils flared as wide as quarters, "… I'd know."

At that point, I decided.

Wonder Springs might have been super cute, but between the mind-reading parrot, the heart-reading hottie Tina with dibs on my irrational crush, and a local murderer determined to torpedo my life, this last little icing of a snuffling sheriff who was somehow also a dog was just one touch too much. I had to get out of this town. Right now.

"Bye!" Keegan chirped.

"Ms. Sassafras?" the sheriff asked, cocking a wary eyebrow. The creep could probably *smell* my fear. "Is there a problem?"

"Not at all," I said, and I grabbed my purse and my cat and I ran.

"Summer, wait!" Tina cried behind me, but I was already halfway down the hall.

As I whipped around the corner, I could hear Tina arguing with Sheriff Jake, but their voices were muddled, and I wasn't going to wait to catch the details. I slammed onto the spiral stairway and leapt my way down, taking the groaning old steps two and three at a time, nearly toppling except for my hand gripping and sliding on the smooth wooden rail. My heart was trying to pound its way out of my chest, and all I could think was, *Get out. Get in your car and just drive. Anywhere.*

I was terrified I'd run into Grandma, or another Pritchett, or even Vladik the chef, but I made it right out to the parking lot and dove into my car. When I touched the wheel, it felt like it had been *weeks* since I'd had that surge of power and freedom. The Inn was *their* world, but this was *mine*. I was a grownup, I had a car, and I could go wherever I wanted.

I hit the ignition, lurched out of the parking lot, drove three-quarters of a block... and the engine died.

"*What?*" I yelled.

Mr. Charm, who'd landed in the passenger seat somehow *still* asleep, finally jolted and cracked open one eye.

"You are *kidding* me!" I shouted. "I'm out of *gas?*"

I was. I tried three more times, but the needle was sunk past "E", and the engine wouldn't budge.

No gas. Of course not. I'd driven half the day to get here, and I hadn't even started with a full tank. And even assuming I could find a station in walking distance that would lend me a gas can, I wasn't going to get far on forty-seven cents.

I was trapped.

And that's when I started to shake.

First my hands, then my chest, then down to my thighs. My pulse was exploding. I was gasping for breath, but each short, shallow pant only made me feel more paralyzed.

In some tiny, rational corner of my mind, I managed to ask, *Is this a panic attack? Is this what they feel like?*

I didn't *get* panic attacks. Ever. Yes, I had reasons to be fearful just now, but this was *overwhelming*.

Was I dying?

What would happen if I died, right here in my car?

Would some tourist find me first? Would she take a photo, promising herself she'd never post it online, but then sharing it with so many "friends" that eventually my corpse went viral? Would someone at least get my beloved cat safely back to Grandma?

My dear cat... my one true friend. With a huge effort, I reached toward the passenger seat and clutched Mr. Charm for what could be a final hug.

At the soft, warm touch of his fur, something *crackled*.

It was like a static shock, but faint, just above the surface of my skin. It reminded me of the jolt I get when I do the Touch, except that I barely felt it. Mr. Charm must have taken the brunt.

But he didn't seem to notice. He just curled up on my lap, then gently licked my hand.

Then I realized. The panic was utterly gone.

What... had just happened?

I sat there stroking my cat, letting the rumble of his purr soothe me back into my skin.

That sudden, mind-crushing terror had felt like... an *attack*.

Oh, crud. Was that a thing? Psychic attacks?

Why not? If the parrot could read minds and Tina could read hearts... what other secret powers were festering in Wonder Springs?

Then I remembered how dear old "eccentric" Uncle Barnaby with his wizard hat had "welcomed" me to Wonder Springs. A single command — "SLEEP" — and I had *freaking gone to sleep*.

What if someone else could make me feel far worse?

"Fantastic," I said. "Am I in some kind of war zone for psychic assault? From an enemy I don't even know?"

Mr. Charm licked his paw. I took that as a circumspect *maybe*.

Then I brightened. "But think about this, Charm. When you touched me, the attack vanished. *Instantly*. You're like a Feline Psychic Protection Unit!"

Mr. Charm yawned. He is occasionally modest.

"Seriously!" I said. "That, or else I'm finally losing my mind."

No comment from the cat on that one.

"Okay. One crisis at a time," I said. "I can ask the others later about psychic attacks, right? First, I've got to figure out this murder. If the killer's planting evidence in my room, maybe that's a *good* sign. Like he's feeling the pressure. Don't you think?"

Mr. Charm closed his eyes, and he settled even more heavily into my lap. He was falling asleep again. Of course.

"Hey!" I said. "Come on, let's take a walk. I've got all these clues bouncing around in my head, I've got to sort them out."

I got out, cradling the cat in one arm. But as soon as I closed up the car, Mr. Charm squirmed, leapt to the ground, and trotted off toward the Inn porch.

"Charm? Wait!" I called. "What if I need you?"

He flicked his tail in a farewell wave.

Great. I braced myself for another panic attack, but nothing came. Hmm. Maybe Mr. Charm had some kind of sense when the psychic coast was clear.

Or, maybe he thought he'd done more than enough owner care for one day, and he wanted back in to his cozy bed. Whatever, cat. I could do this myself.

It was time to take a stroll through Wonder Springs. Find a place where I could think hard, figure out the mystery, and catch this killer.

Before the killer made the next move.

CHAPTER 21

As I walked onto the cobblestones of the main street, the evening sun was bathing everything in a golden glow. The pretty shops along either side glistened, the tree blossoms shone like clouds of tiny stars, and the people walking were backlit with halos like angels.

Even for a perfect spring Saturday evening in a tourist town, there seemed to be a *lot* of people walking this pedestrian mall. Maybe I'd just forgotten how different the feel is when a street's full of people instead of cars.

Then I noticed something that shocked me, even for Wonder Springs.

Right down the center of the street, in a groove set in the cobblestones, ran a stream.

It was only a couple feet wide; an adult could step across it, and a group of kids was having a lot of splashy fun trying. But the gurgle was as lively as if it were coursing through the heart of the forest, and in the low southern evening sun, the water sparkled like dancing stars.

I turned and looked, tracing the water's path back up the slope. It led straight up to the Inn, where a wide front plaza circled a fountain at its heart.

Wonder Springs… had a real spring.

I watched all these people sauntering in a murmur of peace and contentment… an older Asian woman eagerly window-shopping a pottery store with shelves of gleaming vases… a middle-aged white hipster couple holding hands as they studied an outdoor menu… a younger Hispanic couple laughing with their kids as their towering cones of ice cream began to tilt and slide…

… and for the first time, I really worried if Nyle's death could break this.

Something about Wonder Springs was different. I didn't know what it was, but I caught myself caring whether it got hurt.

The mom, who was crouching beside her toddler and his teetering cone, looked up and caught my eye. "Hi there!" she said. "Oh my gosh, I *love* your shirt."

"Thank you!" I said, startled and pleased. "It's a loan, actually."

"Really? From where?"

We chatted for a bit, but I was feeling anxious to find that quiet spot to think. All this sweet Wonder Springs goodness was only giving me *more* to lose if I failed. Besides, I still had that cop in my bedroom, convinced he had the proof that the killer was me.

I excused myself and scanned the shop signs, squirming a bit at the over-the-top cuteness. Finally I settled on a candidate: *Namaste with Natisha (Yoga and Tea)*. A cup of coffee and a solitary corner sounded perfect.

As I hurried up to the door, trying to look preoccupied and unapproachable, I realized what made Wonder Springs feel so different.

Or at least, I realized one of the reasons: a total stranger had talked to me on the street.

I mean, an actual *conversation*, not street harassment. These days, that was kind of weird.

I'd always thought the South had this reputation for hospitality, but the few times before that I'd ventured into these small Southern towns, I'd been lucky even to catch someone's eye. And it wouldn't be some mom enthusing about my shirt; you were way more likely to trade eye contact avoidance with some sullen pasty woman venturing out into daylight with greasy hair, a stained undershirt, huge faded pajama bottoms, and an oversupply of tattoos that she'd probably regret.

But here? It was different.

Why?

I bustled into the *Natisha* shop, and even in my rush, I had to take a second to enjoy the space. The interior was all natural light and walls in soothing blue, with menus carefully chalked on boards that had whimsical frames. A faint incense mingled with a symphony of fragrant teas.

Also, the "yoga" part of *Yoga and Tea* was for real; at the back, a studio was connected by a glass wall, and I could see very mature ladies holding poses that made my muscles cringe.

Behind the wooden counter, a black woman in her forties welcomed me in with a high-watt smile. I guessed this might be Natisha herself; she wore yoga pants and a tank top, and though she was a bit more curvy than me, she was a healthy weight and glowing with vitality. I'm pretty religious with my workouts, but just from how she held herself, I had no doubt that if we both tried to hold a pose, I'd pass out before she even broke a sweat.

Seeing her, I realized something else about Wonder Springs: this crowd was super diverse. Other Southern small towns I'd seen tended to be a sea of white, but there was a mix here of races that was more like what you'd see in the city. It was refreshing, even a relief.

But I had to wonder… how had that ever happened? Out here, that kind of mix didn't seem to happen by accident.

"Hello! I'm Natisha," the woman said, graciously confirming my name theory. "Welcome to Namaste. What can I get you?"

"I was just thinking a coffee?" I said, scanning the menus. At which precise moment, I remembered…

How much coffee did I expect to get for forty-seven cents?

Crud.

"Oh, I'm sorry, honey, the coffeeshop is across the street," she said, probably for the fiftieth time that day. "But if I may entice you… many a coffee drinker enters this realm and discovers a whole new universe of flavor and delight."

"Oh, um…" I hemmed.

But it was too late. Natisha launched into a passionate declaration of the unknown virtues of tea…

… for about thirty seconds.

Then she stopped. She scrutinized my face with a curious stare.

Great. For all I knew, the town was plastered with Most Wanted posters starring the Murdering Redhead Substitute Waitress.

"I feel rude saying this," she said. "But have I seen you before?"

"I doubt it," I said, trying to smile. "This is my first time in Wonder Springs."

"Hmm," she said.

"You know, this place looks busy," I said. "I'm really looking for a spot where I can escape. I mean, be alone! Think. You know. Thanks!"

I turned to go, and nearly plowed into an older woman who'd been hovering two feet from my shoulder.

"Hi!" she boomed, as I managed to regain my balance. "I'm Vivian!"

Vivian had to be in her sixties, but she had such a youthful face and a trim physique that I couldn't be sure. The makeup job on her pale face struck me as… adventurous… and her long gray hair had the casual bounce of a teenager's.

"Sorry!" she said, with a smile, and she took a step back. "Didn't mean to crowd your aura."

"Aura?"

Natisha cut in, talking across me to Vivian. "Not everyone knows your lingo, hon."

"Oh, an aura's your energy field," said Vivian, matter-of-fact, like this was totally normal. "I'm *all* into that stuff. I run a New Age gift store over in Back Mosby."

Back Mosby? I thought. Really? I'd heard my share of goofy town names, but what kind of parents got together and said, *Hey, let's raise our kids with "back" actually slapped into the name of their hometown! Way to boost that confidence!* Had there already been a Front Mosby? Probably... and coming up with a brand new name from scratch might have taken a whole fifteen minutes...

I must have shown more snark than I intended, because Vivian's smile tightened.

"Sounds great," I said.

"I love it," she said. "Though I definitely need my time to recharge in Wonder Springs." She glanced at Natisha, and they shared a smile.

"Back Mosby's not like this?" I said.

Both she and Natisha snorted in unison. It was kind of amazing.

"It is *not*," Vivian said. "But enough about *me*, I came over to see *you*."

"Me?"

"What's your name?"

"Um, Summer, but—"

Natisha cut in. "Doesn't she look familiar?"

Vivian cocked her head. "Maybe... but Summer, you just seem like you could use a friendly ear. I have this *feeling*."

"A feeling?" I blurted. "What, are you an empath too?"

Now both women *startled*. Hard.

Natisha's stare hardened till I could almost *feel* it. She looked inscrutable, a well of secrets.

But Vivian spoke in an entirely different voice, quiet and confidential. "You know an empath?"

I couldn't believe I'd been so stupid. I had half a mind to zap her, but I didn't want to risk it with Natisha watching so hard.

"Forget it," I said. "I didn't mean—"

"You *do*," Vivian said. Her eyes were round with wonder.

"I didn't say that," I blustered. "Please just forget it. It's a freaking secret, okay? She's like the nicest person in the world."

"An empath? Really?" Vivian looked shocked.

I frowned. "Wait, do *you* know an empath?"

Vivian flicked a glance at Natisha, then said, "Summer, I think you and I should get tea. Now."

"Look, thank you, and you're both super great," I said, "but is there anywhere in this town where people aren't so aggressively... friendly?"

They looked confused.

"I'm just kind of in the middle of something," I rushed on, "and I *really* need a quiet place to be *alone* and *think*."

"There's the orchard," Natisha said. "It's private, though."

Vivian lit up. "Oh, the orchard! Yes! It's *beautiful* right now! And the man who works it is absolutely hunkalicious." Her smile faded. "But he does keep to himself."

"Perfect," I said. "I'm sure he won't notice me."

"Oh, you should at least *try*," she said, wistful. "I already did."

At first, I thought she was joking. After an awkward pause, I realized that she was completely serious. She also seemed totally unembarrassed at both the attempt and the fail with a guy who was probably less than half her age.

Well. You go, girl. Maybe if I was lucky I'd grow up to be like her.

They gave me directions, and I thanked them and made my escape before they could ask any more questions. I cut between two shops and found the little mulched path they'd described, wandering away down a grassy slope. Fruit trees soon surrounded me, and in that last golden hour of sunset, the cherry and apple blossoms engulfed me in a luminous, fragrant paradise.

But, like the original paradise, there apparently had to be a dude.

He was crouched by a tree, his back toward me, and at first I couldn't tell what he was doing. Then I saw that the trunk was infested with blight; it looked like a black mold, evil and deadly. The blight had smothered most of the trunk, and some of the larger branches were withered and dead.

The man was moving his hands along and above the branches, not quite touching them, and softly humming. The tune sounded vaguely familiar, but I couldn't place it. It was like some lullaby my mother might have sang that my mind forgot, but could still shake my heart.

My eyes went moist. Though part of me felt silly, the rest of me ached.

The light was starting to die, and the shadows were long, and I stopped a bit too far away from him to clearly see what was happening. It occurred to me that the whole scene was exceedingly odd, even for Wonder Springs. Even if the song was strangely moving, what was a grown man doing out here singing to a dying tree?

Even as I asked that, my skin prickled and warmed. Because I saw.

As his hands passed, the blight vanished.

First the trunk cleared, and the bark gleamed fresh and new. Then the dead branches began to lift and straighten, and buds sprouted and whorled into bloom.

I think I gasped. I made some kind of noise, because the man startled, and he twisted to see me. His face opened with surprise, and I flushed, castigating myself for getting caught there staring when I should totally have known his voice.

Yes, it was Cade.

CHAPTER 22

"I was just trying to be alone," I said, talking fast to fill the sudden silence. "This old lady said there might be some hot guy here, not *you*."

His lips twitched. "Sorry to disappoint."

As he crouched there easily by his miraculously healed tree, he looked *infuriatingly* comfortable. I didn't know why it bugged me so much. After all, it was probably his orchard.

I suddenly wondered if he spent most of his time around trees, if he were more used to plants than people. That would help explain his total lack of a bedside manner; it's not like you could *ask* a tree how it felt about its medical options. At least, as far as I knew.

This would also explain why, in a town that catered to tourists, especially middle-aged and up, he didn't spend every waking hour healing a constant stream of health complaints. Just like with Tina and the parrot, his whole healing thing was secret.

Unless, of course, he spotted me with a zit.

What was I doing defending this guy? And not clamping down harder on this stupid trembly lightness in my chest? *Think*, Summer, I scolded. With your *brain*, not your... other parts. This guy was all about *Tina*. If I was going to survive the rest of my stay in Wonder Springs without further humiliation, I needed to make it crystal clear to this man that I had *zero* interest. None. Nada. Zip. Even if I did keep swiveling back toward his smile.

"Sorry to interrupt your tree magic," I said. "I'll let you get to it."

He frowned and stood. "It's not magic," he said. "Not exactly."

"Right," I snapped. "Tina said the same thing. Super helpful."

Was it my imagination, or when I said *Tina*, did he flush a little? Of course he did. I mean, yes, the sun was setting in earnest now, and his face was partly in shadow. But I was still sure he'd flushed.

"Really, it's not," he said.

"Then I don't know what I'm supposed to call it when you freaking *cure* a *tree*."

He smiled, and he looked over the tree with deep satisfaction. "Yes, she's going to be just fine," he murmured. A tender love softened his lean face, and I glimpsed an affection I'd barely seen on parents rocking their babies, or a girl with her new puppy, let alone a dude with a plant.

Then it flicked out as he turned back to me. I wilted a little.

Politely, he said, "Have you ever heard of morphic fields?"

"Nope."

"Well," he said. "That's kind of a long conversation."

He turned and sauntered ahead on the path, clearly expecting me to drop whatever I was doing and tag along beside him through the twilight. Which I did. But I kept a *wide*, disapproving space between us, enough so that the crackle along all my skin on the side facing him was subdued to a medium throb.

"So, you probably *have* heard of genes," he said. "Thing is, when they first started mapping the genome, what they *thought* they'd find—"

"Hold up," I said. "I'm sure this is super fascinating, but I've got to tell you, I'm really kind of preoccupied."

"Oh?" he said. "With what?"

NOT your dimples, which I now just noticed for the first time, I chided myself. "You might not have heard this out here in your personal Walden," I said, "but up at the Inn, a guest was poisoned. Murdered."

"I did hear about that," he said. "I'm sorry. The tragedy itself is bad enough, but with it being a guest and everything, that must be incredibly hard on you all."

"What do you mean *you all*?" I said. "I just got here."

"Oh. Aren't you with Tina and Grandma?"

"No, I'm not *with* 'Grandma'," I snapped. "Grandma sent me this letter out of nowhere, and then right after I got here, I handed this guy a poisoned plate. So now while Grandma and Tina and you and a gazillion tea-slurping tourists are having the time of their lives here in lovely magical Wonder Springs, *I'm* trying to catch the killer before your butt-sniffing sheriff gets *me* convicted for *murder!*"

To my surprise, he snorted… and even *giggled*. It was so adolescent it was almost not attractive.

"Sorry," he said, as he got control. "Just that bit about the sheriff. An apt description."

"It's funny for *you*," I said, stepping closer as we walked to make the point more aggressive. But my treacherous skin spiked with proximity, and I backed off again. "I'm the one on track to spend the rest of my life in prison."

"Right, I see," he said. "I had, ah, heard a bit about that…"

From Tina, I thought, abruptly seething.

"…but you know, the sheriff's bark really is worse than his bite."

"You did not just say that."

"It's true!" he said. "Trust me. Everything'll be fine."

"A guy got *killed*," I snapped. "Look, I know Wonder Springs is this gorgeous little bubble and everyone lucky enough to live here has this sweet pretty perfect life, but out in the *real* world, everything is *not* fine. People get *hurt.* They lose their job, or their family, or their own health—I mean, honestly, what the heck are you doing hiding out here with trees? For all you know, there are people down the street with cancer!"

I hadn't meant to get so mad, but I guess it had all been building up. I'd been looking straight ahead into the dying sunset as I spoke, but as I finished, I turned. Cade was grim, and sad, and on that final word *cancer*, he winced.

We walked in silence through the deepening shadows.

Then he said, his voice low and quiet, "It's not that simple."

"Why not?" I said, but gently. "Sure, I'm a big hypocrite... I've mainly been using *my* power to sell long-term software contracts with obscene commissions. But I also didn't grow up in Wonder Springs. When I was *way* too young, I lost my mom—"

"Really?" he said. "Me too."

"You did?" I said. "When? How? I'm so sorry."

"It was..." He cleared his throat, and he looked ahead as we walked. The light was nearly gone now, and in the twilight gray, I was losing his face. "It was cancer," he said. "Really bad."

"Oh, Cade," I said. "I am *so* sorry. I can't believe I said that, I didn't know—"

"No no, it's fine," he said. "The thing was... I was ten. So I was only just discovering this whole... talent. I'd found a robin with a broken wing, and my dad kept saying it had healed on its own, but I *knew*, when I'd picked it up, I'd *felt* it... the change..."

"Yeah," I said.

"So when they finally told me Mom was sick, I thought, *I can fix this...*" He gave a short, hard laugh. "Yeah... no. My skills were not up to the challenge. I'm still not sure I didn't make it worse."

"Oh my gosh!" I said, horrified. "Don't *say* that! You were just a kid, you were trying to help—"

"You're right," he said. "Of course. I'm just saying, after that... what's the first rule of medical school? *Do no harm.* Sure, I've picked up some skills, for certain conditions, and a few people know. With you, it was an emergency. Grandma straight up asked me."

"Right, 'asked'," I said. "I'm *sure*."

He chuckled. "You do know Grandma. And your condition was still superficial, which helps a lot. But in general… it's like, if I accidentally kill a tree, I can live with that."

"I understand," I said, softly in the dark.

I ached to reach across the space between us, even just to touch his arm. But his skin was bare, and the only "skill" *I* had was for isolation and loss.

He flicked me a glance, stopped walking, and raised an eyebrow. "No surprise you're in sales, Ms. Sassafras. You can really get a guy talking."

I stopped too. "Summer, please."

"Okay, then," he said. "Summer."

I shouldn't have asked for that.

When he said my name… facing me alone in the cool spring night, with the moon making his face new, and the clouds of blossoms on every side like bridesmaids whispering and waiting…

… what was left of my brain knew I had to get out of there. Now.

"Thanks," I said, lightly, as if his voice weren't still resonating in my chest. I fumbled in my purse to pull out my phone and fake like I was checking the time, then remembered I'd fried the thing anyway. Dang it. "Hey, do you know what time it is?"

"Sure," he said. "Night time."

"*Thanks,*" I said. "I'd better go. I need to… um…" *Get away before I fall so hard for you I break my nose?* "Tina's probably looking for me."

"You heading to the Inn? I'll walk you back. I feel bad, I didn't even hear what happened with *your* mom."

"No no, thanks, it's fine," I said, waving him back and starting to walk away.

"You sure?"

No! "Totally. See you later!"

"See you, Summer."

Tina's got dibs, I chanted in my head as I scurried away. *They're a thing. You saw it. You don't even live here. He was just being nice. Also, moonlight. And cherry blossoms. Hazardous to your heart...*

But when I snuck a peek back, he was still standing there under the moon, watching me go.

CHAPTER 23

Mercifully, the sheriff had vacated my bedroom. Mr. Charm was sleeping peacefully, and the room was quiet; I could finally buckle down and review the case.

So, of course, I went to bed.

I was exhausted! There was no point trying to solve a puzzle when I could barely keep my eyes open. First thing in the morning, I promised, I'd tackle this once and for all.

But I woke up to three sharp knocks.

"It's not even six o'clock!" I said, as I opened the door to Grandma and Tina.

Grandma sniffed. The morning light was still gray and early, but she was already coiffed, with makeup sparkling. "Yesterday, I let you sleep in. You'd had a stressful night."

"Right," I said. *"Now* I'm only being framed for murder."

Tina gave me a sympathetic frown, but Grandma just *humphed* and sat in the room's one chair. That left me and Tina the edge of the bed. I cinched my bathrobe tighter, and wished I'd taken a minute to get dressed before trying to face Grandma. The bathrobe the Inn provided to its patrons was thick and comfy, for sure, but my sole pair of underwear was drying in my tiny bathroom, and I just wouldn't have minded an extra layer of security. If I ever had money again, I was definitely going to stock up on more than one pair.

"I have a job for you," Grandma said.

"A paying job?" I said.

Grandma scoffed. "This is serious, Summer. A matter of life and death."

"I thought I was already working on that," I said. "Doesn't Virginia have the death penalty? You gave me a week."

"I did," she said. "But now you've got until they get that vial analyzed. A day or two at the most."

"Oh, you heard about that," I said, with a glance at Tina. "Don't you think I should stay focused?"

"I believe this is connected."

"I don't understand," I said. "*What* is connected?"

Grandma hesitated. She flicked her gaze down, and twisted one of her glinting rings. "Tina tells me you've learned a bit more about our... gifts."

"You mean your telepathic parrot?" I said.

Tina cringed a little, and Grandma flashed her a sharp glance. Oops.

"Look," I said, "I came down here in the first place because some creep wilted my plant and gave me a magic rash. I'm in on the secret, okay? You can feel free to be candid."

"I am *always* candid," Grandma snapped, the lilt of her accent deepening perilously near a twang. "And the fact is, another person is going to die. Today."

"*What?*" I said. "How do you know?"

"Because," she said, with a glare that bored right to the back of my head. "I had a dream."

"Oh," I said.

There was a tense pause.

I was glad that Grandma didn't also have the power of laser vision. If she had, my face might have been a puddle by now, and that would be problematic, especially with such a nice bedspread.

When it was clear that I had no intention of raising any flippant objections (such as, *Are you claiming you can SEE the FUTURE in your DREAMS???*), she continued. "I didn't get a clear view of the face, but I do know the victim is a young lady, with long dark hair."

"Doesn't that teen girl have dark hair?" Tina said. "Taylor Pritchett? The one with the brother Tyler, about the same age?"

"Taylor and Tyler? For real?" I said. *"Great."*

"You met them?" Grandma said sharply.

"Not exactly," I said, hoping we wouldn't get into details that involved our unauthorized excursion with the parrot. "They didn't say much."

Tina cut in. "What else did you see, Grandma?"

Grandma eyed us both, then said, "Not much. I had a sense that it would happen today, right here at the Inn."

"How?" I said. "A gun? More poison? Did you see the killer?"

She shook her head, and squinted her eyes half-closed. Her eyelids fluttered as she strained her inner sight. "No poison..." she murmured. "Couldn't see who or where... but it was some kind of attack... she was using her phone."

"Oh my gosh, that *is* Taylor," Tina said. "Both those kids are on their phones nonstop."

"And you're sure about this?" I said. "This... dream?"

Grandma's glare flared up again. Even Tina looked at me like I'd farted in church.

"Okay, then," I said. "You have dreams that tell the future."

"We don't have time to chitchat," Grandma snapped.

"Can I just have a moment to take this in?" I said.

"No," Grandma said. "And I hope I don't need to tell you this is *extremely* confidential."

"Got it."

"You'd better. If the wrong people knew, the ramifications could destroy this town. At a minimum."

Despite the woman's flair for the dramatic, something in her voice made goosebumps shiver across my arms. I didn't want to pry for details. Not yet.

Instead, I said, "But why would this killer want to go after a teenager? I thought this was about Nyle and Mercedes. Did you know she used to date his *brother*?"

"Tina told me," she said. "It's a fine theory, but it doesn't mean Taylor is safe. A killer might target an innocent *because* she seemed random, to hide the true motive. Or your theory might be wrong. Did you even talk to all the family yet?"

I squirmed. "Um… no."

"Well, then." Grandma stood. "Looks like you've got a full day ahead."

"But what are we supposed to *do*?" I said. "Follow Taylor around all day?"

"I leave that to you," she said, walking for the door. "I need Tina for meals, but otherwise she's free."

"What about me?" I said. "I'm about to go down for murder, remember?"

She paused in the doorway, incandescent with disdain. "Well. If you're too busy, Summer Sassafras, that's on *your* conscience."

And she shut the door behind her.

"Wonderful!" I snapped, leaping up and starting to pace. "If she can see the future, why didn't she have some dream before *Nyle* died?"

Tina shrugged. "She can't get dreams about *everything*."

"Right, sure, priorities," I said. "It's not like she could have prevented murder."

"I don't think she really controls it," Tina said. "Anyway, maybe we can prevent *this*. And it's probably the same killer, right? All we have to do is protect Taylor, and we'll catch the murderer too."

"Great plan," I said. "Except that if we mess up, some teen might *die*."

Tina nodded. "No pressure."

CHAPTER 24

Even by Grandma's standards, it was still too early in the morning to start interviewing suspects or tailing a teen.

I slipped into another shirt-and-skirt Tina combo (pale green and lilac—two colors I never wore, but Tina assured me I looked stunning), and I hauled my huge purse onto my shoulder.

"Oh, you can leave that here," Tina said.

"Never hurts to be prepared," I said, trying to shift the strap weight off a particularly tender muscle. "Besides, I don't trust that sheriff to keep his nose out of my room."

Then a wince flitted across Tina's face, and I flushed with embarrassment. You know it's time to clean out your purse when your empath friend gets shoulder pain.

"Sorry," I said. "I'll totally clean it out. I've been meaning to for months—"

"Oh, it's fine—"

"Seriously, I've got a fresh trash bag in there, ready to go. I just got *super* busy, you know? And now we've got this *murder* thing—"

"Totally understand," she said, forcing a smile.

We decided to get a cozy early breakfast. I was still supposed to be avoiding the dining room, but Tina thought it would be fine, as long as we were out before the guests came down.

As we crept down the creaky old spiral stairs, I had to admit that the Inn looked good in the pale morning light. The quiet stillness seemed somehow intimate, as if the building itself were a comfy old grandmother wrapped in a robe, about to tell a story over the first pot of coffee.

Tina looked good too, already perky and bright. She peeked in the empty dining room, then beckoned me to follow, eyes shining, like we were two kids playing hooky.

My mind flashed back to Cade in the moonlight, the hum of my name in his mouth...

... yeah, I probably needed to clear the air with Tina on that. Maybe she and Cade were just close friends... *super* close... and that whole lighting up thing had all been in my imagination. Right? All I had to do was ask. Drop a hint. Easiest thing in the world. I would totally do that.

Later.

Then I thought, *What are you worried about? You can always undo.*

Oh, right. Except, hadn't I promised her I wouldn't?

Why? something in me whispered. *She reads* you *all the time. Why are there special rules for Tina?*

It's not *that*, I thought, with an inner squirm. Erasing memories was totally different.

Or was it?

Ahead, Tina pranced into the kitchen, then poked her head back out. "All clear!" she said, in an utterly unnecessary stage whisper that echoed in the empty dining room. "What do you want for breakfast?"

I made an official offer to help cook, but Tina brushed this aside, and I didn't insist. (Call me unladylike.) I *can* cook, sort of, but I never saw the point. Not when I was eating alone.

Standing there in the long, narrow kitchen, just the two of us, it was the perfect time to broach the topic of Cade.

Instead, I paced around, pretending to go all Sherlock Holmes. Maybe if I caught some precious clue, the surge of confidence would be the nudge I needed to risk telling Tina that I was maybe possibly potentially seriously interested in you-know-who.

Yeah, *that* made sense.

No wonder Holmes and Watson never chased the same girl. This was a workplace nightmare.

I tried to focus on actually finding clues. Technically, this kitchen was the scene of the crime. The killer must have snuck in here... this *room*... to lace the food with poison.

A chill crept down my back. He might have stood right *here*, right in the entrance where I was standing now, our feet touching the same stone...

Except... what about the chef? Vladik would have been standing right at the stove, or bustling up and down the long counter that held the dishes. He couldn't possibly have missed a civilian profaning his sacred kitchen.

No. The killer must have snuck in while the chef had left the kitchen empty.

Which meant...

The Matriarch must have been the key. She'd called the chef out of the kitchen.

If the killer had *known* that his ancient Pritchett relative *always* insisted on harassing the chef, he could have waited for her to make her move, then slipped in and out of here in less than a minute.

Damn. That still could have been any of them.

Even creepier... the killer must have walked *right past* where I'd been standing only moments before, at that archway into the hallway. That was the only path into this kitchen.

If I'd stayed there watching the Matriarch, instead of trying to sneak out, would the killer have had to abort? Would Nyle still be alive?

I couldn't think about that. It's not like *I* could see the future.

Besides, what about the sheriff? He'd been right there in the *bathroom* while the killer must have snuck right past. No wonder he was inclined to think I'd done it; not only had I carried the plate, he'd actually *seen* me lurking down the hall from the kitchen.

We really needed that video from Kitty. The whole crime hinged on which Pritchett could *not* be accounted for during the entire time that the Matriarch had kept the chef out of the kitchen.

Sure, it was *possible* that the killer could have snuck in and poisoned an ingredient ahead of time. But that seemed far more risky. He'd have to have known *exactly* what Nyle would order, and also have been willing to kill anyone else who happened to order *anything* with the same ingredient... at his own family reunion.

Conceivable? Yes. Likely? No. I mean, I couldn't say I knew how murderers justified themselves, but the risk of wholesale slaughter seemed like a big jump.

So, what clues could we get besides that video? Anything in this kitchen? The place was fanatically clean. Between the snooping sheriff and the fastidious chef, any possible clue had been scraped away.

But what would I expect to find here anyway? Not the poison. *That* had been kindly deposited in my room.

Although, how had the killer avoided leaving a scent there for the sheriff? I wondered whether the sheriff had sniffed around in this kitchen; maybe even he couldn't track a scent in this wonderland of odors.

What other evidence would a killer have left of poisoning Nyle's breakfast?

I looked around, disheartened. My gaze drifted over pristine empty counters, shelves lined carefully with cookbooks, cabinets glowing perfectly clean...

I frowned.

Something was off about the cabinet in the corner.

Not the cabinet itself. Beneath it, on the old white tile... was that a tiny smudge?

I came close and bent low to look. The cabinet cast a shadow, which made it hard to see much, but there was definitely a round mark on the wall, about the size of a quarter. It was whitish, like some kind of residue, and it reminded me of something I couldn't place.

"Find something?" Tina called from the stove.

"Not sure," I said. "Take a look."

Tina came and got much closer than I had, leaning on the counter to peer in. Then she reached out...

"Hey!" I said. "Don't touch it!"

Too late. "It's fine, he wasn't poisoned with wall gunk," she said, scrutinizing her fingertip. She rubbed it against her thumb. "Hmm. Sticky," she said.

"Would you please wash your hands?" I said.

"NOT IN MY KITCHEN!" bellowed Vladik the chef.

Tina and I both whirled to find the irate chef towering in the doorway, hands on hips, his face flushed with rage.

"How *dare* you?" he roared. "This was safe place, beautiful place..." He marched right at me, jabbing thick fingers toward my face. "Now? Police! Newspaper! And *so much food*, out! In trash! Because *maybe* poison. Precious spices, weeks to replace!"

"Wonder Springs has a newspaper?" I said.

"OUT!" he screeched.

"But if we could just take a picture," I said. "We found a—"

"*NOW!*" he howled. "You too, Miss Tina! Never again put foot in this place! Or else!"

"Or else *what?*" Tina snapped. Now *her* cheeks were flushed... oh great, was she feeling *his* anger now? This empathy thing was nuts. "I work here too, Vladik!" she said.

"Not *here*," he barked. "Not if you bring redhead poison friend. You no like? I go! Let Grandma find new chef with *half* my skills, ha!"

"Come *on*, Tina," I urged, edging toward the door around the culinary volcano. The last thing I needed was to lose Grandma a critical staff member (especially when I'd been forbidden the whole area).

"I have a right to be here!" Tina said. "And *you*..." She furrowed her brows at Vladik. "You're just being *darn* rude!"

"Crushing," I muttered.

But Vladik really seemed to take it hard. Shame flit across his face, and he shrouded it with a scowl. "Humph!" he grumbled, apparently having read it somewhere and thought it was valid English. "Tango takes two. Now out. For permanent."

Of course, now *Tina* was looking shamefaced. "Sorry," she murmured, and she slunk out behind me.

"Now what?" I said, as we scurried across the empty hall.

"No worries!" she said, instantly perky again. "I've got snacks in my room."

"I mean that *clue*," I said. "We don't know what it is or what it means, but if he catches us in there again, he'll quit and Grandma will kill us!"

Tina looked thoughtful. "She wouldn't actually *kill* us. I mean, unless he quit during the rush—"

"You've *really* got to learn that shielding thing," I said.

"I know, I know."

"Oh crud," I said. "Like, now. *Right* now."

"What?" she said, confused. "Why?"

But then she followed my gaze.

The doors to the dining room had just opened.

To a man I'd hoped to never see again...

CHAPTER 25

… that twerp in the turtleneck. Bryce.

He'd scanned the room in a nanosecond, honed in on Tina, and tried to fake a surprised wave. Like he hadn't snuck down here early on purpose to find her.

"Seriously, please at least *try* to block that guy's desperate yearn," I muttered, keeping my voice low. "Last time, you pretty much lost it."

"I'm not going to fall for that guy! He's all the way across the room!" she hissed. "I'm not my mom, remember? My empathy's short range."

With a jaunty, casual air, Bryce sauntered straight for us.

"I hope you've picked a dress for the wedding," I muttered.

"Would you relax?" she muttered back. "Attraction waves aren't that big a deal, and I've got it pretty much under control."

"Oh, like last time?"

"Look, we *have* to talk to this guy, don't we? Isn't he a suspect?"

"Sure. Just don't let him wind up as your fiance."

"That hasn't happened in *years*."

I arched an eyebrow.

"Hey," she said. "High school was rough, okay?"

"*High* school?"

Just then, our clearly unimportant private conversation was superseded by the Arrival of an Interested Male. "Hello, *ladies!*" Bryce said, trying to deepen his voice and mainly sounding like he had a slight cold.

Tina giggled.

Unbelievable.

"Hi Bryce," I cut in, giving him a chance to at least pretend to not be hitting on her.

"Did I ever show you my app?" Bryce said, to Tina. He whipped out the phone-tablet-pocket-monitor-thing and started swiping. "Check this out. This thing's going to kill Tribesy."

You do know Tribesy, right? It's this app that's like if you took the worst parts of Facebook, Twitter, and Instagram, put them in a blender, and made the whole thing ten times as addictive.

I hate Tribesy. And it's the first app I install on every new phone.

Bryce sidled up beside Tina and held the screen so they could both see it together, with at least their shoulders touching.

"Oh *wow*," Tina cooed. "That looks *great*, Bryce!" She tapped the screen, and frowned. "Oh… um…" She tapped again. "Is something supposed to happen?"

Bryce chuckled. "Oh, *this* is just the mockup. An image of how the app will *look*."

"Oh! Wow, so you made this? That's super neat!"

"I'm not a *designer*," he sniffed. "I outsourced. With all the iterations, this cost me over forty thousand dollars."

"For a *mockup?*" I said. "How much did Nyle *give* you?"

Bryce's eyes narrowed, and he glared my way. Beside him, Tina visibly relaxed, flicked him a look of distaste, and edged a step away.

"I don't know where you're getting your information," Bryce said, with stiff condescension, "but although Nyle was initially supportive, he came to prefer other opportunities."

"Really?" I said. "He passed up your fabulous investment returns on a mockup?"

"It's not *my* fault he needed money!" Bryce snapped.

Tina and I both stared.

"Needed?" I said. "For what? Nyle *never* needed money."

"How would *you* know?" Bryce barked. He was flushing now, like he knew he shouldn't have opened his big venture capital mouth, even to save face in front of Tina. "And why are you so interested, anyway? Who *are* you?" He turned to Tina, and abruptly he switched to a fatuous leer. "I mean, I know *Tina*." He clapped a skinny hand on her shoulder, and Tina's guarded expression melted to open interest.

"Would you *please* keep your hands to yourself?" I snapped.

"Seriously?" Bryce said. "What are you, the hall monitor?"

"Summer, please," Tina said. She was flushed, and looking all conflicted.

"Please what?" I said. "Your new masseuse just confessed the perfect motive to kill."

"*Excuse* me?" Bryce demanded.

"Oh, come on. How much did he 'loan' you? A hundred thousand? Two hundred?" I eyed him. "Half a million?"

Bryce winced.

"Half a *million* dollars?" I said. I eyed Tina. "Is that true?"

She scrunched her face. "Um, I'm not sure…"

"Why? You're not close enough?" I snapped. "What's he have to do? Kiss you?"

"What are you talking about?" Bryce said.

"Summer!" Tina said. "Stop!"

I groaned. "I should have just brought the parrot."

"Parrot?" Bryce said.

"*Summer!*" Tina said.

"We're fine," I said, and I zapped Bryce's nose.

The jolt hurt like hell.

Seriously, the pain bit like a bee sting. "*What* the… gyah!" I barked, through clenched teeth. I shook my hand, then clamped it under my arm. "What is *wrong* with this *family*? Do you all have some recessive gene for Psychic Counterzap?"

It was really, really stupid to say something like that *after* I'd wiped his memory. True, the "touchee" was usually too dazed at first to notice much, but still. Dumb.

Not that it mattered.

Because Bryce was clutching both hands to his nose... and *howling*.

That was a first.

After the initial jolt, the people I touched had never seemed to feel a thing. If they *had* felt any pain, they must have forgotten it as part of the wipe.

But Bryce flopped into a chair and started rocking back and forth with his eyes held shut, moaning, *my nose, my nose, my nose...*

Maybe I *did* have a zap.

Tina looked shocked. "What did you *do?*" she demanded.

"That never happened before!" I snapped. "Come on!"

I made for the door. Tina raced behind me, and Bryce's moans chased us all the way out to the hall.

"Where are you going?" Tina panted, as we hustled up the stairs.

"Your place," I panted back. "I wasn't kidding about getting the parrot."

"You shouldn't have said all that," she said, behind me. Without her face, her voice sounded hurt and sharp.

I hated that. "Trust me," I said. "He won't remember a thing."

"That's not what I mean!"

"I was *trying* to get him away from *you*," I snapped.

"I can take care of myself!"

I snorted. "You've got more boundary issues than a plate of yogurt."

"All he did was touch my shoulder!"

I stopped, gripping the banister. Tina stumbled past me, then turned back.

We faced each other in the narrow old spiral.

Quiet and low, I said, "He's some random dude. It's not okay."

She crossed her arms. "And what *you* did? That was okay?"

"I didn't mean to do *that*," I said.

"You didn't?"

"No! And I *promise* my hand hurts worse."

"How do you know?" she said.

"What, did you feel that *he* felt worse?"

"No, I didn't," she said. "That's not how it works. It's unpredictable. And confusing. And I just…" Her voice caught, but she kept on. "It would just be great if you remembered sometimes that you might not know *exactly* how it feels to be me."

We stood in silence.

For once, I shut up.

Finally, I said, "Okay. I'll try to remember that."

"Thanks."

"And if you ever need a human cattle prod…"

Tina snort-laughed, and the air around us seemed to relax. "Look," she said. "You may have a point about boundaries."

"Good," I said. "Now Old Mother Summer won't have to sit up nights worrying over your wild empath ways."

She smiled. "And I won't have to worry about you giving everyone dementia?"

I shrugged. "I only zap if they deserve it."

"Summer, seriously—"

I started up the stairs again. "Let's go get that parrot."

Behind me, Tina sighed.

We retrieved Keegan (and a quick breakfast), then decided it was now late enough in the morning to check in on our possible-future-murder-victim Taylor Pritchett. Tina knew the way to her room, and it was only after we knocked that I realized something important.

"Tina?" I said. "What are we going to say to this kid?"

"Oh, you know…" She scrunched her lips in thought. "Maybe Keegan'll get something."

"No way," Keegan chirped.

Tina eyed me. Then she held Keegan close so he could give her lips a peck. It was weird. (Giving Mr. Charm's nose a nuzzle is *totally* different.)

"It would help if you had some confidence," she said. "He can tell."

"It would also help if he told us something useful. Ever."

The door opened, revealing not a dark-haired teen, but a gray-mustachioed older Pritchett. When he saw us, his eyes boggled, and his jaw literally fell open.

"MURDERER!" Keegan squawked.

CHAPTER 26

"Mr. Pritchett?" Tina asked, with instant solicitude. "Are you all right?"

Why was she worried about *him?* The parrot had just outed the guy as the Mustache Murderer! I sent Keegan warm thoughts of heartfelt apologies. Then I realized I was attempting mystical contact with a bird. Who had just pooped on Tina's shoulder.

Meanwhile, the murderer ignored Tina, and he glared at *me* with open fright. "What are you doing at large?" he wheezed, in a pretentious educated accent like some guy on old-timey radio. "Aren't you the prime suspect?"

"*Me?*" I said. "*You're* the one who... I mean... oh."

This guy wasn't the murderer. He'd *thought* the *word* when he saw *me*.

Stupid parrot.

That was 0 for 2, Keegan. A false-alarm *MURDERER* and the cryptic, useless *GUITAR* he'd squawked with Mercedes.

"Two, two, tutu," Keegan chirped. "Ballerina."

The man squinted at the parrot, apparently distracted from his immediate concern that I would jump at the chance to off another male Pritchett. "How curious," he pontificated. "I would never have anticipated that a modern-day killer would affect the trappings of a literary pirate."

"*Pirate?*" I said.

"There must be a misunderstanding," Tina cut in, with a glowing smile. "We're hotel staff. We're only here to help, Mr. Pritchett."

"And the... *accoutrement*?" he asked, with a nod at Keegan.

"Oh, that's Keegan," Tina said brightly. "He's an old Inn tradition."

"Ah!" said Fitzgerald, and then his eyes went bright as he finally actually looked at Tina. "Please, call me Fitzgerald."

Personally, I'd rather have called him a taxi. But he ushered us in... and I tried not to gag.

Although Fitzgerald Pritchett was presentable enough, draped in an old tweed jacket with English professor elbow patches, his room was a disaster. Even the morning light and spacious architecture of the Inn couldn't atone for the tornado-strewn mess of clothes, bags of chips, boxes of cookies, and bottles of cheap whiskey.

On a lovely couch that had to be Victorian, the two teens slouched, messing with their phones.

They didn't look up, but somehow, they did perceive us. In unison, they rocked up out of the couch and lumbered toward us, still watching their screens.

Before I could say anything, they stood on either side of the parrot (totally ignoring me and Tina), arched out their phones, and snapped a string of selfies.

Then they sat back down, without a word.

Well. At least they weren't going to upload a video of Keegan being all telepathic. I hoped.

"These are my children," announced Fitzgerald, with a ring of paternal pride. "Tyler and Taylor."

Children, huh? The man had to be in his sixties, at least. I wondered whether this was his second (or third) marriage... and if he had a first wife, how did she feel about his new kids? Murderously jealous, perhaps?

"My wife, alas, could not join us," he continued. "She remains at home, unwell."

Tapping her phone, Taylor muttered, "You mean, 'hung over'."

The wrinkles in the man's face contracted with a spasm of shame. Maybe this kid was going to snark her way into an early grave.

"We won't bother you long," I said. "We just wanted to check on a few issues to make sure your experience is top notch."

Tina looked surprised, then granted me a subtle nod of approval.

"We noticed that one of your relatives felt she needed direct contact with the chef," I said. "Is that unusual?"

If it was, it might narrow the suspects a bit. At least to those who were more intimate with the old matriarch, and could rationally *plan* on her calling out the chef.

But Fitzgerald was shaking his head. "Alas, no," he said. "I'm afraid dear Nana puts on rather a display whenever she dines out. She's been in the habit for at least ten years."

So much for that. Looked like every Pritchett in the family tree could have planned on her yanking the chef out of the kitchen.

"What about guitars?" Tina said.

Fitzgerald frowned in confusion.

"Any… family traditions?" Tina pressed.

Fitzgerald's face cleared. "Well… now that you mention it…"

"Yes?"

The older man favored her with a long, bushy wink, then mimed a few chords on an air guitar at his mild paunch. "I used to play a bit myself."

"Yeah, *by* yourself," Taylor muttered.

Grandma must not have met this kid. If she had, she might have been open to letting fate take its course.

Fitzgerald scowled, then cleared his face. "Much as I would love to entertain such a lovely young woman…" he said to Tina, then darted me a quick glance and amended, "… *women*…"

"It's fine, dude," Keegan chirped.

The boy Tyler snorted loud through his nose. But Fitzgerald pressed on, and gestured us both toward the door. "... I should let you resume your duties. We're really finding the service quite satisfactory..."

"Aside from killing Uncle Nyle," Tyler muttered.

Somehow the older man was guiding us toward the door without actually touching us. Tina was already out the door.

I stopped walking, flicked the teen girl a glance, then faced her father. "Sir, I don't want to alarm you, but... is it possible any others in your family might be in danger?"

"Danger?" He frowned. "I don't know what you mean. The owner assured us that the kitchen—"

"Yes, yes, of course," I said hastily. "But if you have any... enemies..."

"Nonsense!" he snapped. "Thank you for concern, but no. Good day." He creaked shut the door...

...until Keegan chirped, "MANSION!"

Fitzgerald froze, and blanched pasty white.

Behind him back on the couch, the boy Tyler piped up, "It's talking about Nana's mansion."

"Obviously," Taylor said.

"Wow," Tina said. "You have a family mansion?"

"We do," Fitzgerald said, with a tight smile.

"*We* don't," Taylor called. "The whole dump's going to Cousin Kitty."

"Along with Nana's millions," Tyler added. "Everything."

Everything? I thought. This matriarch had a whole reunion's worth of descendants, and she was planning to give her entire fortune to *Kitty*?

But Fitzgerald's high forehead was flaming red, and he erupted in a voice so jagged that I jolted back.

"The Manse is *not* a *dump!*" he barked. Flecks of spittle creamed at the corners of his lips. "The Manse has been in the Pritchett family for *generations*. The architecture alone should make it a national treasure!"

"Psycho," Keegan chirped.

The teens giggled, and I wanted to throw that parrot out the window.

Yes, the thought had been mine; the man's sudden passion over an old house struck me as fairly disturbing. Now he was glaring at the parrot with serious venom. I looked to Tina, but her face had gone tight with resistance.

"Ignore him," I told Fitzgerald, trying to sound light. "Sounds like the Manse would be a great place to raise a family."

"Yes! Exactly!" he cried. His cheeks were flaming ruddy, almost feverish. "Yet for some *perverse* reasons of her own, my mother *insists* on living out her days there all alone. She has never shown the *slightest* interest in her youngest grandchildren."

On the couch, the last two scions of the House of Pritchett swiped at their screens.

"Maybe Kitty's been more… attentive?" I said.

"*Attentive?*" he roared. "That woman's not even a real Pritchett! And if you're suggesting that actual *family* need to *fawn* to earn the slightest consideration, well, that didn't work out so well for Nyle, did it?"

"Oh?" I said, struggling to maintain the pretense that this conversation was remotely normal. "Nyle never struck me as the fawning type."

"Is that *so?*" he snapped. I couldn't tell whether he'd made the connection that I'd actually worked with Nyle or he was just too worked up to question the logic of a random maid having an opinion on Nyle's character. "Well, you must have missed his remarkable turnaround in the last few months. Suddenly he was *devoted*. Flying in to the Manse for weekend visits. Entertaining my mother for hours on end."

"Gold digger?" Keegan chirped.

I flicked Tina a private scowl. She needed to gag that thing.

But Fitzgerald laughed, way too loud. "Your parrot is a remarkable judge of character," he said. "I'll give Nyle this; at least he would have kept the Manse in the family. But that little Carter..." His fists clenched. "I expect she'll liquidate the Manse before my mother is cold in her grave."

The dread vision entranced him. He seemed to stare past us, seeing a future where, despite his decades of futile scheming, the Manse would slip past his children into the hands of strangers.

My mind was buzzing with new questions. Bryce had said that Nyle *needed* money. Had he needed it so badly that he'd tried to woo his awful grandmother?

And if he had... had Kitty killed him to keep a grip on the huge fortune?

On the other hand, what if it wasn't *Kitty* who'd seen Nyle as the looming threat?

Fitzgerald was clenching his fists so hard that his knuckles were turning white. I knew *I* wouldn't want to be the one standing between him and his obsession.

More than one Pritchett might be capable of murder.

CHAPTER 27

Tina and I (and Keegan) made an awkward goodbye and scuttled off down the hall. At the corner, we held a conference, whispering beside the wainscot paneling.

"Now what?" I said. "We've got yet another suspect for Nyle, but we still have no idea who'd want to kill that teen."

"We'll just have to stay and watch," Tina said.

"All day?" I said. "Couldn't we post a security camera or something?"

"I don't know where we'd get one." She scrunched her forehead, thinking. "Actually, wait. We might have a camera in storage. Grandma was thinking about an indoor security system, and she ordered one to test it, but then she ran into some hitch. You're supposed to be able to watch the feed on your phone."

"Perfect!" I said.

"I guess." Tina frowned, and peeked back down the hall at Taylor's door. "But wouldn't it feel kind of… creepy?"

"What, and it's *less* creepy to stand around all day like stalkers?"

"Kind of," she said.

"I don't get this. We're trying to save this kid's life. And you spend half your time spying on people's *emotions*."

"Maybe that's why! I'd just feel more comfortable if—"

Down the hall, the door opened.

We darted around the corner, then both slipped our heads out just enough to see. Behind us, hidden by the wall, Keegan clacked and muttered on Tina's arm.

Fitzgerald Pritchett shuffled out, followed by his son Tyler and... that was it. Fitzgerald called something to his daughter, then he closed the door and the two walked off.

"Why's she staying?" I said.

"Maybe she ate already," Tina said. "They've got enough junk food in there to host a convention."

"The others are going to breakfast?"

"Must be," Tina said. "Which reminds me. I need to get down there during the rush."

"What? No!" I said. "Don't leave me here alone! I'll die of boredom!"

She smiled. "No worries. You'll have Keegan."

She tried to hand me the bird, but Keegan squawked and flapped in a panic.

"No! No!" he cried. "Help!"

Tina rolled her eyes, but she took him back. "Fine, you can stew in your cage. Won't *that* be fun?"

"Yes!" Keegan chirped.

"Seriously, what am I supposed to do here?" I said. "Just stand here and watch? I don't even have a phone to play with!"

"Then you won't get distracted," she said. "I'll take a turn after breakfast, promise."

"Wait, wait!" I said. "That stupid bird pooped on your shoulder." I swung my giant purse around front and started digging. "I think I've got baby wipes."

"Baby wipes?" Tina said.

"I've got *everything* in here," I said. "Shoot, they're in here *somewhere*..."

"It's fine," she said. "I'll get a napkin."

And off she sprinted down the elegant hallway. With a handful of parrot.

That's Wonder Springs for you.

I leaned against the corner, watched, and waited. And waited. And waited some more.

I have never been so bored in my entire life.

I don't know how cops and detectives do stakeouts all the time. I would lose my mind.

True, I guess they might have a partner along, and they could trade quips. Or take turns reading. Or knitting. *Something*.

I found myself totally coveting Taylor's phone. What was she *doing* in there? Reading news? Watching videos? Checking Tribesy? Could I somehow sneak in and watch over her shoulder? No, that would probably be weird.

But so would me having a psychotic break out here in the hall.

What are you so anxious about? I wondered. I was pacing now, making a tight circle on the old plush carpet, stirring up the dust motes in the musty stillness. *What's wrong with a bit of reflective solitude? Don't you have a few life questions you could be sorting out?*

Of course I did, you priggish neocortex. That's exactly *why* I was anxious.

I wish I could report that I had some big personal breakthrough, just me, myself, and the loving old grandmotherly Inn.

But mainly, I obsessed about whether the Sheriff had a warrant yet to haul me off to jail. For all I knew, that tox report on the vial from my room could be coming any minute.

When Tina finally came back to me, after about six months, I'd worked myself up pretty bad.

"We can't spend all day doing this," I hissed. "We've got to keep talking to people and figure out who got Nyle."

"I thought we'd catch the killer when he came for Taylor," she said.

"You mean *if*," I said. "And we don't even know it'll be the same person. There's no conceivable motive to get both Nyle and Taylor. Maybe the Pritchetts are all homicidal maniacs."

"What about the will?" Tina said. "Maybe there's more going on there; maybe 'Nana' is having second thoughts about that Kitty woman after all."

"Good point," I said. "We haven't even talked to her yet."

"Go ahead. I'll stay, you go."

"By *myself?*" I blurted. Tina smiled, and I hastily added, "No empath drama? No cryptic parrot?"

"You're welcome to try getting Keegan."

I shuddered. "No thanks."

"Text me when you're done," Tina said. "I'll tell you where I am; Taylor might have moved."

"I broke my phone, remember?"

"Oh. Then try not to take too long. It's fine, I doubt she's going anywhere."

"Where is this Nana woman?"

"Second floor, first door left of the elevator, because she can't walk so well. Her name's Priscilla Pritchett."

"*Priscilla?*" My stomach twinged with dread, and I recalled her stentorian abuse of the usually intimidating Vladik.

Tina frowned with concern. "Are you all right?"

Of *course* I was all right. I was leaving Tina alone to maybe tackle a killer, while I jaunted off to chitchat with an old lady. I had no excuse to feel so intimidated.

So tell that to my cold sweat.

CHAPTER 28

"*Enter!*" boomed Priscilla Pritchett.

I fumbled open her door and slipped in. I blinked; the room was large, the largest suite I'd seen yet, but shrouded in shadow. The wide curtains were drawn, and a single lamp cast a dim pool of light around the grand old matriarch.

Priscilla was settled in an easy chair, her bulk at rest. Her body seemed to have turned against her. Her calves were swollen, poking out beneath her elegant dress, and I noticed that across the long room, on a counter in the kitchenette, a massive pill box was stocked for at least three weeks. The pills were the size of jelly beans.

She was flipping through papers that had dense, difficult print, and looked like financial statements. And when she snapped me a glare through her glasses, her gaze was clear and sharp.

"What do you want?" she said. "I didn't call for room service." She squinted, searing me with even greater scrutiny. "Or for anyone to poison my meal."

Great.

I considered trying to be clever, but this lady struck me as the type who enjoyed eviscerating any efforts to persuade. The sort who wants the price up front, and woe unto you if you slip in any fees.

Kind of like Grandma, come to think of it.

"I want to clear my name, Mrs. Pritchett," I said. "I didn't kill your grandson, and I want to know who did."

The matriarch cocked her head, bemused. I calculated that my candor had bought me, at most, an extra sixty seconds. Maybe less. I hate hard sells.

"I see," she said. "And what makes you think that this tragedy would have any connection with me?"

I steadied my breathing. Why was this woman getting so much under my skin? "I was just speaking with your son Fitzgerald," I said. "He seemed to think—"

"I know exactly what he thinks!" she snapped. "The man's only had one thought for the last twenty years. And if he'd ever bothered to make something of himself, he wouldn't have gotten himself into a bidding war with his own nephew."

"Bidding war?" I said. "You mean Nyle wanted… your *house?*"

"Of course he did," she said, contemptuous of my slow wit. "Just like his uncle, he had it in his head that he was going to carry his wife over the threshold and raise himself a little brood of Pritchetts, right there in the ancestral home. The difference was, Nyle was willing to pay for it."

"Fitzgerald wanted your house for free?" I said.

"Not *free*. But the man couldn't wrap his mind around the concept of *market value*. He's been badgering me for decades for a 'family discount.'" She sniffed. "I worked very hard to get where I am, young lady. And you can't pay insurance premiums with filial affection."

"Couldn't you have rented him *part* of the house?" I said. "The Manse sounds pretty big."

She fixed me with a gimlet glare. "I prioritize my privacy."

Maybe she wasn't quite like Grandma after all. Grandma's "house" was an Inn; she literally took in strangers. This woman couldn't even stand to share a mansion with her own family.

Granted, this was Tyler and Taylor we were talking about.

But still. It's not like they were loud or disruptive. If someone kept their fridge stocked and the electricity running, those kids might not emerge from the basement till they were thirty-five.

Then I realized a problem. "Why didn't you mind Nyle and Mercedes moving in?"

"I did," she said. "But Nyle was willing to be... generous. I could have bought myself an even more suitable home."

I didn't even want to know how much money Nyle had promised to throw around. No wonder he'd been leaning on Bryce to get his money back. I wondered whether Mercedes even knew she'd inspired all this domestic strain.

"But what about Kitty?" I said. "Wouldn't she want the Manse?"

Priscilla scowled. Softly she said, "Fitzgerald *has* been chatty, hasn't he? He always had a weakness for a fresh young thing."

I bristled. "Actually, it wasn't *me*—"

"I'll tell you a little secret," the matriarch said. Her scowl deepened, till it was positively venomous. "My family has been one lifelong disappointment."

"Oh," I said, stunned. "I'm... sorry to hear that."

"Thank you. But the *one* exception, in all that brood, has been Kitty." A small warmth crept into her face, a distant hint of affection. "Kitty's more Pritchett than the rest put together. Of all the family, she's the most like me." She frowned again. "And I can *assure* you, Kitty couldn't have cared less who owned the Manse. She knew that she'd be *very* well taken care of."

"So does that mean...?" I trailed off. Kitty *couldn't* have killed Nyle. What had I been thinking? She'd been doing that video call the *whole time*... she was the *one* Pritchett who had an actual documented video alibi. The only one automatically disqualified.

Well, aside from Priscilla herself. Not only had she been publicly arguing with Vladik the whole time, but even if she hadn't, she could never have nipped in and out of the kitchen on those swollen legs. She'd have needed five or ten minutes just to cross the dining room.

Who did that leave? Fitzgerald?

A disappointed old man, on the verge of losing his dream... to Nyle?

But if *he* was the killer, who was coming for his daughter?

Could Fitzgerald have some deranged scheme to move Priscilla to pity? Like, if Taylor was killed, Priscilla would finally see how much she *really* loved her grandchildren, and the least she could do was welcome the surviving Tyler into the Manse?

That... was a stretch.

A more likely option: now that Fitzgerald had killed once, he figured he might as well take care of his annoying daughter while he was on a roll.

Then I felt terrible for thinking that. Truth was, I was jealous of her for having a doting dad.

"Would you care to share your fascinating reflections?" Priscilla asked, jolting me out of my ill-timed reverie.

"I apologize, I got distracted," I said. I very much did not want to overstay my welcome. "Thank you so much. I appreciate your time."

"And what is your name, may I ask?" she said, her beady gaze boring up at me.

"Oh," I said. I hesitated, but I couldn't very well refuse. "Summer. Summer Sassafras."

"I see." She set down her papers, and folded her thick fingers across her lap. "I don't believe I've ever heard that name."

I shrugged. "It's not very common," I said.

"I won't forget."

I had the urge to reach out and make sure she did.

But that was pointless; it was *way* too late to wipe the whole conversation. And she could easily get my name from Tina or anyone else.

Plus, she had to be pushing ninety, and she clearly had health issues. I'd never done any real damage with the Touch (assuming Bryce had recovered), but I didn't want to push my luck if I could possibly help it.

Besides, what could she really do to me? Sure, she sounded wealthy enough to hire five separate assassins, but that was just paranoid.

Still, as I walked away, my back could feel the prickle of her gaze.

As I pulled the door shut, my hand on the knob, I realized that I'd forgotten to ask her one key point. Fitzgerald clearly believed that Nyle had wanted her fortune, rather than the house. What if other Pritchetts had made the same mistake? If Nyle had been killed to get access to the fortune, but Kitty was innocent... who stood to inherit *after* Kitty?

What if Kitty was the next target?

I popped back into the room. "Mrs. Pritchett?" I called. "I just had one more quick—"

"*Out!*" shrieked Priscilla, in a terrible voice that skewered me right in the chest.

I froze. Why on earth was she glaring like that, her eyes wide and wild with rage? My gaze dropped to her hands, but she wasn't counting piles of cash or drugs or anything; she was just fumbling with that huge pill box. Was she that ashamed of her meds?

"I'm sorry!" I said. "I didn't mean—"

"Now!" she roared. "And don't you *dare* invade my privacy again!"

I scooted back out, my heart pounding. As I hurried back to the hall where Tina was keeping watch, I kept cycling those final moments through my mind. What the heck was *that* all about?

Priscilla had to be hiding something. Something huge.

But I couldn't shake the feeling that whatever it was... I'd already seen her secret. Somehow, it was right in front of my face.

Frustrating.

I was still mulling this over as I panted back to the hallway corner where I'd left Tina.

She was gone.

"Relax," I muttered, as I fast-walked down the empty hall to Taylor's room. I listened at the door. Nothing. I knocked, waited, and then tried the knob, and to my surprise, the door creaked open.

The room was empty. And trashed.

"Tina?" I called. "Fitzgerald? Taylor?"

No answer.

Now my pulse was pounding in my neck. I ran to the spiral staircase and leapt down two at a time. "Tina?" I called. *"Tina!"*

What had I been *thinking*, leaving her alone with some psychopathic killer? If anyone had hurt that girl, I would hunt them down and zap them senseless.

I tore through the lobby and over to the dining room. Maybe Taylor had finally moseyed on down for brunch?

Nope. Empty. The breakfast crowd was long gone.

Where could they be? I tried to focus on the options that weren't lethal. What about shopping? The town was practically one big walking mall; she must have drifted out there, right? Of course. I ran back to the entrance, rushed outside and across the front plaza...

... and plowed right into Sheriff Jake.

CHAPTER 29

"Ms. *Sassafras*," he intoned, with a deep, noisy sniff. "Just the person I was hunting down."

"Have you seen Tina?" I panted.

"I have not," he said. "But I'm going to need you to turn around and put your hands behind your back."

From a work belt crammed with cop tools, he slipped out a pair of cuffs.

I drew back. "Wait! No! You don't understand, she's in danger!"

"Ms. Sassafras, as a courtesy to the Inn, I'd prefer not to make a scene. However—"

"Do you even have a warrant?"

"Of course." He showed his teeth in a grin that was freakishly doggy, like a mutt so pleased with his catch that he couldn't stop wagging his tail. "We expedited that report. The evidence is in, Ms. Sassafras. And the judge agrees you're a flight risk."

"Flight risk? I can't even buy gas! And there are *multiple* suspects that actually make *sense!* His whole toxic family is festering with motives!"

He scowled. "Do you really expect me to take advice on a murder investigation from an amateur? Who is *also* the prime suspect, with the *murder weapon found in her room?*"

"It's not my fault you're too lazy to actually investigate," I snapped. "Did you even know that Nyle's fiance used to be in a relationship with his brother?"

The sheriff frowned, but I caught his face flicker in a microexpression of doubt.

"Please," I said. "I promise I'm not going anywhere, but we *need* to find Tina. Or that teenage girl, Taylor Pritchett. She really is in lethal danger."

"Excuse me?" he said. "And how would you know that?"

I hesitated. Was Sheriff Jake in the Inner Circle that knew Grandma's secret?

"Ms. Sassafras," he snapped. "You're stating a serious threat."

"And *you*," snapped Grandma, "are being a serious nuisance."

Both the sheriff and I startled, and we turned to see Grandma glowering beside us, her arms crossed tight.

The sheriff wilted slightly. Then he rallied and drew himself up. "I've got a warrant, Christina," he said. "I'm sorry."

"What you're going to have is another murder on your hands," she said. "Not that I expect you to listen to sense."

The sheriff stepped closer and hissed in a lower voice. "That's not fair and you know it, Christina. In my world, there's a little thing called *evidence*."

"Oh, of *course*," she said, and she tapped him on his big nose.

He sneezed, then angrily wiped his nose with the back of his hairy hand. "Christina Meredith!" he yapped in frustration. "When are you going to respect that this is a delicate instrument?"

"Perhaps when you decide to supplement it with mental activity."

But I no longer cared about their bickering. At the full name, *Christina Meredith*, that strange tingle had quivered again in my chest, as when I'd first read the last name in her letter. *Christina Meredith.* The name made me ache, like when you wake up haunted by a dream that you know was piercingly beautiful, and you know that it's lost forever.

Then, at the front of the Inn, someone caught my eye.

Beside the oaken double front doors, an arch of white blossoms framed a sign on the stone wall: *The Inn at Wonder Springs*. It was clearly designed as a selfie trap, and a woman was standing by the sign, holding out her phone and posing.

Her phone.

It was some kind of attack, Grandma had said. *She was using her phone.*

But the woman was… Mercedes.

The hair was all wrong. Grandma had dreamed of long dark hair, but Mercedes wore her hair shaved short on the sides and dyed bright pink. There she was, rocking a new punk outfit, puckering for the camera and checking the screen…

…except, as I watched, she frowned at her photo, reached up behind her head, and *shook out her long black top hair.*

Oh crud.

"Mercedes!" I shouted.

Both Sheriff Jake and Grandma shut up and stared at me.

But Mercedes hadn't heard. She raised her phone for another shot.

"Mercedes!" I called again. I started fast-walking across the plaza, then broke into a jog.

Behind me, the sheriff thundered for me to stop, but Grandma said something back, and I didn't even catch it because now I could *feel* that something was horribly wrong; every hair on my limbs was standing straight up, full-body alert, right here in the sunny pretty plaza, and I wondered if this was how targets felt, in that last second before the sniper fired, and I was calling *Mercedes! Mercedes!* but she just kept looking at her stupid phone and I was jogging faster and I thought *snipers are high* and I finally looked up and *oh my gosh this huge thing was falling…*

I ran and tackled her. Rolled.

The thing smashed. The sharp crash was piercing, like the shatter of glass. Bits hit my back, both dirt and fragments of something hard. But also the brush of something creepy and soft.

I twisted back to look. It was a tree.

An ornamental tree, three or four feet long, prone amid the dirt and ruins of a pot that must have been enormous.

And way too damn close. The blossoms were brushing my calf.

I realized I was on top of Mercedes, and I heaved myself off and sat on my knees. "Sorry," I said.

"Sorry?" she gasped, still lying on the cobblestones. "Oh my God, you saved my *life*."

"I guess I did," I said. "If you're feeling grateful... I could really use some gas money."

Mercedes looked confused.

Then she looked past me, up, and her face froze.

I twisted back to follow her gaze.

On a rooftop veranda, three or four stories up, at the top of the Inn, a man was leaning over the railing and looking down.

Lionel.

But though his face was far away, and the high sun cast him in shadow, I could still have sworn that he looked... surprised.

Even horrified.

PART IV

CHAPTER 30

Before I could even get up off the plaza stone, Grandma was at my side.

"Are you all right?" she demanded. Her piercing gaze probed my face, then flitted across me in an instant triage. Her care was ferocious, like a mama panther.

"I'm fine," I said, staggering to my feet. "Really, I promise."

Her frown softened into a warm smile.

"Well done, sweet pea," she said, her voice husky. "Well done."

Yes, this felt amazing. I felt like I was five, and the teacher had just given me every gold star in her desk.

Across the plaza, the sheriff hollered up to the roof. "Lionel Pritchett!" he barked. "Stay right there!"

Lionel bolted out of sight.

"Dang it!" he yelled. "Christina, where's his room? What floor?"

She told him (she knew, of course), and he took off toward the Inn. He ran *exceedingly* fast for a man with his age and paunch... he was practically *loping* like a hound.

It's these little surprise details that keep freaking you out. Even if you've just dodged an early death by a plummeting pot.

"Go!" Grandma snapped at me. "I'll care for Mercedes and lock down the Inn."

So I tore after the old man, panting to keep up and clutching my massive purse so it wouldn't thud against my side. At least I was still wearing the stupid sneakers, not the sandals or high heels that would have looked like, you know, a grownup. I barely managed to keep the sheriff in sight as we pounded up the staircase.

I'd worked very hard to catch this killer. No way I was going to let him slip out now.

The sheriff burst through Lionel's door, and I rushed in right behind. Lionel's side of the room looked even more disastrous than before, with multiple suitcases disgorged on his bed. But he was hunched on a pile of clothes, feverishly scraping the touchpad of a laptop.

"Hands in the air!" barked Sheriff Jake.

"Wait! Please!" Lionel gasped. He was panting, his face flushed and his jowls quivering, like his run down here from the rooftop veranda had been the most exercise he'd had since high school. Honestly, I was feeling the burn myself. The sheriff didn't even look winded.

"I've got to show you this!" Lionel gasped. "Evidence!"

The sheriff unsnapped his side holster. "Evidence of what?"

"I didn't do it," Lionel said, still frantically swiping and clicking. "I don't know how that pot fell. I was only there because I got a message. From Mercedes. To meet."

"*Mercedes?*" I snapped. "Why would she want to meet *you?*"

Lionel scowled. "She didn't say!"

"Isn't *that* convenient—" I started, but the sheriff cut in.

"What kind of message was this?" he said. His eyes narrowed. "Email? Text?"

"It was an email, but it said something about how it would self-destruct... you had to click through to the browser to see the actual message... oh, thank God!" Lionel exhaled, suddenly exhausted. "It's still here."

"Let me see that!" I snapped, and I grabbed the laptop.

On the screen, a web browser showed a short message that was just what he'd said it was. A typed note to meet on the rooftop veranda, "right now, this can't wait," with the signature *Mercedes*.

Then the laptop croaked a loud *BEEP*, and the screen went black.

Oh, come *on*.

I made a mental note: next time a murder investigation hinged on evidence on an electronic device, let someone *else* touch it.

(So dumb.)

Sheriff Jake leaned in to look. "This computer's dead," he said.

"What?" Lionel shrieked. He lunged and grabbed it back, fiddling with the keys. "No! No no no no *no*..."

He rebooted the machine, and it seemed to start fine. But when he launched his browser again, the message was gone.

"It was here! I swear!" he cried.

Sheriff Jake eyed me with a suspicious glare, and his nostrils quivered. But whatever he'd heard about my "power", if anything, it didn't seem to include the part about sporadically frying electronics. (I wasn't sure even Grandma knew that part yet.) And all he'd seen me do was *take* the machine, not press any buttons. So despite his obvious intuition that it was my fault, he turned back to Lionel.

"I'll take that computer," he said. "I've got a tech guy who can take a look."

"You do?" Lionel said. He eagerly handed it over.

"Absolutely. And I'll need you to come with me."

Lionel blanched. The flush drained right out, leaving him pasty white. "But I swear, that pot just *fell*—"

"Don't worry, we'll get your full statement," the sheriff said, as he bent and took Lionel's arm.

Lionel winced at the meaty grip. But he rocked up to his feet. "I'm calling my lawyer!" he warned. "He'll come down and slap you with a lawsuit so fast—"

"That'll be fine," the sheriff said, as he urged him out into the hall. "Tell him we've got great fishing here in Wonder Springs."

As I watched them go, I felt torn. On the one hand, even that glimpse of the message had me convinced that Lionel was innocent. I'm not super techie and I knew that, in theory, he could have faked it... but Lionel just didn't seem the supervillain type. He also didn't seem *that* stupid, and what kind of idiot fakes an alibi that'll vanish if he reboots?

On the other hand, if Lionel was clear, that might put me back in the hot seat. Without Lionel, I lost my handy fall guy for whoever'd planted the poison in my room. Then it would my arm trapped in the sheriff's mitt.

And the *real* killer would still be out there.

At the door, Sheriff Jake turned and gave me a gruff nod. "Don't go anywhere yet, Miss Sassafras," he said. "But, for now... good job. I think you saved that young woman's life."

"Thanks," I said.

But inside, I thought... she's not saved *yet*.

I had to find Mercedes and get the whole truth. Someone had gone to a lot of trouble to crush her skull.

Someone who would certainly strike again.

CHAPTER 31

I rushed to find Mercedes' room. Even though I was in a hurry, I still avoided that creepy old elevator. I'd have to ask Grandma what the deal was with that thing.

Mercedes wasn't in her room.

Then I remembered that Grandma was probably feeding her. This was the South, after all. When in doubt, bring out the comfort food.

I totally nailed it. When I crept into the dining room, unsure whether Lionel's public arrest meant I could now safely show my face, I found Grandma there, tending to a sparse lunch crowd. She caught my eye, then nodded across the room toward Mercedes, who was sitting alone in a sunny nook and digging into a teetering stack of pancakes.

Pancakes...

"Nice," I said as I walked up, stealing a hungry glance at her plate and a heavenly whiff of warm syrup. "Maybe someone'll try to kill *me*."

Mercedes frowned. "You can have the pancakes."

"Sorry." I sat across from her, and her fork and knife clinked in the silence.

Finally, without looking up, she said, "Did you get him?"

"We did." I hesitated. "But I'm still... concerned."

"*You're* concerned?" she demanded. Now she did look up, incredulous.

"Someone sent him a message. Claiming to be you."

I watched her carefully, but it didn't take an empath to see that she was shocked.

"So that means..." she faltered. "Whoever did it... they're still..."

She was starting to freak out, and I decided to take a chance. Besides, she wasn't a Pritchett, so if things went sideways, the Touch might just actually wipe her memory, like it was supposed to, instead of blasting us both like a cattle prod.

"Mercedes, listen to me," I said. "I don't know if it's connected, but could this possibly have anything to do with... a guitar?"

She stared. Then she blasted out a laugh.

First it erupted. Then it fizzled into cascades of giggles, the pent-up stress spewing until she was gasping for breath.

I waited, fingers at the ready.

At last she could manage to talk. "That stupid parrot. What the hell is that about?"

"It's complicated," I said. "But if someone's trying to kill you over a musical instrument—"

"No, no." She sighed, and fiddled with her napkin. "This is so stupid," she muttered.

"If you're sure it doesn't connect to Nyle—"

"Oh, it does. But it's just..." She flickered with sudden sadness, wiped a finger across one eye, and took a deep shuddering breath. "None of this had to happen."

"How? What do you mean?"

She straightened up and steadied her voice. "So... a *very* long time ago, I was... involved... with this minor celebrity. Punk rock."

"Really?" I said, trying to sound flatteringly surprised. She'd put her black top hair back up, so her pink sides made her look ready to jump on stage and sing backup. "Who?"

"I'd rather not say," she said. "Because when things didn't end well, I kept a souvenir."

I laughed. "Wow! And he never knew?"

"No way. He would have prosecuted to the full extent of the law. Trust me. Which is why it was incredibly stupid for me to tell Nyle."

"Huh," I said, sensing where this was going. I decided to make another risky probe. We were still alone in the dining room, right? The Touch was still on the table. "Don't take this the wrong way, but I was kind of curious why you went for Nyle."

She scowled. "Is there a *right* way to take that question?"

Crud. I eyed her bare hands, slicing away at the pile of carbs… I might be able to reach her wrist before she noticed…

But she tossed her head. "Nyle could be smooth. In some ways, he was like an improved version of his brother. Who, by the way, was a *totally* different person before he went all corporate. You'd never guess it now…" She frowned, thoughtful. "Honestly? There's definitely a perverse rush in getting with your ex's brother." She paused, and forked another syrupy mouthful. "Or maybe it was just the perversity of Nyle."

"How so?"

"Let's not go there," she said. "I was done. I wanted out."

Shocker, I thought. "And he really thought he could use the guitar thing to make you get *married*?"

"We didn't really start fighting until after the engagement," she said. "And he got so damn excited to announce the wedding date *here*, at the stupid reunion. Lionel and Deanna would have to take it in public, in front of the whole family."

"Sounds like Nyle," I said.

"The last straw was that creepy old Pritchett Manse. Have you seen any pictures? That place is like a Civil War nightmare; it's falling apart, maybe the ghosts are chewing it to bits. I don't know what family fantasy he thought he needed to act out, but I was not going to be the woman on his arm."

"So were you really going to do it? Marry him?"

"No! I don't know." She rubbed her face. "I wasn't thinking that far ahead. It was like, just get through this stupid reunion, let him lord it over Lionel, and then figure out some way to break it off." She shrugged. "Or get some dirt to blackmail him back."

Yikes, I thought. "It sounds like this guitar thing was a long time ago. Are you sure you'd have even been arrested?"

"I don't know. At a minimum, I'd have lost my job. My department head is a stickler."

I startled, trying to imagine her walking into an office building.

Mercedes smirked, and let down her hair. To my amazement, as she shook it out, the pink was entirely hidden. Her face was framed in a respectable corporate cut.

She eyed me. "I really am pathetic," she said.

"No, not at all..." I said, weakly. I found myself remembering my own corporate suits, the ritual mornings preparing my battle garb.

For the first time since I'd landed in Wonder Springs, I realized how utterly I was *not* missing that life. Not the endless sales calls, not the traffic and the urban blight, not a single one of my "colleagues". If I had to choose, I'd much rather be broke here in this bizarre pretty town, having fun... chasing a killer.

"So if Lionel didn't attack you," I said, "who do you think did?"

"Who else?" Mercedes said, weary. "His wife."

"Deanna?" I tried to picture the beady-eyed neat freak as a killer. It was pretty easy. "But why would she have targeted *Nyle?* I could see Lionel wanting revenge, but his wife?"

"She *hated* Nyle. He... we... were humiliating them *both.*" She shook her head, and slunk back in her chair. "The irony is, if she'd just waited a couple weeks, she'd have gotten all the payback on Nyle she could have wanted. I would never, *ever* have gone through with that wedding in the end. But I kept my mouth shut, procrastination won... and now he's dead. And I might be next."

She looked so sad that I wished I could hug her. "I doubt it," I said. "You don't think she'd try again?"

"I don't know. Where *is* Deanna?"

Crud. That was a very good question.

She hadn't been in the bedroom with Lionel. She could be anywhere.

And the sheriff was busy hauling off the wrong suspect.

CHAPTER 32

I left Mercedes to finish her pancakes under Grandma's watchful eye, and I raced off to find Deanna. But as I hurried out into the hallway, I realized a couple things.

One, if Deanna really was a murderer, maybe I didn't want to apprehend her all by myself, and two, since Taylor had never been the target, Tina could drop guard duty.

These were two great reasons to find Tina first. The problem was, I had no idea where she might be either.

If she were still following Taylor, she could be anywhere in Wonder Springs. But if she'd heard about the attack on Mercedes, she might be looking for *me*... or she might even have gone back to work. I was still pretty hazy on what exactly Tina did all day, besides greet and seat people during meal times, but once or twice she'd mentioned helming the front desk. I might as well start there.

Just like the first time I'd seen it, the wide old desk and the wall of cubby holes made me feel like I was walking into a classic film. Cary Grant might stroll up and give me a mysterious wink.

Thinking of dishy movie stars reminded me of Cade.

I really did need to clear the air with Tina.

True, the whole physical-contact-zaps-your-memory thing had always made romance... problematic. But who knew? Maybe a guy who could cure blight was the one man who'd be able to handle my Touch. I mean, yes, he hadn't actually touched me *yet*... his healing seemed to operate with a tiny bit of airspace, hands hovering instead of skin-to-skin contact. Still, a healer had to have some special power here, right?

Or maybe that was "magical thinking". Literally.

I leaned over the counter, craning to see through a door to the back office. I opened my mouth to call, "Tina?" but her name died on my tongue. Something else died too. Hope.

Because through the crack of the open door, I did see Tina.

In Cade's arms.

They were facing each other, eyes closed, smiles soft. His strong arms enfolded her, his hands were moving gently down her back…

My stomach clenched, and a splitting headache seared down my skull. In that moment, I wanted someone to die. Maybe me, maybe Tina. Maybe both. I felt utterly shut out from the world… abandoned, untouched, and alone.

Then Tina cried out and clutched her own head, exactly where I hurt.

Damn it. I skittered away around the corner and huddled out of sight. The last thing I needed was the Perfect Couple catching me in my desperate yearn.

Though their voices were muffled, I heard Cade making solicitous murmurs of concern, then Tina replying with reassuring sweetness. *Don't worry, I'm fine*, I could imagine her saying. *Must have been some passing loser.*

Well, no. Tina would never *call* you that. Even in private, that would be beneath her. Like everything else.

I heard the door creak open, and Tina spoke. "Hello?" she called. "Is someone waiting?"

I steeled myself. I had a killer to catch, remember? Make that *we*. Tina had treated me just about perfect; it wasn't *her* fault I'd come down with an Insta-Crush on her boyfriend. Or that he was into exchanging soulful personal stories with near-strangers in his orchard by the moonlight, or that he might be one of like five guys on the planet who might have some magical ability to touch my skin without literally losing his mind. Plus, for all I knew, my four other options were probably stringy old creeps... but Tina could have any guy she wanted...

Okay, STOP, I thought. Just stop. Tina was with Cade, that was how it was, and I was going to put this all behind me and be Tina's friend. Or at least cordial acquaintance. She'd never even know; I'd never need her pity.

I took a deep breath, and I sauntered around the corner.

At the counter, Tina was radiant, eyes sparkling. I don't know about Cade, because I couldn't even look.

"Summer!" Tina called. "I heard about Mercedes! I'm so glad you're okay!"

"Me too," Cade put in.

"Thanks," I said, ignoring Cade and bracing myself against Tina's torrent of honest affection. I stayed focused on Tina. "We've got to talk."

"Sure," she said, with a cryptic glance toward Cade. She frowned. "Are you sure you're all right? You feel..."

"I'm fine!" I snapped. Against my better judgment, I flicked a look at Cade, and his surprise at my outburst twisted in my gut. *Dodged the bullet with me, didn't you?* I thought. "Really, I am," I added, with forced calm. "I mean, I did do a flying tackle, so I might be a little sore."

"I bet," Tina said. "And nothing bad happened with Lionel, right? Sheriff Jake just took him away."

"He did," I said. "But I don't think he got the right guy."

"You don't?" Tina said.

"Neither do I," said a new voice, close behind my shoulder.

I turned in surprise. It was Kitty Carter.

Her mousy little face was grim, and she met my gaze with a level stare. "After what happened with Mercedes, I decided to watch that video after all."

"You did?" Tina chirped, excited.

Kitty nodded, her eyes still fixed on me. "I think you should take a look."

CHAPTER 33

Tina tried to invite Cade along, but I cut in, and he took the hint.

I considered asking Kitty to wait until we'd found Deanna, but on consideration... what exactly did I plan to *do?* It's not like I could arrest the woman. Would I just start following *her* around? I had zero proof, just the obvious fact that if she were a vengeful wife, she'd be highly motivated to kill both Nyle and Mercedes, and frame her loser husband. Not quite grounds for arrest, even in Wonder Springs.

But if Kitty had spotted something on this video... real proof would change everything.

Mercedes would be safe for now. But we had to make this as quick as possible.

As Tina and I hustled down the hall after Kitty, I tried to talk like everything was normal.

"Whatever happened with you and Taylor?" I asked Tina. "When I came back, you were gone."

"Oh, right!" Tina said. "Sorry about that. She came out right after you left, and she went down to eat."

"You mean nothing happened? I was worried sick! The room was trashed!"

"I know." Tina scrunched her nose. "They must have a maid at home."

Oh right. The room had looked ransacked when I saw it empty, but in my panic, I'd forgotten that it had *already* looked ransacked when we'd been interviewing Fitzgerald and the teens. Oops.

"Anyway, I followed Taylor down," Tina said, "and then I was like, why don't we just hang out? It's way easier, and the killer might back off if she's not alone."

"You *hung out?* With that teenager?"

"Yeah, she's actually pretty neat."

"I thought she was glued to her phone!"

"I know, right? But get this: she was *editing* a *movie.* Can you believe it? I had no idea you could do that on a *phone.* It's this short film she shot herself, a documentary. She and her friends went around interviewing these senior citizens who lost their spouses to this new pharmaceutical. They're hoping to get the drug pulled; there's this nonprofit putting together a class-action lawsuit, and they said a video like this could be a *huge* awareness boost."

"Great," I said, trying to sound enthusiastic. What was the world coming to? You turn around, and even the twerps turn out to be activists saving lives.

Kitty led us up the stairs (I was glad to see she shared my feelings on the elevator) and bustled into her room. Last time I'd been here, she'd locked me out, so now I finally got to see her place.

It was... underwhelming. Of all the Pritchetts, Kitty seemed the most capable of just staying in a hotel room like a normal human being. Everything was tidy; even the nightstand was clear.

She pulled a chair over to a vintage dresser and set up the laptop on top. Tina and I stood behind to watch.

The picture was better than I expected, and the audio was pristine. A ripple of excitement surged up my back; would this be the evidence that finally caught our killer?

Apparently... not any time soon.

For several minutes, we slogged through what was, after all, an awkward video call between failing young entrepreneur Bryce and the ailing Aunt Delilah. Actually, she turned out to be his *mother*... but he'd moved out to San Francisco and hadn't even talked to her since the video call at the *last* reunion. Which neither of them seemed to think was weird. This family, I swear...

... though who was I to talk? When was the last time I'd called *my* dad?

The whole time, Kitty was on-screen. Mostly just her shoulder and elbow, but every so often she would lean in to make a comment. When she did, she would inadvertently show that she was also holding her phone (and perhaps not entirely invested in the conversation).

Finally, on-screen Kitty told the talkative Bryce that he should hop off and let someone else have a turn. He slid out of the chair... but he didn't actually *leave*. He just walked back behind the chairs and leaned against the wall... watching across the room.

"What's he doing?" I said. "What's he looking at?"

Real-life Kitty arched an eyebrow. "I think you mean *whom*," she said, and nodded at Tina.

Tina's face flickered in a slight wince, and she took a discreet step away from the seated Kitty. "He might have just been watching for his food," she said.

"Nope. Kitchen's the other way," Kitty said.

"He was just standing there? Staring at her?" I said. "How long did he stay there?"

"The whole time," Kitty said, shortly.

I felt a tug of sympathy for her. Not that I got the impression she was actually *into* Bryce (which would have been weird, on multiple levels), but it had to be hard to watch women get those adoring, hungry looks you'd never get yourself. I mean, who was I kidding? It was hard for *me* to watch, and I certainly got my fair share of glances. Though not whenever I was with Tina.

(Unless you counted that creep Lionel. Ugh... I considered letting the sheriff have him after all. He had to be guilty of *something*. Besides, if he could have reached Tina, he'd have grabbed her first.)

Speaking of Lionel, he was next on the screen. Along with Deanna.

"Whoa, they came on then?" I said. "While the chef was still in the kitchen?"

"They did," said Kitty.

"Did *they* stay the whole time?" I said. "Is this their alibi?"

"No," said Kitty. "Watch."

And then, with sweet mercy, she finally sped up the playback.

When Lionel and Deanna got up, they both moved off-screen. Then came Fitzgerald and his mustache, along with both Tyler and Taylor. Soon after they came on, Kitty played it again at normal speed, and off-screen, Priscilla bellowed for the chef. We could hear Vladik calling as he walked out.

The kitchen was empty. The window had opened for the killer to strike.

And which Pritchetts were accounted for? Priscilla, of course, and Kitty... and Bryce in the background... and Fitzgerald and the two teens.

Everyone but Lionel, Deanna, and Mercedes.

And if the attack on Mercedes proved both her and Lionel innocent... which wasn't certain yet, but extremely likely...

"Is Fitzgerald there the whole time the chef's out?" I said, getting excited. "And the kids?"

"Yes," Kitty said. She jumped ahead a few minutes, then played Priscilla finishing off her harangue. Vladik bellowed promises of satisfaction, and then his voice vanished into the background chatter.

"He couldn't have taken more than a minute or two to get back to the kitchen," I said. "And look, Fitzgerald and the kids are still there! They're in the clear! It's *got* to be Deanna!"

Kitty nodded, her eyes fierce and bright. A Pritchett had fallen, and vengeance was near.

Plus, I realized, Deanna had married in. She wasn't even a "real" Pritchett. Not that it mattered to *me*.

"This is it!" I said. "We finally have proof!"

But Tina said, "Shoot."

"What? What is it?" I said, sensing doom.

"It can't be Deanna," Tina said. "She was talking to me."

Both Kitty and I cried out in dismay.

"You?" she said.

"The whole time?" I said. "You're sure?"

"I'm sure. Grandma had told me to take over at the hostess stand, and Deanna came up and started asking me about the history of the Inn. I know she came over *before* Vladik came out, because we both stopped talking when Priscilla started shouting. Deanna was super embarrassed; she started apologizing to me, as if it were *her* fault."

"But how are you certain she didn't slip off to the kitchen?" Kitty said. "The chef was out for a long time."

"Before this, I *wasn't* sure," Tina said. "But now I am. Deanna couldn't have left me before the chef went back to kitchen."

"Why not?" I said. "I don't hear Deanna on here; you two were on the other side of the room."

"I know," she said. "But she *didn't* leave. Not until Bryce came over."

"Bryce?" we both echoed.

"He came over and 'rescued' me," Tina said, with a wry frown. "Look."

And as we watched, Bryce finally straightened his shoulders, pulled out his own phone, checked his hair on the screen (with an app, I guess?) and strode off.

Long, long after Vladik had to be back in his kitchen.

Crud.

We'd watched the video, and we had proof all right. All the proof we'd ever need.

Proof that this mystery was impossible.

CHAPTER 34

Defeated, I slouched with Tina out into the hall.

At the door, I turned. "Hold onto that video," I told Kitty. "We've got to show the sheriff."

"I will," she promised, and she closed the door.

"Hey," Tina said, gently. "How about I make some tea?"

"Why not?" I said. "Nothing magically solves impossible puzzles like a gratuitous beverage."

"You never know."

We climbed the stairs to the top floor, slipped down toward the bright bare Quaker side hall with the red begonia door to her ladder… and at the corner, met Sheriff Jake. Frowning.

"You?" I said. "Here?"

"Pleasure to see you too, Ms. Sassafras," he said. "I hope we can finish a conversation without you sprinting off like a hare."

Of course, at that, my adrenalin surged, and my major muscles tensed. "Why would I?" I said. "I thought you'd be interrogating Lionel."

"I did," he said. "Turns out his lawyer is quite the crackerjack."

"You mean Lionel's in the clear now?" I said. "Just because of his *lawyer?*"

"I didn't say that," the sheriff said. "But his lawyer raised an interesting point. If you don't mind my asking… how *did* you happen to be right there, in the exact right place, at the exact right time?"

"Sheriff Jake!" Tina cut in. "That's not fair and you know it! Grandma told me she'd already talked to you and straightened that out."

"She did admit that she'd asked you two to keep an eye out," he acknowledged. "Though she was mighty parsimonious of details."

"That's Grandma," Tina said, with crossed arms.

"Indeed. But as I understood it... she'd asked you to watch an entirely different person."

"Hold up," I said. "Are you trying to say that I *staged* the attack on Mercedes? So I could *pretend* to rescue her myself?"

The sheriff shrugged. "It certainly is convenient how it seemed to clear your name."

"But we weren't even looking for Mercedes," Tina said.

"*You* weren't," the sheriff said. "In fact, Ms. Sassafras could be reasonably certain that you'd be otherwise occupied. All she had to do was keep a close eye on her real target, and send a quick message to Lionel Pritchett once she was in place."

"Oh *come* on," I said. "How do you think I made a pot fall from the roof? At the exact right time?"

The sheriff frowned.

"See?" I pressed. "Not to mention that that thing crashed like three feet from *my head*. If I were going to stage some fake rescue, trust me, I wouldn't put myself in the line of fire."

The sheriff cleared his throat. He looked... troubled.

"This whole murder mess is a Pritchett family disaster," I said. "Has been from the start."

"Kitty Carter has a video," Tina added helpfully.

I nearly jabbed her with an elbow. Why the heck was she bringing *that* up?

The sheriff snapped to attention; his droopy mustache bristled. "Video? Of what?"

"The whole thing," Tina said. "They were making a video call to an aunt, and she has the recording. All the way through until Nyle... um, you know..."

"Did you watch it?" he demanded. His nostrils were flaring. "Where is she?"

Tina told him, and the sheriff bounded off. She turned to me with a pleased smile.

"That should keep *him* busy," she said.

"Maybe for twenty minutes," I said. "The whole point of the video is that *none* of the Pritchetts could have done it. The second he figures that out, he's going to be sniffing me out and carrying cuffs."

"You don't know that," she said. "He might see something we missed."

"Like what?" I said. "Every Pritchett in that room is either assumed innocent from the Mercedes attack or else totally accounted for. They *couldn't* have gotten in and out of the kitchen to poison that dish. Not without some magical power."

"Except you," she said.

"Thank you, yes," I snapped. "I'm still the one plausible suspect. Plus, I actually *have* a magical power…"

I froze.

My mouth literally hung open.

"Summer?" Tina said.

"Magical power," I murmured. "Oh my *gosh*…" Tingles of realization were rippling down my skin. "How did I not see this?"

"See what?"

"I forgot to tell you this," I said. "When I went to see Priscilla, she had these pills. On the counter."

"Okay…?"

"She was in her chair, and the counter was across the room," I said. "I stepped out for maybe two seconds, and then I walked back in and the *pills were in her lap.*"

Tina's brows hunched close… then her eyes went wide.

"You're sure?" she said. Her voice was low. Was she… scared? "It was that fast?"

"Absolutely!" I said. "She hadn't moved, she *couldn't* have. You saw her legs. She was sitting right there the whole time... because *she got the pills with telekinesis.*"

Tina stared. She was turning pale.

"What's wrong?" I said. "It's a thing, right? Just one more psychic power? Didn't you say you have a relative with telekinesis?"

"Not a nice relative," she said softly.

"Neither is Priscilla! Don't you get it? She called the chef out of the kitchen on *purpose*. She wanted him out of the kitchen so *she could use the poison herself.*"

"If that's true—"

"What do you mean *if?* It's the only possible explanation!" I said. "I might even have *felt* it... I was standing right there in the hallway, and I got this weird faint prickle, like a tiny jolt, emanating from the kitchen."

"How faint?" Tina said. "I get those too sometimes, but they're *totally* unreliable. It could mean anything—"

"But she could have been doing it *right then*, Tina! While everyone was watching her argue with the chef, Priscilla was *lifting the vial through the empty kitchen and dumping it on Nyle's plate.*"

"We would have seen it," Tina said stubbornly. "It would have had to fly across the whole dining room. Which would be *crazy* hard—"

"No, you're forgetting," I said. "All she'd have had to do was sneak down the night before and hide the vial in the kitchen. She'd only need to move it a few feet, and no one would ever see."

"But—"

"Tina! Face it! There's no other option!" I said. "Priscilla Pritchett has telekinesis, and she used it to kill her own grandson."

The words hung in the small hall, like the crack of a judge's gavel.

At last Tina spoke.

"If that's true," she said quietly, "how can we ever prove it?"

CHAPTER 35

It didn't take long for me to remember Grandma's camera.

"You want to hide a *security camera* in Priscilla's *room?*" Tina demanded. "That's so *creepy!*"

"It won't take long," I said. "I couldn't even get out the door before she lifted something. We just need to catch her on camera. Once."

Tina frowned and paced in the tiny bright hallway, passing the bare doors with their pretty painted flowers. "This sounds *super* illegal," she said.

"So's poisoning your grandson!" I said.

She quit pacing, and then rubbed her forehead and ran her hands through her thick hair. "Shouldn't we ask Grandma?"

"Are you kidding? Forgiveness is *way* better than permission."

"Not with Grandma."

"Tina, listen. We'll give it a half hour, tops. If nothing happens, we quit watching and no one has to know. But what if we *do* catch her? We can show it to Grandma, the sheriff... we could save Mercedes' *life.*"

"You think Priscilla tried to kill her too?"

"Who else?" I said. "She's got *telekinesis.* Who knows what she'll throw next?"

"If she's really powerful enough to lift that pot..." Tina crossed her arms in a tight self-hug. She shook her head.

"What? Is that bad?" I said.

"It's... unusual."

"Like, you'd rather we were sending in a SWAT team?"

She nodded.

I shrugged. "Who needs a SWAT team? We're an empath and a... um..."

"Disruptor," she said, automatically.

"*Disruptor?*" I frowned. "That's what you guys call it?"

"It's just a technical term—"

"Is it super common?"

"Oh no, not at all," she said. "We were kind of surprised that one had been sent to get you."

"*What?*" I demanded. "That creep who killed my plant? And tried to give me cancer? That was... that's me?"

Cold dread iced my chest. Whole new vistas of horror were opening for my future.

"Summer! No!" Tina said. "It's not like that. It's... it's all how you use it."

"But it *could* be? I could do that?"

"Forget it." Tina took a step back toward the main hallway. "Come on. Let's get this over with."

I walked with her, and we headed for Grandma's office, where the indoor security camera was still in storage, unopened in its box. I could tell she really didn't want to talk about this "Disruptor" thing, so I let it drop. For the moment.

But there was no way I would just *live* with my possible future as a carcinogenic plant assassin. Words were going to be spoken. And soon.

But first we had to install hidden surveillance on a nonagenarian Jedi on the Dark Side of the Force. Just another day in Wonder Springs.

The plan was simple. First, Tina would sneak into the office and nab the camera from a closet. Then, Tina would check in on Priscilla. If luck was with us, she'd be out, and we could get in and get out in a few minutes. Once the camera was set up, we could watch the stream with a special app for it on Tina's phone. (A phone which I would be very careful *not* to touch.)

The app could record, too. So the minute we caught Priscilla moving anything through the air, we'd have proof. Solid proof.

It wouldn't hold up in a court of law, but that was fine. All it had to do was convince the sheriff. I wasn't thrilled with him knowing I *had* done anything illegal, but Tina was positive that the man wouldn't even think to give us trouble; he'd be glad that, for once, someone *else* had done the line-crossing in pursuit of justice. And once Sheriff Jake got obsessed with the *actual* killer… we could all finally relax.

That was the plan.

At first, our luck held. Grandma's office was clear, and Tina nabbed the package with ease and we climbed up to her room. Getting it all set up was a struggle, but after several failed attempts, and some existential questions about whether the writers of instruction manuals are actually human, we finally got the feed showing on Tina's phone.

(And by "we", I mean "Tina", since I couldn't risk frying our only tech. At least the manual was paper.)

The feed image was grainy and blocky, but as Tina swept the tiny camera around her tower room, you could clearly pick out the details on her screen. This thing might really work.

Then we snuck down to Priscilla's room. For once, my bulky purse came in useful; it had ample room to stash the camera out of sight. (Although, since I couldn't risk touching and frying the camera, this did mean that Tina got an actual glimpse of the inside of my purse.)

At Priscilla's door, Tina gave a soft knock. No answer. The door was locked, so she keyed her way in. The wide curtains were drawn, and the spacious room was dark and empty…

…or not. In the easy chair, in the shadows, sat Priscilla.

We both froze.

Then, in the silence, above the jackhammer of my heart, I detected another sound. Breathing, rhythmic and slow.

"She's asleep," I whispered.

Tina nodded. And we both crept forward like Jack to the sleeping giant.

I couldn't touch either the camera or Tina's phone, so I felt frustrated and helpless as she fiddled with the tech.

"Could you put the camera here?" I whispered, pointing to the corner where the waist-high paneling made a slight ledge.

Tina shook her head. "Too small. It might fall," she whispered.

"Can't you stick it?" I whispered. "Didn't the package have some adhesive?"

She literally recoiled, her face open in frank horror. "Can you imagine what Grandma would say?" she hissed. "This wallpaper is older than the Civil War!"

"I'm trying to prevent a *murder*."

"So am I!"

We kept hunting, while Priscilla stirred and snored. Her sleep seemed fitful.

"Come on, come on," I urged. "She's not going to last forever."

"Don't be stressed," she whispered, as she tried to prop the little camera on the dresser beside an ancient TV. "When you're stressed, I'm stressed."

Since the suite was posh, the TV was huge... for the mid-90s. No flat screen here; the dresser had been pulled forward from the wall so that the massive cathode-ray casing could hang off the back.

"Just stick it to the TV," I hissed. "Or is that also a national treasure?"

She stuck out her tongue in a silent raspberry, but she reached in the box for the little white strip. When the camera was attached, she brought up the feed on her phone... and gasped.

"It's too dark," she whispered.

"She'll turn on the light eventually," I whispered.

"I thought you said we'd only do this for a half hour!"

I smothered a frustrated groan, then slipped to the window.

"Wait, don't!" Tina whispered.

But I eased the curtains open, letting in the light.

Priscilla startled and stirred. I froze, holding my breath.

Then her face relaxed, and she settled back to sleep. Slowly, I opened the curtains all the way. I crossed back to Tina and leaned beside her to check the feed on her phone.

"Perfect, that looks great," I whispered. "Anything she moves, it'll fly across the screen."

"Yeah," Tina said. She smiled. "We did it."

"What on *earth* are you *doing?*" demanded Priscilla Pritchett.

Her bulging glare pinned us both.

I could have tried to explain. Maybe.

But without thinking, I lunged and zapped her.

This jolt was the worst ever. The pain seared completely up my arm to my shoulder. It was so bad that I stumbled back and tripped into the TV.

"Summer!" Tina shrieked. "She's hurt!"

"And I'm not?" I growled. But I forced myself to focus.

Priscilla was slumped in her chair, her head hanging to one side. She looked confused, and she was muttering. Dread prickled in my gut.

"Should we call someone?" Tina said.

"She'll be fine!" I snapped. I was feeling scared and guilty, but there was also some legitimate peevage—had Tina really not noticed my body slam? Did she think I liked to fake all this pain? "She's breathing," I said. "Talking, too."

"She looks delirious."

"She's just confused! In fact…" I drew close to the trembling ancient woman. "Mrs. Pritchett?" Her head jerked, and her bleary, bloodshot eyes locked with mine. "Mrs. Pritchett," I demanded, "how long have you been able to move things with your mind?"

The bleary eyes went wide.

"Summer?" Tina hissed behind me.

"You're recording, right?" I snapped. "We can just do this now."

"But—"

"Mrs. Pritchett," I said again. "When did you first use telekinesis?"

Priscilla's head was still bobbing, uncertain. But her eyes went narrow.

"I don't know what you're talking about," she rasped.

"Tina!" I said. "What's she feeling?"

"Summer, *don't*. The camera—"

"You can feel that she's lying! Right?"

"I don't know!"

"Why not?"

"I wasn't paying attention—" Tina said.

"What kind of empath—"

Priscilla croaked, "Empath?"

"*Damn* it," I groaned. I grit my teeth and clamped a hand on Priscilla's sagging forearm.

This time I made myself watch. Her head threw back, and her swollen legs kicked out and slammed my shins. This hurt, but I didn't notice it much, since my whole arm was on fire.

"Summer, *stop!*" Tina yelled. "You're hurting her!"

"She's a freaking murderer!" I yelled back. "She tried to frame me! She nearly bashed my head in with a tree!"

"I know! But we don't use this stuff to hurt people! We can't!"

"People like you never *had* to hurt anyone."

Tina gaped. Like I'd spoken some curse that could never be unsaid.

"Now," I said. "Pay attention this time!"

"No," she said, and her voice was iron. "I'm leaving."

She strode for the door.

But I lunged up and grabbed her by the back of the shirt. The movement sent fresh pain shooting up my wounded arm.

Tina gasped and gripped her own arm in the same place, right where I was hurting, and then she whirled on me, bewildered and furious.

"Just one more minute," I pleaded. Still gripping her shirt, I craned back toward Mrs. Pritchett. "Did you use your mind powers to poison Nyle?" I barked. "Did you?"

Priscilla's head was shaking hard now, losing control. But she clamped her lips tight shut.

"Why are you doing this?" Tina said.

"You're not the one in line for prison," I panted. "I won't get another chance. If the camera doesn't work, at least Grandma might listen to *you*. Can't you tell what this woman's feeling?"

"All I can feel is your hate."

She looked so accusing, so judgmental, that part of me wanted to scratch her perfect face.

But maybe she also looked frightened, and sad. And another part of me thought, *What the hell am I doing?*

I released her shirt and took a step back.

"Camera?" Priscilla croaked. "What camera?"

Damn.

"Summer, *please*—" Tina gasped.

But I touched Priscilla's skin for a third time.

I hadn't done three zaps so near to each other for a long, long time. The pain was stunning. Imagine your leg falling asleep, with "pins and needles", except it's your entire body… and you start thrashing, hard, because you're also drowning. I would much rather have done that.

Then I saw Priscilla, and I forgot the pain.

Because she went still, and her eyes rolled up until they were only bloodshot white. She looked dead.

And I passed out.

CHAPTER 36

I woke up to Cade.

He was leaning over me, his eyes soft and kind, with the low golden sun kissing his cheek.

Our eyes met. That touch, at least, I was allowed. In that moment, I could even believe he was touching back.

Then Tina leaned in.

"Summer!" she cried. "You're okay!"

Cade broke contact and leaned back, looking awkward. Whatever, dude. Why was he crouching? Was I on the floor?

"What happened?" I asked Tina. "Where are we?"

"Downstairs. In a linen closet," she said, and as I glanced around the tiny room, we were indeed shelved in by neatly folded sheets. This being the Inn, even the closet smelled of lavender, and the window was a circle of golden stained glass. Is that why the light in here was golden? Maybe it wasn't as late in the day yet as I'd thought.

Either way, Cade certainly looked good in gold.

"We would have carried you to the couch in the front office," Tina said, "but if there were guests at the desk, you know—"

"*Carried?*" I said. "You carried me?"

"Not *me*. When you fainted—"

"I didn't *faint*—"

"When you shocked yourself into oblivion," Tina said, "I was stuck there in Priscilla's room with two people unconscious. I tried to wake you up, and then I tried to drag you out, but it was super awkward and I was afraid I might accidentally touch your skin, so I texted Cade."

I covered my face.

"Don't worry," Cade put in. "I used a thick blanket."

Mortified, I looked down and realized I was still partly wrapped in a bedspread. Lying on the floor.

Had Cade really carried me all the way downstairs? The thought made me flush... of *course* I'd had to go and be unconscious right *then*. Not that he cared either way.

"I wore long sleeves, see?" he said, holding up his flannel arms. "Just in case."

"Great," I said.

"Oh, and here's your purse," Tina said brightly, dropping it onto the floor beside me with a massive thunk. "And I popped up to your room real quick to make sure you'd fed Mr. Charm—"

"What about *Priscilla?*" I cut in. "What happened to her?"

Tina frowned. "She still hasn't woken up."

"What? How long has it been?"

She checked her phone. "At least half an hour."

"Oh my gosh!" I lurched to sit up, then swayed as dizziness hit. I almost grabbed at Cade's safely sleeved forearm to steady myself, but at the last millisecond I held back. Maybe to punish myself. "Tina, that's never happened before. We've got to get a doctor—"

"Relax, hon. We already did," Tina said. "We were worried about you too, but you were breathing and seemed okay, and by the way, do you have a primary care physician? Because how does that work with the Touch thing?"

"Not. Very. Well," I snapped, as a fresh hot flush of embarrassment flooded my cheeks. Maybe Cade wouldn't notice if I didn't look at him. Sure, that is totally how it works. "What about *Priscilla?*" I said. "What are they doing?"

"Not sure," Tina said. "The family's debating whether to take her to our local hospital or risk a transport back to 'real' doctors."

"We can't let her go!" I said.

Tina's face hardened.

I held up my hands, placating. "Look, I know I was way out of line. I'm really sorry."

Tina arched an eyebrow.

Sometimes I hate empathy.

"I'm sorry *intellectually*," I clarified. "Which counts for something. But I *feel* like Priscilla is a creepy old killer, with telekinetic powers, and if we let them fly her out of here, someone else will die."

Cade cut in. "Maybe so," he said. This was a relief, because at least Tina must have filled him in on *why* I felt compelled to keep zapping a ninety-year-old woman until we both passed out. "But we can't *prevent* them from moving her out."

"Sure we can," I said. "You heal her."

Cade pulled back. Sitting on his heels, he crossed his arms. "Sorry," he said. "Too many people around."

"I'll distract them," I said. "She *can't* leave yet; she might be the killer."

"I can't heal her," he said. "Not in public."

"What if she gets away with it?" I said. "You're going to have the Murder at the Inn that's *never* solved. What'll that do to Grandma? To Wonder Springs?"

"She's right," Tina said.

Cade scowled. "Tina!"

"We can do this," she said.

Their eyes met, and some unspoken understanding arced in the space between. I looked on from a mile away.

"Fine," Cade said, and he leapt to his feet. He stepped around Tina, with a hand on her shoulder, careful to avoid touching me.

Well. At least he listened to Tina.

We hustled out into the hall, and we made for the front staircase by the desk. Cade was leading, until he stopped and hung back against the wall.

"Check it out," he said, with a nod ahead. "Company."

On either of the staircase, Tyler and Taylor Pritchett were standing and staring, arms crossed, as still as stone lions. Except that unlike statuary, they were glaring right at me.

"What did you tell them?" I asked Tina.

"We didn't even see *them*," she said. "But we did run into Kitty on the way down."

"With me unconscious?" I hissed. "*Great.*"

"Maybe she'll assume it was a coincidence," Tina said.

"Sure," I said. "And maybe those kids just want to ask us out for coffee."

"I could go for some coffee," Cade said.

"Totally," Tina said. "I'm feeling it."

I groaned. "That's the one time you get to say that."

Then I marched right up to the teenage gate.

As we approached, the glares intensified, an open cold rage that made Tina contract. She huddled closer to Cade. I walked alone, but I could almost feel the icy bite myself.

We hurried between them and up the stairs, and I thought we'd seen the last of the Pritchetts. But no, around the first curve, I nearly plowed into Bryce. He looked up from his phone, and his boyish face crinkled with disgust. He barely made room for me to squeeze past.

You wouldn't think this would have affected me. I mean, Bryce? What a tool. But anyone can club you with true contempt.

At the top of the stairs clustered a final Pritchett threesome: the mustachioed Fitzgerald, the portly Lionel, and his apparently not-murderous wife, Deanna. When they saw me, they fell silent, and they stabbed me with stares. Clearly, none of them shared Priscilla's psychic powers, or I'd probably have burst into flame.

But when I saw Kitty, I knew the worst was yet to come.

She stood at the open door to Priscilla's bedroom, arguing with a woman I couldn't see. The unseen voice was piercingly intelligent, with a faint Southern lilt that was flavored by another accent I couldn't place. Both women sounded politely incensed.

"This should be a non-issue," Kitty was saying. "My grandmother has a *very* intimate relationship with her physicians, and both they and we would be *much* more comfortable—"

"You'll be much *less* comfortable if she's dead," the woman snapped. "So unless I get a direct order from someone with power of attorney..."

She stepped into view.

Wow.

Behind me, I could almost *feel* Cade tense. Seriously. His energized muscles must have charged the air even hotter.

"Didn't think *she'd* be here," he grumbled.

Great. I'd been wondering how a guy like him had stayed single for so long. Odds were looking high that he hadn't. This local Wonder Springs doctor was drop-dead gorgeous. And I placed that extra accent: Jamaican.

When she saw Cade, she lit up with a gleaming, radiant smile. Then she cocked her head, questioning, and her tight, abundant black braids rippled like water.

Cade leaned toward me, and his heat touched my neck. "I can't do this," he whispered. "Not in front of Kenise."

"Oh, please," I hissed, with sublime hypocrisy.

"Hey, it's because she's a *doctor*," he whispered. "Not because of any ancient history—"

"Hello, Cade. Tina," said Kenise the knockout doctor, with courteous nods. "I don't think I've met your friend."

She stretched out her hand.

There must be some subculture *somewhere* where the whole handshaking thing is outdated and quaint. Maybe some hipster borough in New York City, where introductions end in a mutual glare. I would love that.

For once, I was at a loss. And wouldn't you know it, Kitty did me a solid. Sort of.

"*You!*" she snarled. "What are *you* doing here?"

"Oh, hi Kitty," I said, as the doctor retracted her hand in surprise. "We heard your grandmother was sick."

I peeked around the doctor through the open door. Priscilla still lay in her chair in the wide empty room, unmoving and alone. They'd turned all the lights on, but it only made the room look like a funeral home.

"*Did* you?" Kitty snapped. "*I* heard you both *happened* to go unconscious at *exactly* the same time."

"Really," the doctor said, her sharp eyes giving me a thoughtful scan.

"Did we?" I said. "Huh."

"I'm very curious what she'll say when she wakes up," Kitty said.

"*If* she wakes up," the doctor said.

"Is it that serious?" I blurted.

The doctor frowned. "She's a very old woman, and her health is poor. If she doesn't wake soon, I'll be gravely concerned."

Behind her, in the too-bright room, Priscilla stirred.

At the same moment, a movement from Cade caught the corner of my eye.

I turned to see him rigid with concentration, his jaw clenched… and by his side, his left hand open and subtly aimed toward Priscilla.

My skin tingled with wonder.

And relief. Even if the woman turned out to be a murderer, I could never have lived with myself if I'd caused her death.

Then I saw Cade's *other* hand.

He'd slipped it onto the small of Tina's back… underneath her shirt.

Tina was concentrating too, eyes closed, deeply focused, with Cade's fingers on her bare skin.

Let it go, Summer, I thought. *Just look away.*

But I just kept staring, burning in the bitter memory.

"Kitty!" Priscilla croaked. "Who's that doctor?"

Kitty cried out with relief, and the doctor rushed back to her patient. Kitty turned to follow, then twisted back and jabbed a finger in my face.

"Whatever you did to her," she said, "you're going to pay."

She slammed the door in my face.

CHAPTER 37

"Come on," Tina said, nudging Cade and giving me a nod. She and Cade hustled down the hall, away from the Pritchetts who were rushing up to investigate Priscilla's cry. I tagged after them, the rickety third wheel.

Around the corner, we stopped to catch our breath. Tina and Cade were positively glowing, both talking at once in excited whispers.

"You were *amazing!*" Tina gushed. "You tuned her *across* the room—"

"Only with a boost from you!" Cade gushed right back. "I was tapping into your chakra, I could *feel* it—"

They were so *happy* together. Two special people, with special magic that could share how you feel or save you from death.

Meanwhile, *my* magic consisted of nearly killing an old woman.

An old woman who, incidentally, might be downstairs reporting me for assault. True, no one else I'd touched had ever remembered... but no one else had ever passed out, either. (Well. Not for a very long time.)

"Hey," I said, and the two lovebirds stopped chirping and turned toward me. "What do we do next? About Priscilla?"

"What do you mean?" Tina said. "I thought we were going to watch the camera."

"You left the camera *in* there?" I said.

"Of course. That was the plan."

"It *was*, and then I accidentally knocked out a ninety-year-old woman and Kitty managed to guess it was me!"

"How was I supposed to know Kitty would see us in the hall?" Tina snapped. "*I* can't see the future!"

Cade cut in. "If the camera's on, let's just take a look. We'll know exactly whatever Kitty finds out."

He was so calm, and collected, and rational.

It might have helped that he wasn't the one who'd been caught on camera zapping a ninety-year-old woman into oblivion.

Tina pulled up the feed on her phone. The screen showed only Priscilla, still slumped in her chair but looking only exhausted, not comatose (or dead). Even with the blocky, low-quality image, her face had enough detail to show her expression: annoyance.

"I don't remember," Priscilla was saying, irritated. The sound quality was also low, but even the tinny rendition resonated with her matriarchal thunder. I unclenched a bit with relief; she certainly sounded unharmed.

"But they were here?" Kitty said, off-screen. "In your room?"

"Yes. I think so. But I don't remember why or what happened, so you may as well stop asking. Get my Scotch."

Kenise the doctor interrupted, stepping into the frame. Since she was standing, the shot only showed her from below the shoulders down. "I'm afraid that's a bad idea," she said. "Not so soon after—"

"Kitty!" Priscilla barked. "This isn't my doctor. Get her out."

"I *insist*—" Kenise began, but Kitty came on-screen and actually grabbed her elbow. Polite but firm, Kitty escorted Kenise off-screen. The doctor's protests faded into the distance, then died behind a door slam.

Silence.

My heart was pounding out of my chest. Now was the moment; Priscilla was alone. What would she actually *do*?

As we watched, Priscilla looked off-screen, toward the shut door. Then she took a deep breath, grit her teeth... and started to get out of the chair.

I was crushed. She was totally normal. How could I have been so delusional?

Priscilla struggled to rise, but she collapsed back into her chair, exhausted. She scowled, and flexed her fingers.

And a bottle of golden whiskey floated right into her hand.

It happened so *fast*, right there on the grainy phone screen, that it almost looked normal. But it was also terrifying. Even though I'd thought I'd been expecting to see this, the raw power of real magic still freaked me right out. The implications of what she'd done made my skin creep.

Tina and Cade weren't any more chill.

"Oh my *gosh*," Tina breathed.

"It's only a bottle," Cade said, trying to sound resolute, but with a faint tremor.

"It's *huge*," Tina said. "And I bet it was in the kitchen; that's *across* the *room*—"

"Nana!" came Kitty's voice, in sharp rebuke.

On the screen, Priscilla lowered the bottle she'd jammed to her lips. She was blinking hard, like her eyes were watering. "Mind your own business," she said. She wasn't slurring yet, but her voice had slightly slowed and turned nasty.

"Nana..." Kitty said, more gently, and she came on screen. She crouched by the chair to meet Priscilla's eyes. "Are you hungry? Can I get you something?"

"Let me be." Priscilla looked away and took another long sip. I imagined the Scotch setting her throat on fire.

"What about a movie?" Kitty persisted. "I can stream something for you, or there might even be something on TV." She nodded toward the screen—and then frowned.

"Oh no," I said.

Oh yes. Kitty rose, still frowning, and walked straight toward the camera. Then the image swung wildly as she plucked the camera from its perch, finally resting on an immense closeup as she scrutinized the lens.

"I'm dead," I said.

The screen went black.

"Don't panic!" Tina said, sounding panicked. "She can't see the videos, remember? She doesn't have the app. We had to set up that whole account—"

"The files are on the *camera* too," I said. "All she has to do is plug it into her laptop!"

"Wait," Cade said. "You actually *recorded* yourself disrupting her memory?"

"I was trying to get her to confess!"

"How was *that* supposed to help?"

"*Clearly* it *didn't!*" I snapped. "Feel free to jump in anytime here with *your* brilliant ideas. Maybe you can heal the woman's murderous heart."

"I'm not a *therapist*," he sniffed.

"Summer, listen," Tina said. "Even if she sees the videos, what can she do? We just caught Priscilla on camera flying that whiskey."

"We also caught *me* zapping her grandmother. And *you* admitting you're an empath. What do you mean, what can she *do?*"

Tina gaped.

Then her phone buzzed with a text. Tina checked it, and her lips clamped tight.

"It's her?" I said. "How'd she even get your number?"

"It was before all this," she said. "We were chatting." She shrugged, as if all normal people exchanged numbers to close every conversation.

She held up the screen. Kitty Carter had sent a single text.

We need to talk. Now.

PART V

CHAPTER 38

Tina, Cade and I peeked around the corner, back down the hall toward Priscilla's room. Kitty had bustled out and was charging past her relatives at the top of the stairs.

"Where's she going?" I said. "Her room?"

Tina checked her phone and nodded. "She says to meet her there. Come on, there's another stairway."

"You want me too?" Cade said, looking at Tina.

Don't we all, I thought.

But before she could answer, I heard a phone vibrate, and Cade frowned and pulled his phone from his pocket. He glanced at the screen. "Shoot," he said. "Sorry."

"Is that Una?" Tina said.

He nodded, then gave me an apologetic smile. "My boss," he said. "At the orchard. She tends to be... urgent."

"We'll be fine," Tina said. "Besides, Kitty probably doesn't want extra company."

"You sure?"

"We're big girls," I snapped. "I've talked my way out of much bigger disasters."

"I believe it," he said, eyes twinkling.

"Hey—"

But he hustled off before I could get him back. Whatever. Right now, I had much worse problems.

Tina and I hurried through the halls, panting back and forth with attempts to make a plan. But by the time we reached Kitty's room, all we'd figured out was that she could use that footage to wreck our lives.

As we ran up to her door, Kitty stood in the hall, arms crossed and glowering.

"I changed my mind," she said, her voice cold. "All things considered, I don't quite trust my room to be private."

"Please, I assure you—" I said.

"Drop it," Kitty said. "Let's go."

She shoved past me, nudging me with a monstrous purse that was even bigger than mine. Some sharp corner in there *poked* me; she had to have some serious junk in there. Then again, who was I to talk? I hiked up my own heavy purse, and I promised myself that if ever got this murder solved without landing in jail, I truly would clean all the trash out once and for all.

Kitty marched ahead of us, stone silent, until we reached the old elevator.

I tried not to cringe. A musty old semi-dilapidated elevator was the least of my problems. Or so I tried to tell myself.

And then, at last, Kitty spoke.

"I imagine you're worried about that footage," she said, watching the old floor indicators blink above the closed doors as the elevator crawled down the shaft. "If I were smart, I'd use it against you. But the truth is…" She sighed. "I don't want anyone to see it any more than you do."

"Really?" I said. I was dumbfounded; the relief was blistering. Was this even possible? "Why not?"

Kitty glanced around, but the hall was entirely deserted. In a low voice, she said, "Did Nyle ever tell you *how* we got so wealthy?"

Something in her tone made my back prickle.

But Tina was way ahead of me. "The telekinesis!" she said, in a hushed whisper.

Kitty nodded. "Gambling." She made a wry smile. "It's amazing how the odds improve when you can tweak the dice."

I stood there speechless. The sheer simplicity of it all was stunning. Priscilla Pritchett had had decades and *decades* to amass wealth by manipulating high-stakes games. Card games wouldn't have worked for her, but anything with dice, a roulette wheel, even slot machines before they went digital… she must have been *astounding*.

"That's the family fortune," Kitty said. "That is, it *was*." She flicked me a sharp glance. "But just so you know, there's not much left to extort. The so-called 'Manse' is mortgaged to the highest spire. And about to be foreclosed."

"Why?" I said. "What happened?"

"She got old," she said, and her voice was small, like there was still a kid inside there who'd believed in a grandmother who would always be rich and strong. "Her skills declined, but not her lifestyle. When she started losing, she'd double down to make it up on the next round…" She shook her head. "I'd thought I was the only one who knew."

"About her finances?" I said.

"Yes, but also the other thing. The… power. But now I'm thinking…"

"Maybe she told Nyle?" Tina said.

Kitty fixed her eyes on the closed crack of the elevator door and gave one short, sharp nod.

"And maybe she regretted her decision?" I said.

Kitty didn't reply.

The doors rumbled open. We stepped inside, Kitty pressed a button, and the doors whined shut.

Once again, the ancient machine lurched and creaked and sloshed (seriously, the slosh thing could *not* be good), but to my surprise, on this second ride, the elevator didn't seem scary, just old. Maybe it helped to be in there with two other people.

Or maybe the narrow escape just now from having my entire life wrecked had put outdated elevators into perspective.

"I'm not ready to accuse her with certainty," Kitty said. She was fighting to keep her composure, and I wondered what it would feel like to discover that your grandmother had murdered your cousin. "But the problem is... the whole truth might come out. Everything. And the estate's already nearly gone."

"What do you mean?" I said.

"I mean the casinos," she said. "If there's even a *chance* that they could launch some crazy clawback lawsuit, our whole *family* would be devastated. We'd all be on the hook for a lifetime nightmare of debt."

"I can't imagine an actual lawsuit," I said. "Prove telekinesis? In court?"

"We're talking *millions*," Kitty said. "They'd try."

"But what if it *was* her?" Tina said. "What if she hurts someone else?"

"I know," Kitty said. "That's why I need your help. Hypothetically, if she is... guilty, how could we expose her, but keep her power secret?"

"I don't think we can," I said. "That sounds... impossible."

Silence.

Except for Kitty muffling a sharp breath, like someone trying not to cry.

The moments dragged, and the strain tightened as the elevator crawled. At last, Tina said, "Oh. I think we're going up."

"Sorry," Kitty said. "I must have been mixed up, I meant us to go down to the lobby."

She reached to press the button for bottom floor, but Tina was reaching too. The tips of their fingers touched.

Tina gasped.

"Oh!" she cried, jolting back and literally touching her heart. "Oh, Kitty! You *loved* him."

Kitty recoiled. Her face flashed stricken, then grieved, vulnerable...

"Oh, Kitty," Tina said again. "This must be so *hard*..."

Nyle? I thought, reeling. *Kitty was in love with NYLE?*

Then I remembered.

The very first minute I'd met the woman, when she was setting up her video call and Nyle was across the dining room... what had happened? Tina had seen Nyle and had thought he was cute, *because she was feeling it from Kitty.*

Kitty's attraction had been so intense, it had empathically infected Tina, several feet away. Wow.

"He never knew, did he?" Tina said. "And he was your *cousin.*"

Kitty frowned, and Tina winced.

"I mean, no judgment," Tina said quickly. "But that must have been super awkward."

"Yes," said Kitty, and she hit the big red button marked STOP.

The elevator lurched. Both Tina and I lunged for the ancient side railings to catch ourselves. I was too surprised to think straight, but I did wonder why no alarm was sounding. Was that not a thing with these old elevators?

Instead, a grating clattered to the floor.

Where had *that* come from? I looked up to see a gaping hole in the ceiling.

"What's that?" I asked Tina, but she just shrugged, bewildered.

Both Tina and I had fallen toward the elevator's back wall, but Kitty was leaning on the opposite side, four or five feet away, staring at her phone and frowning with concentration.

"Kitty?" I said. "What is it?"

Tina shrieked.

Because a tray was unsteadily lowering through the opening. By itself. In the air.

The tray was clear plastic, like a casserole dish, but larger and deeper, and it was full nearly to the brim with a liquid that sloshed yellow. The tray teetered above Tina and me, hovering over our heads.

Tina reached up to try to take it, but Kitty spoke in a tight voice that made us both freeze.

"Careful, sweetheart," she said. "That's bleach."

CHAPTER 39

We were trapped in an elevator, on the top floor, with a telekinetic woman who was holding a tray of bleach over our heads.

"You," I said, dumbstruck. "It was you."

"You killed the man you *loved?*" Tina gasped.

"How *dare* you," Kitty snarled. She'd slipped the phone back into her huge purse, and she was glaring at Tina with eyes on fire. "You can have any man you want. You have *no idea* what I've been through."

To my utter shock, I felt the impulse to agree. My mind crowded with images of Tina and Cade, so happy and perfect together, and me the lonely exile.

Then I thought, don't even *try* to tell Kitty you've been in the same boat.

I might be lonely, but I still had enough in the looks department to catch guys giving me glances. Even with all my career priorities, and no matter how much I loathed getting come-ons from creeps, there were still days where I lived on the secret assurances that I was still mildly hot. The honest truth was that if those looks ever stopped, I wasn't sure how I'd survive.

Meanwhile, Tina just stared. I could tell she was wrestling with the waves of Kitty's hatred, but she was also trying to wear a look of compassion.

Bad move, Tina. Kitty only scowled in deeper rage.

"I've wanted Nyle since I was *twelve*," she hissed. "I *lived* for these stupid reunions; they were the only time we got to meet. He brought girl after girl, but we'd still talk, we had *real* conversations. I always thought, give it time, one day he'll see. But Mercedes... she was the one to get the ring. He wanted to buy *my* future house, the *family* house, to have *her*." Her pale face was splotching red.

"That tool didn't deserve you—" I started.

"Shut up!" she screeched. Above our heads, the tray wobbled, and the acid lapped. "She didn't even love him! Why did she *pretend?* This was all *her* fault!"

My mind was shrinking to a single loop—*get out get out get out*—but I strained think logically, step by step.

Yes, she was telekinetic, and yes, she was raging out. I still wasn't sure how the magic stuff worked, but my guess was that the less control she had over her emotions, the less she'd be able to control the bleach. Great.

If she'd been holding a gun, I could have chanced rushing her and zapping her out. But this was a floating tray of bleach, in a tight space. If I zapped her now, the acid might splash us all.

She had planned this way too carefully. Just like the murders.

"Just so I'm clear," I said, all calm and normal, like I was reviewing the details on a contract. "The poison thing with Nyle was before you knew Mercedes didn't want him?"

"Of course!" she snapped. "Didn't you *see* her? Taking damn *selfies* the *day* after he *died*."

"Oh, I saw her. That potted tree almost hit *me*, by the way."

"No one asked you to butt in."

"Trust me, I'd rather not have been involved," I said, still sounding nonchalant, although every muscle in my torso was shaking. "But I had to do *something* about that poison in my room. No biggie, but you did frame me."

And I realized now that she hadn't even had to sneak *into* my room. No wonder the sheriff hadn't smelled her. She must have stood outside and just floated it up through the open window. That time I was with Cade in the solarium and she'd walked in... she'd probably done it just before then.

"So what if I did frame you?" she snarled. "Didn't you *want* him dead? That was the first thing you said to me. So much *contempt* that anyone could even *think* of being attracted to him."

This hurt my brain. But from her perspective... maybe she had a point?

"Okay," I said. "That's fair. I apologize."

"Because I've got a tray of bleach over your head," she said. "Industrial strength, by the way. This isn't the lightweight kitchen crap you can rinse off without a burn."

"Okay," I said again, wrenching my voice to keep sounding normal. "But you haven't dumped it, right? Because you want something. There's something we can do for you. What can we do?"

Kitty's face spasmed with some fresh lethal passion... envy? Hate? Humiliation? I had no idea who she'd first planned to torture in this tiny prison, but in this moment, she had ultimate power over two women who were stand-ins for all the pretty flirts who'd ever stolen away Nyle.

The power didn't seem to be easing the pain.

I glanced to Tina for help, but I cringed. Tina was terrified, her face distorted with both her own fear and also the horrors she was feeling from Kitty. She was visibly trying to shield, her brows clenched in concentration and her face shining with sweat, but she looked like she was failing.

Losing Tina scared me.

"What can you *do*?" Kitty said. "Nothing! You keep wrecking everything that *I* try to do. I had this *brief* hope that your crazy accusation of Nana might satisfy the police, but I'm realizing now that that's ridiculous. Why would *Nana* want to kill Nyle? And how would she have *seen* into the kitchen to add the poison? I needed a camera in there, or I'd have been lost."

Oh... I'd completely forgotten that, that a telekinetic out in the dining room would still need to see what she was doing in the kitchen.

That explained the sticky gunk under the kitchen cabinet. I'd used the same stuff to attach our camera to the TV.

And just as we'd watched our camera feed on Tina's phone, Kitty must have been watching *her* feed on *her* phone... all while she was chatting it up with her Aunt Delilah on the video call. That entire time, she'd been watching her phone screen for the right moment to tip poison into Nyle's breakfast.

This woman was a psychopath. And she was freaking out again.

"Nana couldn't have set up a camera!" she cried. "Not in a million years! *I'm* the techie... they'll *know*... if it ever comes out that Nana's got the power, they'll start checking the rest of us..."

The tray was wobbling hard now, like a raft slipping into harder waves. A tiny bit of bleach sloshed over and splattered out, an inch from my sneakers.

"Kitty, listen, you're overthinking this," I said. "That sheriff just wants this over. Make his arrest, get the town off his back. No one has to know about the telekinesis. Wait... what about the chef? *He* could have done it, and your Nana could have *paid* him."

"That's true!" Kitty cried, with a sudden, awful hope.

But Tina was horrified. "Summer!" she said.

I wanted to stomp her foot. *Of course* I wasn't *actually* planning on sacrificing two innocents to save myself... right? This was hostage negotiation. I was only thinking as far as getting both of us out of this death room.

But Kitty turned to Tina and snarled across the small space. "You *really* don't get it, do you? You still think you're a princess in a magic bubble... nothing *really* bad can ever *really* hurt you. I'm sure everyone's always been so *nice* to you, so *kind* and *caring* to a pretty little girl..."

The tray lurched sideways to hover directly over Tina.

It moved *fast*, too fast, and more bleach sloshed over the side. The acid splashed the tip of Tina's shoe, and she cringed and drew back with a yelp of terror.

I hate to say it, but some dark part of me felt a rush of satisfaction. Because Tina really *had* had a pretty perfect life.

Sure, she might have *tasted* lots of other people's problems. But she could always come home to a gorgeous body, a sweet personality, and a family who loved her. For her, that was the real world.

Then I realized Kitty was eyeing me with interest.

Oh, crud. Sometimes I really forget to keep a poker face.

"You *want* me to," Kitty said.

I blustered. "I don't know what you're—"

"You hate her too, don't you?"

"I do *not*—"

"I bet she makes you feel fat. And boring. And ugly." Kitty cocked her head, bemused. "You really don't think you're pretty. I saw how you were looking at that Cade guy in the sun room when he *deigned* to tell me hello. I bet Tina here could snap her fingers and he'd come running."

My face was burning.

"Wait, what?" Tina said. "Summer, what happened with Cade? Did you—"

"*Shut. Up*," Kitty barked.

The tray angled up, until the bleach was pooling a few millimeters from the rim.

Tina blanched and froze.

But Kitty turned to me and smoothed her face into a smile. "I have an idea."

I couldn't speak. My mouth was dry.

Kitty kept talking. "I know you're telling yourself that I'm this insane serial killer, but this was supposed to be a one-time thing. It's not *my* fault you two kept hassling me. And I know that sweet little Tina here would never keep her mouth shut… but you? I might be willing to take a chance. If I have leverage."

I worked my tongue, trying to get enough spit to speak. "What kind of leverage?" I rasped.

She nodded at Tina.

"Bleach won't kill her," I said. "She'll still report you."

"Not if someone wipes her memory."

Oh, I thought. Damn.

"I saw what you did to Nana," Kitty said. "You can make Tina forget this *entire conversation*, that the three of us ever met here... and also the real reason why she's not quite so pretty anymore."

I realized I was starting to breathe faster. Too fast.

"Imagine it," Kitty said. "You go out for drinks, and the guys find her *repulsive*. All they want is you."

It was horrifying. Right? Yes. Absolutely.

Also, the whole plan was flawed. Kitty didn't know how the Touch worked. She thought I could erase whatever memories I wanted. In reality, this conversation had been way too long; there was no way I could prevent Tina from remembering that Kitty was the killer.

However... Kitty didn't know that.

She thought that after my Touch, Tina really wouldn't know she was a killer. She also thought that I'd never say anything about it, because if I did, Kitty could tell everyone how I'd joined her in torturing Tina with acid. Or at least, that I'd sacrificed Tina to save myself.

Kitty was wrong. No matter what I did, Tina would remember she was a killer.

But... I realized... Tina wouldn't have to remember about *me*.

If I went along with the bleach, and then wiped Tina's memory, Tina could still wake up with no idea precisely *when* the tray had dumped, or why only *she* had been horribly scarred, and not *me*. It could look like an accident, or Kitty's crazy whim.

Tina would never have to know why the Universe had finally come to collect on her lifetime of unfair princess luck... and women like me could finally be around her without hating ourselves.

I mean, this wasn't *my* idea, was it? If I tried to refuse, we'd just *both* get disfigured for life.

"Your call," Kitty said. "Say the word."

"Summer?" whispered Tina.

CHAPTER 40

At Tina's voice, Kitty scowled, and the tray dipped. Tina whimpered and tried to shield her head.

"You'd better decide," Kitty said, frowning and glaring at the trembling tray. "This thing's no potted tree, but I've been going for awhile now, and I'm getting tired. I've got maybe a minute left, two max."

"You'd really let me go?" I said.

She shrugged. "If you ever talk, I'll talk. But I can also just kill you both. All three of us, actually. I'm not leaving this elevator until I'm 100% certain that I'm never going to rot in jail."

"Kill?" I said. "That sounds... messy."

"Not with the *bleach*," Kitty said. "Why do you think I took us to the top floor?"

Still eyeing the tray, she dug into her huge purse, fished around, and pulled out a detonator.

It was black and blocky and old-fashioned, like an ancient walkie-talkie. It looked absurdly prosaic and real. Which made it terrifying.

Kitty admired it. "You'd be amazed how easy it is to rig the brakes and cables on these old elevators."

My vision went tight, a narrow circle pinpointing the black device that could kill us all. My legs and arms tensed, and my whole body coiled for a desperate lunge.

But Kitty yanked the detonator close, clutching it to her chest. "Stay back, Summer. No sudden moves. We can both walk out of here, but only if you wipe Tina's memory. And first you have to you help me dip her, so I know you'll stay discreet. You've got ten seconds. Call it."

"Summer, it's okay," Tina murmured. Her eyes were nearly shut and she was wincing. Her hands were up by her face, defensive, but whether she was bracing against the bleach or Kitty's onslaught, I couldn't say. She swallowed, then said, "It's stupid for us *both* to die."

I seethed inside. Of course Tina *would* say that.

"Five seconds," Kitty snapped.

"All right!" I said. "All right, fine!"

Tina gasped. Shocked. That I'd actually taken her at her word.

"Excellent," Kitty said.

"But what about me?" I said.

Kitty frowned. "Just come over here and stand by me. There's room. I'll be careful."

"I mean, *after*. I have to *touch* her, remember? How am I supposed to touch her if she's covered in bleach? Oh! Wait, I have a trash bag."

I dug frantically in my disaster purse.

"You don't need a *trash* bag," Kitty said. "I've got gloves—"

"No, it's fine." I yanked out a massive black plastic bag and shook it out. "I'm *never* going to clean out this damn purse. I bet your purse is all organized and spotless, right?"

"What?" Kitty said, glancing down at her open purse.

That's when I struck.

I whipped the bag over Tina's stunned head, and yanked it down past her shoulders as far it would go, barking, "*Stay down!*" Then I twisted on my feet and lunged for Kitty.

My fingers closed on the detonator. I tugged with both hands, but Kitty's grip was iron.

Behind us, the tray crashed, out of control.

The bleach splashed everywhere with a sickening *whoosh*, and I felt it spatter all down the back of my clothes. Below the hem of my skirt, a few drops hit my calf and burned.

Ahead of me, Kitty *screeched*.

She covered her face with both gloved hands, howling. I'd only seen her face for a split second beforehand. I wished I hadn't.

But now I had the detonator.

"Tina!" I said, as Kitty rocked and moaned. "You okay?"

"I'm fine!" Tina said, crouching beneath her bag. She rustled to get up.

"Don't move!" I said. "It's all over the bag—"

"You *bitch!*" Kitty shrieked.

I whirled back, but it was too late. She'd already lunged and whipped the detonator from my hand.

"You did this to me!" she panted, her face a nightmare of reddening rage. "I'm not going to live like *this!*"

I froze, in total panic.

She slammed the button.

Nothing happened.

No explosions. No sudden plunge. We just stood there, gulping for breath.

"What the *hell?*" she roared, and mashed the button again.

Then I saw it. The detonator was leaking a thin trail of smoke. Nice.

"You!" Kitty gasped. "What did you *do?*"

"Forget it," I said, and I reached behind her neck and squeezed hard.

CHAPTER 41

Like all the rest of her messed-up family, contact with Kitty blasted a jolt that set my arm on fire. But I grit my teeth and held on until she passed out.

She tumbled to the floor, and I nudged her on the way down to avoid the worst of the puddled bleach.

Then I slumped against a dry wall, breathing hard. With bleach splattered everywhere, including over Tina's bag, I really, *really* didn't want to pass out myself.

As the pain in my arm started to subside, it occurred to me that since at least two Pritchetts had psychic powers, that might be the reason why touching them was so painful. Maybe touching other psychics, or potential psychics, caused extra pain.

Or, maybe they were just a bunch of jerks.

"Summer?" Tina said, in a small voice. She rustled inside the bag. "What happened? Is she…"

"She'll be fine," I said. "Don't move! Hold on."

With ginger care, I slowly worked the bag up over Tina's crouched body, turning it inside out. The droplets glittered and shook, like they were just *waiting* to flick up and hit me in the eye, but at last we got the bag off and safely tied.

Tina carefully rose and stretched, groaning with relief. Then she turned on me with arms outstretched. "You saved my life!" she cried.

"No hugs!" I snapped, raising my sleeved arms in a posture of defense.

Tina managed to stop herself mid-swoop. But her face was a freaking furnace of gratitude. If I'd had shades, I'd have worn them.

Great. The kid sister I'd never had.

I could maybe get used to that.

"Now what?" Tina said.

"First things first," I said. I stepped to the prone Kitty, and cautiously dug through her purse. It really *was* organized. I pulled out our camera, and checked for the data card with the footage.

"Sweet," I said. "It's all here. I think we're good."

"What about her?" Tina said. She bent over Kitty and gasped. "Summer! Did you see her face?"

"I'd rather not."

"We have to get her to the hospital!" Tina whipped out her phone.

"While you're at it, text the stupid sheriff," I said, as she dialed. "He needs to sniff around this crime scene and get the hell off my back."

Tina placed a quick call. Kenise the doctor had already left the Inn, but she could be back with help in less than ten minutes. Then Tina texted Sheriff Jake. "He says he'll come right over," she said. "He'll meet us on the ground floor."

She reached for the red brake button.

"Wait a sec," I said.

She eyed me in surprise, and then her face creased with sudden compassion. "Oh, Summer... you don't have to feel like *that*."

I squirmed. "Can you at least *try* not to do that? *I* don't even know how I feel!"

But I pretty much knew.

Awful. Ashamed. Exposed.

Tina winced. Great, now she was feeling *that*. She really did literally feel other people's pain... emphasis on the *other*.

Kitty and I had hated her for being so happy, but what was the alternative? If she were miserable like us, it's not like she'd have the bandwidth to care about much else.

"Listen, when she was ripping into you..." I said. "Saying that stuff about me hating you... I don't know what you picked up—"

"Oh, honey," Tina said. "It's just feelings."

She was so warm about it, so utterly nonchalant. My throat went tight.

"Seriously," she said, "if you knew the junk I pick up... especially dudes, oh my *gosh*. All that *matters* is what you *do*."

"Cool," I said, suddenly very interested in studying a minor hangnail. "Thanks."

"I mean it! What you did... you could have been *splashed*."

"Actually, it did hit my calf."

"Summer! Oh *no*—"

"It's okay, it's okay! I'm fine. We're all good." I pressed the red button, and the elevator lurched, then began to creak its way down.

But I still had one last thing to say. And it wasn't going to get any easier later.

I sighed, and pushed the brake again.

The elevator thunked to a halt, and Tina swayed and eyed me with caution. "Summer? The doctor *is* coming—"

I cleared my throat. "That other thing she said. About Cade—"

"Oh, Summer!"

"No, wait!" I said. "Don't even *think* about some kind of Tina self-sacrifice move. I've seen you two together, okay? You freaking light up."

Tina made a show of looking confused. "What?"

"Listen, it's not a big deal, I'm not like..." I was talking too fast, and my cheeks were warming. Dang it. I took a slow, mindful breath. Like a real grown-up. "The last thing I want to do is intrude, if you two are a thing."

"We're not a *thing*—"

"Would you just let me say this?"

"Say what?"

"I'm saying, if you *want* to be a thing—"

"Why would I want us to be a thing?"

"Seriously? You're going to make me spell this out?" I snapped. "*Why* would you *want* some sweet, ridiculously handsome hunk with *not only* a magical healing power but also strong indications of a functioning brain?"

"Hmm." Tina's eyes were sparkling. "You'll have to explain further."

"I *saw* you two, Tina! He was all *over* you, rubbing up your back."

She frowned. "When we revived Priscilla? He needed my *help*. He was tapping into my chakra!"

"I have no idea what you're talking about," I said, "but what I was *thinking* of was the other time… I didn't mean to spy, but I was standing at the front desk, and the door was freaking open—"

"Oh!" Tina cried. "That's *right*. I had a backache."

"*What?*"

Tina reached behind her back and massaged her lumbar. "Yeah, it was really bad. He totally took care of it."

She reached and pressed the brake, and the elevator shuddered into descent. That was that, apparently. Problem solved.

"Hold up," I said. "Does he always do a full frontal makeout hug? Or is that a special for the hotties?"

"Not usually," she deadpanned, dodging the barb with effortless grace. "But this time, the pain was super resistant. He was struggling to penetrate my aura."

I literally palmed my face.

"Oh, come *on*," she said. "I've known Cade and his family since I was, like, six. He's like my goofy big brother."

"Goofy?"

She crimped a half-smile. "Oh, he's got a goofy side."

"Tina, I don't know what you're telling yourself, but I've been here for *two days* and the guy keeps finding excuses to come over and see you."

Tina erupted into giggles.

I crossed my arms and affected unconcern. "I'm glad you're so used to male attention—"

"You *goose!*" she gasped. She panted a bit more, then managed to get her breath back. "He was coming to see *you.*"

I burbled. The sound was something like, "Mwah?"

"He told me all about it," she said, as the doors finally groaned open. "He kept hassling me to drop all these hints about whether you were interested, and I'm like, boy, that has *always* been against the rules, I'm not going to break the code now just because you're all smitten. But holy cow, Summer, you hid it *well*, I had no idea till now that you're practically… burning… oops…"

She trailed off.

Because yes, Cade was standing right there. Right outside the elevator. Two feet away.

Locked into my gaze with a bewildered joy.

Around us, Kenise the doctor bustled into the elevator car and crouched over the prone Kitty with exclamations of dismay. Two other people wheeled over a stretcher and started hoisting her in, and I didn't quite catch whether they were EMTs or doctors or escaped inmates, honestly, because I was floating in a sea of Cade.

"Hey," he said, as they wheeled Kitty away. His voice squeaked, because apparently he wasn't adorable enough already, and he cleared his throat and regained his manly rumble. "Do you maybe want to… uh…"

"Yes," I said.

"… go watch a coffee? Or something?"

"Yes."

"Wait, I mean—"

"It's fine."

"Okay." He smiled, radiant again with confidence. My vision may have blurred. He nodded toward the hotel entrance. "Want to go?"

"Not so fast!" growled a voice behind him.

Sheriff Jake, in all his nos(e)y glory. He bustled in between us, mustache bristling. His nostrils flared, then he stifled a gag. "Is that bleach? Oh my word. This is a crime scene, people. And these two women are suspects."

Cade groaned. "Seriously? Come on, Dad!"

I shrieked. "HE'S YOUR DAD??"

Both men stared. Even Tina looked surprised.

"Um, *yeah*," Cade said.

"He's never quite had my looks," the sheriff quipped, with possible sarcasm, "but the family resemblance has always been striking. To the *observant*."

By now, the initial shock had worn off. Oh. I *could* see it. A little. Maybe.

That made another reason the sheriff had always looked familiar. Besides that whole thing about shifting into a bloodhound.

Wait, what if the shifter thing skipped a generation? What if Cade and I got married, and we had a family, and he got me pregnant with a litter of *puppies*...

Okay, stop, I thought. Slow your roll, Summer. The man just asked you to watch a coffee. That's it. And in case you should contemplate any premature displays of affection, kindly recall that you can't even shake the man's hand without possibly knocking him unconscious.

That's me. A real knockout.

Ugh. What a stupid joke. Oh no... of the few "dates" I'd ever had, he'd be the first who *knew*... which meant he might make that joke *all the time*. I bet he already told stupid dad jokes. Because he'd make such an amazing dad.

Down, Summer. *Bad* Summer.

"Ms. Sassafras?" the sheriff snapped. "Are you with us?"

"She's exhausted!" Tina said. "This crazy murderer lady attacked us, and Summer zapped her out!"

"Really?" Cade said. "Wow. You *are* a knockout."

Yep.

It was probably too early in this relationship to have the conversation about dad jokes. So I took it out on Tina. "Tina!" I said. "Can we be discreet?"

"It's all right, Summer," said Grandma, who had somehow materialized. I jumped, but the others didn't seem even startled by her instant appearance. "We can trust the sheriff and his brood…" The very slight warmth in her voice chilled. "… to a point."

The sheriff huffed, but Grandma gave him a small smile, and then turned back to me. Her gaze was steady and deep, and more… *open*… than I'd ever seen her. A prickle of dread crept down my neck… dread, and maybe longing.

"There's a time for secrets, child," she said. "And a time for welcoming family."

"Wait, what?" I said. "What are you saying?" My throat went tight again, my eyes burning with the sudden threat of tears. "You're not saying… *you're* not my…"

"I am," she said. "I'm your Grandma, baby. Welcome to the family."

"We're *cousins!*" Tina squealed. "I've been waiting to tell you *forever!*" She threw wide her arms and clobbered me in a hug.

And got zapped.

Technically, she only got as far as her hand brushing my arm. Which was good, because apparently she'd also forgotten about the bleach spatter on the back of my shirt.

Even with just a brush, though, the jolt still hurt. That lump in my throat vaporized.

A psychic power really can wreck the moment.

Tina staggered back, woozy and confused. Grandma took her arm and steadied her.

"Whoa… what happened?" Tina said, looking around.

"I was *trying* to tell Summer about her family," Grandma said.

"Yay!" Tina cried. "We're *cousins!*"

She lunged at me again. This time, Grandma held her back.

"Oh, right," Tina said. "But you're going to live here, right? And help with the fight?"

"Fight?" I said.

"That's right, sweet pea," Grandma said. "There's a lot you need to know."

CHAPTER 42

Of course, Grandma still couldn't bring herself to just spit out her secrets, right then and there. There was work to be done, what with the Inn's elevator sprayed with industrial bleach.

Honestly, I didn't mind the delay. I needed time to myself, to think.

By which I mean, I crawled up to my room and crashed.

Yes, I said bye to Cade first. Geez. But there was only so much warmth we could put into our smiles, with *not only* Grandma *but also* the scowling sheriff *right there*, who was apparently Cade's freaking *dad*. (That is going to take me a *long* time to get used to.)

Still, even at quarter-power, Cade's smile kept me toasty.

Anyway, when I woke, a low sunset was shrouding my room in glows and shadows, and Tina was gleaming by my bed. She was bouncing on her toes with little hops of excitement, and the moment she caught my eyes open, she dashed to a dress draped over a chair.

"Look at *this*," she breathed, and she lifted the emerald-green dress like it was fine gold. Perhaps it was; it might have been the light, but intricate designs flashed gold in the sparkling green. I'd never seen an outfit so lovely in real life.

Then I realized that Tina was wearing a stunning dress herself, glittering royal blue with silver lines that swirled like honeysuckle vines.

"Who's getting married?" I said.

She laughed. "It's just a family dinner. We all dress up for... special occasions."

I hesitated. "Will the sheriff be there?"

Now she giggled. "You mean, will Cade? No. They're allies, sort of, but not family. And he's definitely *not* your cousin."

I eyed the emerald dress. I *yearned* for that thing, to feel it glimmer across my skin. The ache was almost painful. But... "Is that yours?" I said. "It's never going to fit me."

"Sure it will," she said. "It's not mine. It belonged to your mom."

I caught my breath.

"Maybe later," I said. I got up and swooped the dress into the closet. I tried to only touch the hanger, but the soft fabric brushed my arm, and even that touch was its own kind of pain. "When's dinner?"

I expected some pushback over the dress, but instead, she just beckoned and made for the door.

"Now!" she yipped, with an eager grin. "Come on!" And she pranced out into the hall.

I couldn't believe she was missing my turmoil over the Mom issue. Maybe when Tina got excited enough about her *own* feelings, she stopped noticing mine. That would be... awesome.

Especially because I had a feeling I'd be the focus of the evening's conversation. The murder was solved, I was officially innocent... now what?

Now I was utterly broke, with no job, no home, and all my worldly belongings burned to a crisp.

Also, with a sudden extended family who had serious wealth and secret psychic powers. There was that.

It didn't take any prophetic powers to see that they'd already made plans for me. But what if I had ideas of my own? Or questions they didn't want to answer?

Only one way to find out.

"Come on, Charm," I said. "Family dinner."

He was napping, of course, his white furry body luxuriating in his basket bed. I scooped him up, cradling his warm weight, and his purr rumbled against my heart.

I scuttled out and caught up with Tina, who led me down right into the wide dining room. I had to admit that, now that I was here to eat, not be a substitute waitress or a murder suspect, the place had a decent vibe. On a side wall, she slipped through a set of French doors I hadn't noticed. The glass panes were curtained with velvet red, and after I followed her through, she shut the doors behind us.

So. Welcome to a family dinner.

Grandma had not yet arrived; the long oak dining table that filled the room was vacant at the head. Candles flickered all down the table and glowed in sconces on the wood-paneled walls. The dark old wood exhaled the scent of centuries. But high on the far wall, a small round window was open, breathing in the fresh evening blossoms of spring.

To Grandma's left (I mean, where Grandma *would* be), sat a grave wizard. Actually, no, that was Tina's Uncle Barnaby. Wait, I guess he was *my* Uncle Barnaby? Oh boy. At least the robe looked a little less ridiculous by candlelight, with symbols and constellations glinting silver against the dark.

He snapped me a curt nod. "Good evening, Summer."

"Hey," I said. I hesitated, then forced myself to add, "Uncle Barnaby."

He scowled, and beside me, Tina smothered a giggle.

"*Barnabas*," he said, enunciating with stentorian flair. His huge white beard rippled with indignation. "Please. Let us commence our long-delayed relations with mutual courtesy. *Barnaby* sounds like a circus clown."

"Right," I said. "Sorry."

Seated across from him, a woman and another man twisted back to greet me. The woman rose first, and I startled at the "touch" of her wide, dark eyes. I remembered her, of course; the same woman who'd first greeted me when I parked at the Inn. Now she was beaming.

"I'm your Aunt Helen," she said. "Tina's mom."

She sounded so... *normal*. She looked normal too, like any middle-aged mom dressed up for a meeting. She could have been an accountant. I wanted to hug her and not let go.

But I held back, and not just because of my Touch. Watch out, I thought. *Another* empath. And this one's a pro.

My new aunt cocked her head, and her eyes twinkled. "Don't worry, sweetheart. I'm off duty."

"Really? You can turn it off?" I said. "Wait, then how'd you know what I was feeling?"

"You have a very expressive face."

"Mom!" Tina said. She gave me a rueful look. "I can't stand when she does that."

My aunt made a mock look of prim rebuke, then patted the shoulder of the man who'd risen beside her. "And this," she said, "is your Uncle Denny."

If she looked normal, he looked positively rumpled. His gray suit was baggy, even on his overweight frame. His top hair had thinned to a few wispy fronds that floated like sea ferns. Even his mustache looked like he'd found it in a thrift store.

But his bright smile shone all the way to his eyes. And from the way his wife touched his shoulder, and the glance Tina gave him, it was clear they both adored him.

He gave me a nod and a polite wave of his thick fingers. "Pleasure to meet you," he said. "Tina's told us very good things."

"I *highly* doubt that," I said. "So what's your secret power? Laser vision? Talking to ghosts?"

He rumbled in a deep chuckle. "Pumping septics," he said. "I clean up the mess."

"He's *really* good," Tina said.

"Cool," I said, mortified. "So is this everyone besides Grandma? The whole family?"

"Oh no!" Tina said. "You should see us at Thanksgiving! It's *packed*."

"But I mean, that lives here? At the Inn?"

Still seated, Uncle Barnaby (Barnabas? Barnabossy?) sniffed. "I'm afraid you may sporadically encounter your Aunt Trudy."

"I love Aunt Trudy!" Tina cried. "She's so fun!"

"She is *exceedingly* eccentric," Uncle Barnaby intoned.

"I don't know why you mind her so much," Tina said. "Lots of people talk about their past lives."

"Um," I said.

"Her *own* supposed past lives, I could stomach," said Uncle Barnaby. "But everyone *else's?*"

"Barnabas!" snapped a brisk voice that was all too familiar.

My white-bearded uncle zipped his mustached lip and made his face a stoic mask.

Grandma had taken her place. She stood at the head of the table.

The relatives (*my* relatives) quickly shuffled to their seats. Tina hesitated, but only a moment, and then took the empty place by Uncle Barnaby. I slipped to the seat beside her, reflecting that, although I had saved her life, she had saved me from sitting next to Uncle Barnaby. We were probably even.

Without a word, Grandma closed the round window, and glanced through to the outside as if to check for any lurking eavesdropper. Then she sat on her cherrywood throne.

"So, Summer?" she said, in a tone that was formal even for her. "What is your decision?"

My relatives murmured in confusion, but I knew exactly what she meant.

"You mean about staying?" I said.

She inclined her head in a micro-nod.

"Well…" I said. Over the years, I'd presented in hundreds of conference rooms, burning in the crosshairs of every gaze. I'd hardly ever even broken a sweat. But now, under the table, I was clenching my fists.

"You can't *leave!*" Tina said. "I thought you left your job!"

"I can't just stay at this Inn indefinitely," I said.

"Why not?" Tina said. "We do!"

Aunt Helen cut in, confident and grown-up. "Don't worry about money, Summer. There's always work to do here."

"I appreciate that," I said, focusing on her and avoiding Grandma. "But as a long-term plan, I'm not sure that minimum wage—"

"You're griping about your salary?" boomed Uncle Barnaby. "Have you no sense of the bigger picture? The larger fight?"

"Not really," I said. "You all haven't said much. Or anything."

"But they already attacked you," Tina said. "That Disruptor was Uncle Enoch! From Great-Uncle Vincent—"

"Wait, *what?*" I said. "You know that guy's *name?* And what do you mean *uncle?*"

Everyone around the table fell silent.

Aunt Helen spoke first. "Our... extended... family is a long story," she said. "But Summer, you can handle them. You're a Meredith."

There it was again. The thrill at that forgotten, remembered name. Here and now, at this table, the thrill was stronger, almost unbearable, as if all the others were feeling it too.

"You're family now," Aunt Helen said. "One of us."

"Yeah, *now*," I said.

The silence went cold.

Very quietly, Grandma spoke. "Would you care to elaborate?"

"What's to elaborate?" I said. "I'm in my late twenties! If you all care so much about *family*, why'd you wait *decades* to contact me?"

"I can see why you'd ask that," Grandma said. "But the reasons are various, and cannot all be explored here. To begin with, we wanted to keep you safe."

"*Safe?*" I said. "That Enoch guy nearly killed me!"

"We were not aware you'd been located," she said. "Not until the last minute."

"You mean *you* didn't even know where I was?" I said. "How is that possible?"

"It's a long story," she said, and her eyes dimmed. "There were certain… incidents. Your mother broke off contact. She changed her name. So did your father."

"What?" I said. "Dad's last name wasn't really *Sassafras?*"

"No," Grandma said, with a dry snort.

I know you're thinking, *That name was made up? Shocker!* But I'd grown up with it; it sounded just as plausible as any other random last name. At least this explained Dad's complete lack of relatives.

Oh, crud. If Dad had been lying… I could have a whole *other* set of relatives on *his* side.

I was not going to think about that.

"But why didn't you look for me?" I said. "Did you even *try?*"

"Of course," huffed Uncle Barnaby.

"But we didn't have much to go on," Aunt Helen said. "We'd never even *met* you, sweetheart."

"We were *also* thinking of *your* best interests," Grandma said. "It was highly likely that you did *not* have an unusual gift. In that case, contact with us could only be a liability."

"Of course I had a stupid gift!" I said. "I've had it since I was a kid! But I had to figure everything out *myself*… do you understand? Completely *alone.*"

Grandma furrowed her brow. "Summer, I truly regret—"

"No, listen! By the time I had any *clue* what was going on… I mean, I was *twelve*, I tried to tell Dad, when I managed to catch him sober, and he listened to the whole thing and he was like, he made me swear it, *Never tell anyone. Not even me.* Then he grabbed my hand…"

Crud, my eyes were burning wet. I was *not* going to cry in front of these people.

No one spoke.

I managed to keep my voice. "And now you all are like, Welcome to the family! You're a Meredith, hooray! But you wouldn't even take me *now* until I'd passed some stupid test. I thought *family* was supposed to mean unconditional love!"

"It does, child," Grandma said. "More than you've ever known."

"Then *why?* Why'd you wait so long to tell me?"

"Because the Merediths have people we have promised to protect," she said. "And each of us is free to choose. To help or to hurt."

"What do you mean, *choose?*" I said. "Is that what happened to my mom?"

Grandma's face closed. Her lips pressed firm, and she seemed to wilt into her biological age. She looked ancient and sad.

Then the French doors rattled.

Grandma snapped them a fierce glance. Uncle Denny was closest to the doors, and he leapt up, lunging toward them with surprising speed. But they'd already opened, and a man had burst through, leading with his nose.

"Jake!" Grandma cried, scowling at the sheriff. "I believe I've made it *crystal* clear—"

"It's that woman. Kitty Carter," he said. He was literally panting. "She's dead."

CHAPTER 43

My little *poor-neglected-Summer* drama instantly evaporated. Which, honestly, was for the best. For now.

"Dead?" Grandma barked. "How? Where?"

The sheriff shut the doors, then crossed his arms and planted himself facing Grandma. "The *official* story," he said, "is that she jumped out a three-story window at the hospital. Suicide."

"Oh!" Tina said, with a hand on her mouth. "That's *awful*."

"Yes, well..." The sheriff frowned. "I saw the body before we sent it off. The woman's face was terrified. What was left of it."

"She jumped," Grandma said. "Of course she was terrified."

"Also," the sheriff said, "her hair was *white*. Complete and perfect white. And the grass where she landed was *completely dead*."

No reply this time.

I don't know what the others were thinking. But all I could think of was a cadaverous man touching my houseplant and wilting it to death.

Finally, Grandma said, "Go on, Jake. You must have a theory. What would he want with her?"

"A very interesting question," said Sheriff Jake. He turned to me with a glare of inquisition. "I haven't had the pleasure of your statement yet, Ms. Sassafras, but according to Tina here, the late Kitty Carter had become privy to your unusual... gifts."

"Not to mention that she had her own," Grandma put in.

"That's right," I said, still dazed by this whole conversation. "But why would they attack her? Wouldn't they want to recruit her, like they tried with me?"

"I found this among her effects," the sheriff said. He produced a plastic evidence bag which held a single piece of paper. "Recognize this?" he said, handing it to Grandma.

Grandma frowned. "It looks like one of our old promotions. For the Inn."

Tina hopped up and went to look over Grandma's shoulder. "That's right! I remember she showed it when she checked in. Got a big bulk discount for a bunch of rooms."

"She did?" Grandma snapped. "We haven't run this promotion in years."

"I didn't think so," Tina said. "But I checked the expiration. It still had time."

"That's not possible," Grandma said. She held the bag close, scrutinizing the paper's fine print. She grunted, then tossed it down in disgust. "It must have been faked. Unbelievable."

"Faked?" I said. "Why would anyone fake a coupon to your Inn?"

"Not *anyone*," she said. She slipped off her glasses and rubbed the bridge of her nose. "This is new," she muttered.

"I don't understand," I said. "Are you saying that this... this 'Great-Uncle Vincent' guy, he *enticed* Kitty to come here?"

Tina piped up. "She *was* the one who planned the reunion."

"But I mean... did he *know*? That she was planning to kill someone? Does he have the power to do that?"

"Oh, yes," Grandma said, and she donned her glasses like a helm. "Never underestimate Vincent. He has *devoted* himself to... self-improvement... over a very long life. And more concerning still, he has chosen to enlist... help."

"So he hires psychics? Like Enoch tried to hire me?"

"He does. And also others."

"What *others*? And why would he even *care* that she was planning to kill Nyle? Did he know Nyle too?"

"Not personally, I'm sure," she said. "But depending on exactly what your clients said about you when they asked to cancel their contracts—"

"You think this Vincent guy heard about *that*? And figured out my power? But how would he ever—"

"He has… associates, Summer. Dark entities."

The air in the room chilled. No one would meet my eye, not even the sheriff.

I swallowed. "Are you saying… not human?"

Grandma nodded. "They can offer him services available nowhere else. Even with his extensive connections. In return, however, they always expect…" She hesitated. "Payment."

"So *that's* what happened to Kitty? He sent that Enoch guy to do some kind of… ritual?"

The sheriff grunted. "Wouldn't be the first time."

"No," said Grandma. "But this is the first time he's attacked us directly. Here."

"It's not technically an *attack*," put in Uncle Barnaby. "Kitty Carter was the one to do the act. Technically, the Truce remains intact."

"Truce?" I said.

"I don't care about the niceties," Grandma snapped. "He sensed that this woman Kitty was contemplating murder, and he *deliberately* lured her to our Inn. Possibly with the added hope of entangling Summer, if she refused to go with Enoch and instead came here, with the murder of her own co-worker."

"So your Truce thing doesn't really work?" I said, though it was kind of a relief to find out there was a *reason* that the Pritchetts had just *happened* to show up, of all places, at my family's Inn. "I thought this place would be safe."

"It *is* safe," Tina soothed. "The hospital where Enoch got to Kitty is down the road. It's not in Wonder Springs."

Uncle Barnaby frowned. "At the hospital, Enoch might not even have had to enter her room," he said. "They could have used a telempath."

"Telempath?" I said. "Is that like, *making* you feel something?"

"Exactly," Uncle Barnaby said, with the smile of a patronizing professor. "Telempathy is my own particular specialty. Recall how I used it to guide you to sleep."

"Guide? You knocked me out!"

Aunt Helen cut in. "We needed to, sweetheart. For the healing."

"You didn't even *ask*," I said. "What else can you 'telempaths' make people feel? When I first tried to drive away after the sheriff here found that vial, I'm pretty sure someone 'guided' me into a freaking panic attack!"

Even just *remembering* the attack as I said this, I could feel myself starting to freak out.

Up by Grandma, Tina winced. Then she gasped.

"Is that how you *felt?*" she said. "Oh my gosh! *Mom!* Can't you tell?"

Aunt Helen frowned. "What are you talking about?"

"The feel! Summer's right, she got attacked. By *Malice Alice*."

My relatives all muttered in shock. Even the sheriff looked grim.

"Who?" I said. I was partly terrified, but also partly hoping *Malice Alice* might just be a local 80s metal band. Actually, no, that might be worse.

Aunt Helen pursed her lips. "One of Vincent's telempaths. Probably his best. But she wouldn't be able to strike from outside. We have a shield."

"A *shield?*" I said. "Around the whole *town*? How? Why?"

"Because we're at war," said Grandma.

"It's a long story," Aunt Helen said smoothly, clearly regretting that she'd brought this up. "But the Shield does keep us safe, Summer. It repulses almost all of our known enemies. Enoch, for instance."

"So then how could this Alice person make me freak out?"

Aunt Helen frowned. "She's a highly skilled telempath. If she were *amazing* at shielding her own presence..."

"No!" Uncle Barnaby cried. "It's not possible."

"I believe it is," said Aunt Helen. "She could walk right through. And strike from within."

Aunt Helen closed her eyes, tensing with concentration. After a few seconds, she shook her head and grunted with frustration. "If she's near, I can't tell. And I should."

"He wouldn't dare," Uncle Barnaby said. "Her presence past the Shield *would* violate the Truce."

"But only if we proved it," Grandma said. "We can't base that charge on Tina's impression." She gave me a piercing look. "Where did this attack happen? The Inn has its own additional... protection. Were you outside the Inn?"

I nodded. "In my car. It was the first time I'd left the Inn since I got here."

Now my family hubbubed with concern. *Another attack... Malice Alice... grave danger...*

"You all are freaking me out!" I said. "You're telling me some demented psychic in this *perfect* town wants to drive me insane?"

"Don't overreact," Grandma said. "Clearly, you resisted her."

"Because I held my cat! The feelings only went away when I touched his fur."

I instantly realized how ridiculous that sounded. But of course, this being my family, most of them just nodded.

My family. Had I really just thought that?

"Fascinating," said Uncle Barnaby, abruptly academic. "I've heard of mild assistance from animal contact, but a *complete* defense?" He eyed my cat with interest. "I must have a closer look at this specimen."

"Don't you *touch* him," I snapped, holding Mr. Charm close.

"Summer, listen to me," Grandma said. "Kitty Carter had committed murder. And attempted more."

"I saw that pot falling," the sheriff put in. "You got the jump on her, but only just. That woman had time to nearly shove that pot onto your head instead."

"You mean you saw the pot fall *towards* me?" I said, freshly horrified. "Like, sideways?"

"Thank you, Jake," Grandma said. "The point is, Kitty didn't make those choices in a vacuum. She changed. She made herself more resonant to... other voices."

"Great," I said. "So I'm safe from these 'associates', as long as I don't plan to murder anyone. Awesome. All I have to worry about are *random panic attacks.* Wow! What a lovely town!"

"We can fix this," said Aunt Helen. "You can stay here, Summer. You just need to learn how to shield."

"Or," said Sheriff Jake, "there's also witness protection."

My entire table of relatives gaped at him. Even Tina's mellow dad, Uncle Denny, who hadn't said a word, twisted to glare in surprise.

Sheriff Jake affected not to notice (though his mustache may have quivered). He kept his gaze fixed on me.

"I'm listening," I said.

He shrugged. "You're a smart young woman. That's clear. I looked into your background. Not even thirty yet, and you were making six figures, almost all on commission. That tells me you can get a job in any sales department, anywhere, and land on your feet. All you need is a fresh name, a fresh city, and a few months' cash. If you're not stupid this time with your power, he might never catch you again."

Now *I* gaped. How had I not thought of this myself? To be fair, the last few days hadn't left much time for reflection. But still.

He was absolutely right. Sure, at the moment, I had less than a buck, but I wasn't *trapped* here. I could start all over anywhere I pleased.

Well done, Summer. If I did say so myself.

Grandma cut in. "That *may* be true," she said. "Except for one inconvenient fact. He *has* found you, Summer. His empaths know your feeling signature. As long as they're looking, you'll be far, far easier to find again."

"Perhaps," the sheriff said. "But I think the young lady should *also* know that people can evade you empaths for a long time." He eyed Aunt Helen, who flushed and looked away. Then he faced Grandma, who did not. Softly, he said, "A *long* time. Decades. No matter how well you knew them."

The two elders locked their gaze. Neither spoke, but unspoken memories and accusations swirled in the silence.

Finally, Grandma turned to me. "What he says is true. You *are* free to go, Summer. And if you so choose, the least we can do is gift you enough money to make a fresh start."

Standing behind Grandma, Tina stifled a yelp of protest, but she did give me an imploring look. The rest of them made a studious effort to look indifferent.

I considered my options.

Option 1: Stay here, in a (cute but) tiny room, making *maybe* minimum wage while I got embroiled in some epic psychic family war with a gruesome ancient uncle who got a kick out of inflicting terror on innocent people, including me.

Option 2: A complete fresh start, in a whole new city. With actual cash savings! I'd do it right this time, find a solid woman to work for and *forbid* myself the Touch. No glass ceiling, all honest sales, and a super-strict budget *for real*... and I might just finally fly.

The table of gazes was starting to burn me, so I squirmed up out of my chair and affected a thoughtful stroll. As I came around the table, I noticed that the sheriff's entrance into the room had jostled the curtains on the glass doors. Desperate for distraction, I leaned toward the dining room and took a peek.

The remaining living Pritchetts had drifted in, haggard and grim.

It was clear that they had heard the news of Kitty's death, but the bombshell had fallen like a real explosion; they hadn't drawn together, only scattered. Except for the dyad of teens, each Pritchett sat as far from the others as they could, hunched over a menu. Even the married couple, Lionel and Deanna, were encamped in opposite corners.

My gaze fell on Priscilla. She was just settling herself in the center table, huffing and muttering and alone.

She seemed to have fully recovered from our last encounter, and I felt a mixed pang of remorse and relief.

Then I thought about the wounds she had to carry that might not ever heal.

For one thing, despite her decades of cheating, she was careening toward poverty. Once the sheriff heard the whole story, he'd want to make some discreet calls to the major casinos. He wouldn't want to reveal anything psychic, so he probably couldn't give them enough info for them to press charges about her past, but at a minimum, I was sure he could spin them enough of a tale that she'd never be able to gamble again.

But worse than any money troubles... she was nearing death in utter isolation. And the only relative that she ever might have cared for had turned out to be a murderer, perfectly willing to throw her under the bus. Priscilla Pritchett didn't even have a cat.

I *did* have a cat. A wonderful cat. And so much more...

I turned back to the Merediths, clustered around the table and trying not to stare. Tina, who was looking out the round window and biting her lip, put her hand on Grandma's shoulder. Without even looking, by sheer reflex, her grandmother reached up and patted her hand.

Who was I kidding?

Yes, they were far from perfect. But hey, I *could* have gotten a family like Nyle's. Seriously. The truth was, I'd had some *major* unfair princess luck.

Not to mention that whole Cade thing. There was also that.

"Okay, okay, everybody breathe," I said. "I'm in. For *now*. Who do you want me to zap first?"

Tina made this little gasp of delight, and I tried to smile all nonchalant, but I couldn't even look at her. Actually, I couldn't look at any of them. Someone started a cheer… was that Uncle Barnaby? Or Tina's dad? Oh man, if I went and cried *now*, in front of that stupid sheriff, so *help* me…

"Thank you," Grandma said. "Welcome home."

AFTERWORD

Dear Reader,

Summer's found her family in Wonder Springs…
… but what if Wonder Springs hates Summer?

They're about to blame her for murder… when the prime suspect is Cade.

In a small town, everyone smiles, but old feuds run deep. Land is scarce, and when the stubborn owner of a prime piece is found dead, almost everyone could have a motive. But none more than Cade.

Summer thought that clearing her own name was hard, but clearing her new boyfriend is a perfect nightmare. The whole town knows they're an item. And the jealous are whispering that she's a mastermind killer.

Who can Summer trust?

Because behind the smiles, people hide secret powers…

If you enjoyed this first book in the series, you'll love *Murder With a Psychic Zap*. The stakes are higher and the family has even more surprises.

Continue your journey now.

Get *Murder With a Psychic Zap* at:

https://billalive.com/wonder-springs-2

More Books by This Author

The Empath Detective Cozy Mysteries
Murder Feels Awful
Murder Feels Bad
Murder Feels Crazy
Murder Feels Deadly

BOX SET! Save a bundle with this special box set:
Murder Feels Awful, Bad, and Crazy: Books 1-3

FREE NOVELLA!
Get the secret story of Mark's first case for free:
High-Rise Demise: The Empath's First Case
https://billalive.com/free-empath-mystery

The Wonder Springs Cozy Mysteries
Murder With a Psychic Touch
Murder With a Psychic Zap
Murder With a Psychic Kiss
Murder With a Psychic Gift

Other Mystery Short Stories
The Affair of the Hideous Vase

Fantasy and Science Fiction
Beware of Mortals and Their Birthdays
The Punctuality Machine (And Other Tales of Time Dysfunction)

For Children
How to Talk to a Rock
Julie and the Wishing Rock

Want easy links to these books, free books, and more? Go to:

billalive.com